24 FRAMES PER SECOND

THREE HOLLYWOOD HORROR NOVELLAS

TIM WAGGONER, ANDREW NADOLNY, GARY A. BRAUNBECK

DARK **T**IDE

BOOK 21 IN CRYSTAL LAKE'S DARK TIDE SERIES

Published by Crystal Lake Publishing
Where Stories Come Alive!

Crystal Lake Publishing
www.CrystalLakePub.com

**Follow us on
Amazon:**

WELCOME
TO ANOTHER

CRYSTAL LAKE PUBLISHING
CREATION

Join today at www.crystallakepub.com & www.patreon.com/CLP

THE LAST CANNIBAL MOVIE

TIM WAGGONER

"I'M JUST SAYING it doesn't look like a jungle, that's all," Alan says.

I try to keep the irritation out of my voice as I respond.

"If I had an unlimited budget, I'd fly us all to South America. But since I don't have *any* budget, the woods are going to have to do. Don't worry. I'll shoot the scenes so it's not so obvious."

"If anyone can do it, Toby can," Becky says. "He's an auteur."

I glance back over my shoulder at her, and she gives me a wink and a smile.

I don't think Becky is making fun of me, but everyone laughs anyway. I want to tell them to shut up, but I say nothing. It's the director's job to create a good working environment on set, and I don't want to start things off with a tense atmosphere. Besides, I don't want Becky to think I'm mad at her. We've made a real connection this semester, and I don't want to fuck that up.

Plus, everyone here is helping me for free, and if I piss them off, they might leave. I didn't help any of them with their films—I'm a director, not a fucking crew member—and they have no reason to put up with any of my bullshit. I just need to get this shoot over with, edit the film, and have it finished in time to show the faculty during finals week, along with all the other first-year students. Afterward, the professors will meet and decide which of us get to move on to the second year of the program, and which do not. I'm determined to be in the former group, and if that means ignoring the others teasing me, fine.

It's an early Sunday afternoon in May at Marcum University—sunny and warm, but not *too* warm—and the seven of us are walking across the parking lot of the Creative Arts Center. It's empty for the most part, just a few cars, probably music majors who came to use the practice rooms. A couple of the cars belong to members of my crew, but most of us live in the dorms—including me—so all we had to do was walk here. We're headed toward the woods on the far side of the lot. The school was built back in the late 1960s, and there are a *lot* of trees on the north side. I don't know if that was because of some back-to-the-earth hippie thing or if the university's administration thought having large woods

3

with hiking and biking trails on the grounds would be a draw for students. Honestly, I'm surprised the school hasn't cut down all the trees and put up more buildings or parking lots. Lucky for me and my movie they didn't. Alan's right about the woods being a piss-poor substitute for the Amazon jungle, but when you're a no-budget student filmmaker, you work with what you can get.

I'm in the lead—I *am* the director, after all—and my actors are following me. Becky is right behind me, and she's carrying the scripts. Stephanie's walking beside her, carrying a large cardboard box full of props. Then there's Alan, who's carrying more props, and Celia, who's also carrying a large cardboard box, this one with costumes, wigs, and makeup in it. Justin and Randy bring up the rear, both empty-handed. None of us have camera equipment or boom mikes. That shit's twentieth century filmmaking. All I need is my phone and Adobe Premiere Pro on my laptop back in my dorm room, and I can make a movie that kicks as much ass as anything you could make with old tech.

I hope.

I *have* to get into the second year of the program.

Whatever it takes.

"I got a really good one for you this time, Toby."

I'm eight, dressed in my pajamas, even though it's only seven o'clock. My mom and dad have gone out to dinner and a movie, and they got my favorite sitter—Tara—to watch me. Tara is nice and she's pretty, but what I like about her the most is she brings scary movies for us to watch together. *This one isn't* too *scary,* she said when she brought over the first one, a DVD of an old black-and-white movie called *Frankenstein Meets the Wolf-Man. But don't tell your parents,* she said. *Parents always think their kids are too young to watch scary movies, but we know better, right?*

I enthusiastically agreed with her, of course—and I *loved* the movie, even if it was kind of slow in places and the two monsters didn't fight until the end. She continued bringing scary movies over after that, going from Universal Monsters to Hammer Horror to America International's Edgar Allan Poe films.

"I brought something special tonight," she says. She holds up

THE LAST CANNIBAL MOVIE

the DVD box for me to see. The movie is called *Flesh-Eaters of the Amazon*, the letters bright red and dripping blood. Below the title is a painting of a wild-eyed, brown-skinned, naked man with long black hair. His lips are drawn back from his teeth, and he's gnawing on a severed human hand. Blood streams from the corners of his mouth, splashes onto his chest. The man is framed by plants with green leaves on either side of him, and next to his face, in yellow letters this time, are two words followed by an exclamation point. *Eaten Alive!* Beneath the wild-eyed man, also in yellow letters, are the words *Based on True Events!!!* with three exclamation points this time.

Tara made me chicken fingers for dinner, and I think I may have eaten too many because my stomach suddenly feels funny. She sees something in my face—confusion, fear, disgust—because she frowns, and says, "You're my horror movie buddy, Toby. You can handle a film like this, can't you?"

Sometimes I imagine the two of us getting married after I grow up, and I don't want Tara to think I'm a *baby*. I start to answer her, but an acidy burp comes out instead. For a second, I think I'm going to vomit half-digested chunks of chicken at her—which would be *way* worse than having her think I'm too scared to watch the movie, but I clamp my mouth shut, swallow hard a couple times, and I feel better. A little, anyway.

Tara turns the DVD around and examines the cover.

"It *is* a little bloodier than anything I've shown you before." She looks away from the cover, smiles at me. "But it's fake, right? Just pretend."

I get off the couch. My legs feel a little wobbly as I walk over to Tara and touch my index finger to the words beneath the wild-eyed man's image. *Based on True Events!!!*

She laughs.

"That's bullshit, Toby. Filmmakers say that kind of thing to make their movies seem extra scary, but no one really believes it. You don't believe it, do you?"

Normally, it makes me laugh when Tara swears—Mommy and Daddy never swear around me; I'm not sure they even know how—but this time I give her a faint smile and shake my head. But inside, I'm thinking, *They can't put something like that on the cover if it's a lie, can they?*

"All right!"

Tara holds out her hand for a high five. I think about the severed hand the wild-eyed man is eating on the DVD cover—Is it a woman's hand? I think it might be—and my stomach does a flip. I manage to complete the high five, but I only touch her for the briefest of moments. She looks at me, eyes narrowing, and I get the sense that she's reconsidering showing me the movie.

Please, please, please don't show it, I think.

"All right, you get cozy on the couch, and I'll pop this bad boy in. You want me to microwave some popcorn before we start?"

Another acidy burp.

"No thanks."

"I don't care that the woods don't look like a jungle," Stephanie says. "What bothers me is the *other* reason you chose the location."

Back in the late '70s, a student named Cathleen Halloway was raped and killed in the woods. It was several days before campus police discovered her body, and her killer was never caught. Over time, Cathleen became a campus legend, and a candlelight vigil is held each October on the anniversary of her death. I didn't go this year, and I regret that. It might've given me more inspiration for my movie.

"No one who sees the film will ever know exactly where we shot it. I picked the spot because Italian cannibal films often marketed themselves as being based on a true story."

"A lot of horror films still do that," Justin says.

"And that's one of the many reasons why those films suck," Alan says. "It's a cheap ploy to get asses in seats."

Alan is thinking about dual majoring in filmmaking and film criticism—assuming he makes it into the second year, which he will. I've seen his finished film, and it's good. So good, it pisses me off.

"I'm not doing it to exploit what happened to Cathleen," I say. "I'm doing it as a way of satirizing how exploitive those films were."

"I don't know," Randy says. "Seems like a *really* thin line, Toby."

"And why bother?" Celia says. "If you aren't going to let the audience know, what does it matter where your film is shot?"

What I haven't told them is that while I have no intention of directly saying what "true event" my film is based on, I plan to put *For Cathleen* at the end of the credits and allow the students and faculty at the showing to make the connection themselves. Like Becky said, I *am* an auteur.

I go on. "Besides, at this point, no one remembers the exact location where Cathleen's body was found. It's just *in the woods*. People gather in this parking lot for the vigil every year, but that's only because it's the closest one. I honestly don't give a shit where we shoot, so long as there are some trees and bushes around."

This is a lie. I thoroughly researched Cathleen's case on various true crime websites, and I got the exact coordinates of the crime scene. Using a GPS app on my phone, I came here Friday afternoon, found the spot, and left a rock to mark it so I could find it again without my phone. I know, I know, it's morbid, but that's the vibe I'm going for, right?

I've got to be true to my art.

We reach the end of the parking lot. There's twenty feet or so of grass before the woods begin, a transition zone between our world of classes and tests and weekend parties and whatever waits for us within. Not bad. I've been thinking of adding narration to my film. If I do, I'll put something like that in. I'll leave out the school part, but the idea of a transition between civilization and the woods? That shit's gold.

I step onto the grass and lead the way into the wild.

It takes less than two minutes for us to reach the location where I put the rock. It's not too big, a little smaller than my fist. I left it at the base of an oak tree. Cathleen's killer positioned her naked body so she was sitting against a tree like this, maybe even this exact one. None of my research indicated which specific tree it was, but I figured this one's close enough. Later, after the shoot's done, I'll come back and get the rock. I'll keep it as a souvenir. Someday, when I have a shelf at home for all my awards, I'll put the rock on it with them.

We're in a small clearing which looks even smaller to me now that there are seven of us in it. I'll have to make sure everyone who's not in a scene is out of the way when I shoot.

I point to the side of the clearing opposite Cathleen's tree.

"Put everything down over there. We'll do makeup and costumes, and then we'll rehearse the first scene and film it."

Everyone gets busy. Becky lays the scripts on the ground and goes to help Celia with makeup. Celia has put down her box, and I watch as Becky bends over to reach in. God, her ass is *perfect*. . .She turns to look at me, as if sensing that I'm staring at her butt, and she smiles. I smile back, then I pull my phone out of my pocket. When I was here Friday, I decided how I wanted to block the scenes, and I wrote notes on my phone. I pull them up to review them, but I'm so nervous about the shoot that the words don't make any sense. I pretend to read them anyway and watch as Becky and Celia sit cross-legged on the ground, and Becky starts doing Celia's makeup. It's kind of hot—Celia's pretty too—and I keep sneaking glances at them as I go over my blocking notes.

Alan comes over and stands next to me. He looks up, shades his eyes with one hand.

"You going to have enough light?" he asks. "The leaves are pretty thick up there."

"I think we'll be fine. Besides, I *want* the light to be diffuse. I'm going to use a program to make the film look dark and grainy, like it really was shot in the 1970s."

Alan gives me a skeptical look. "Yeah, but you don't want it *too* dark, do you?"

I try to keep my tone even as I reply. "Like I said, I think we'll be fine."

"Okay. It's *your* movie."

I want to tell him to go get ready, but he doesn't need makeup—only the cannibals do—and he's already in costume: short-sleeved yellow shirt unbuttoned over a white T-shirt, jeans, brown boots.

"I know we talked about this already," Alan says, "But are you sure you want to go with your original casting? I mean, I get what you're going for, I do. But. . ."

"You don't think the professors will understand," I say.

"No, I'm sure they will. It's just. . .well, don't you think it's a bit *obvious* race-swapping the cannibals and explorers?"

The cannibals in my film are going to be played by white people—Becky, Celia, and Randy—while the explorers will be people of color. Stephanie, who's Hispanic; Justin, who's Asian; and Alan, who's Black.

THE LAST CANNIBAL MOVIE

"I'm satirizing the original films," I say. "Indigenous people were portrayed as monsters, and the protagonists were always portrayed by white people. I'm commenting on colonialism, white savior narrative, modern-day racism. . ."

"Yeah, like I said, I get it but. . ." Alan shrugs. "Obvious."

I'm starting to get irritated now.

"It's *supposed* to be obvious. The point is to show how obvious it was in the original films, but even today people don't see it."

Alan holds his hands palms up in a placating gesture and smiles. "Hey, whatever you want. It's your film, right?"

He heads over to help Becky apply cannibal makeup to the actors. I try not to look jealous.

Celia comes over to me then, walking in bare feet. Her makeup is finished—black around the eyes, cheeks shaded with brown to make her face look hollow and hungry, lips rusty-red, as if they have dried blood on them. It all looks fake, which is exactly what I wanted. A black fright wig is supposed to complete the look, but she hasn't put it on yet. She's holding it at her side, as if it's some unidentifiable furry creature she's killed. She hasn't changed clothes yet, is still wearing her T-shirt and shorts.

"I need to talk to you about my costume," she says.

"Is there something wrong with it?"

In answer, she drops the wig to the ground, pulls off her T-shirt, and tosses it aside. Instead of a bra, she's wearing a zebra-print scoop-neck swim top. Becky has the same style swim top underneath her shirt, only hers is a leopard print. I can't wait to see her in it.

She gestures to the top. "Look at this thing!"

I'm not sure what's bothering Celia. The top is a modest one, revealing no cleavage and covering half her midriff.

"I don't—"

"It's like something my grandma would wear. There's absolutely nothing sexy about it."

"I didn't want you and Becky to feel uncomfortable during the shoot. And the tops are supposed to be a comment on the sexualization of women in film—especially exploitation films. The idea is that viewers will wonder why you and Becky aren't in skimpy outfits, and that'll make them question *why* they want that, make them think about what societal forces unconsciously shape their expectations and desires."

Celia puts her hands on her hips and cocks her head to the right.

"Dude, you're making a fucking *cannibal* film, and that's all people will see. No one is going to get your symbolism and subtext. Hell, they won't even *notice* it."

"Maybe not consciously. . ."

"It's intellectual masturbation, Toby. And the skirts are even worse than the tops!"

She pulls down her shorts and steps out of them. She's wearing black thong panties, and when Alan and Randy notice she's taken off her shorts, they cheer, whistle, and applaud. Justin shouts, "Strut your stuff, girl!"

Celia ignores them, walks to one of the carboard boxes, grabs something green and gauzy, and comes back to me. She slips the skirt on, then picks up the fright wig and plops it on her head. The "skirt" is really part of a Halloween costume—green shorts with gauzy fake palm leaves attached to the waist band. Becky has one of the same kind. The tops and skirts are part of a Halloween outfit called Queen of the Jungle, and I bought them off Amazon the same time I ordered the props.

She reaches down with both hands, gives the leaves a flip, as if to emphasize them.

"This fucking thing makes me look like I'm goddamned Tinkerbell!"

I'm tired of explaining the aesthetic choices I've made for *my* film. Plus, the outfits were twenty percent off since Halloween is five months away.

"It's just a ten-minute student film," I tell her. "Not a big studio blockbuster."

She scowls. "You won't make it to second year with *that* kind of attitude, Toby. Remember what Mercedes taught us: There's no such thing as a small film because *all* films are important, even if only to a few people."

I hate professors who insist students call them by their first name, like we're all best buddies.

"I'll try to keep that in mind."

Celia looks at me for a long moment, as if she's unsure whether or not I'm being sarcastic. (I am.)

"Why don't you help Becky with her makeup?" I suggest.

Celia glances at Becky. She's finished Randy's makeup, and

she's starting her own. Randy has removed his shirts and pants, and now he's wearing only a fright wig and brown loincloth. He's rummaging around in the box of props, trying to choose one of the plastic weapons.

Celia smiles. "Maybe I'll go see if Randy needs any costume adjustments."

She heads toward him, hips swaying, bare feet moving across the grass. I realize then that her toenails are painted purple. Fuck it. There's no time for her to remove the polish. We'll just film with her as is, and if anyone watching the final film says anything, I'll say it was intentional, another statement about the pressure American society puts on women to adhere to patriarchal standards of beauty. That's the great thing about being an auteur— you can claim anything in your film is an artistic statement, whether it actually is or not.

"Get ready—this next part is really gross."

I cover my eyes. I don't want to—Tara will think I'm a baby for sure—but I can't stop myself. Just like I can't stop myself from peeking between my fingers.

There are five explorers in this story, all of them white. Four men and one woman. The men are all the same—brave, strong, in control of their emotions. The woman is young and pretty, dumber than a box of rocks and given to emotional outbursts at the most inconvenient times. I don't really understand why they've traveled to the Amazon. They work for some kind of company, and they've been sent there to do something or find something. I'm not sure if this was covered earlier in the movie. It must have been, but I have no memory of it. The next time I'll watch this film, I'll be fourteen, and I'll realize that I was right. The script—or at least the English-dubbed version—is unclear on exactly what the company wants our heroes to do.

The movie has been on for a while, and so far, the explorers haven't encountered any cannibals. They've had a run-in with bandits who tried to rob them—and who wanted to take the woman for some reason that I sense is bad, but I don't fully understand— and they've survived a jaguar attack. After I watch the movie again at fourteen, I'll research it on the internet, and I'll discover the stock footage the filmmakers used was of an African leopard.

But now the explorers have stumbled upon a small village—a dozen huts made of tree limbs and thatched-leaf roofs—and they're hiding at the edge of the jungle and watching the natives conduct some kind of ritual. All the natives in this scene are male adults with brown skin and long black hair, and they're wearing only loincloths. The men are armed with spears, and they're gathered around a fire they've built in the middle of their village. One man near the fire holds a baby goat in his arms, while another man next to him—one wearing a headdress made of dry grass and a cattle skull—holds a wooden club. The one with the club, who I guess is the chief or maybe a priest, chants something in a language I don't recognize. Then the man with the goat puts it on the ground and lays it on its side. It squirms, but he holds it in place, and the chief/priest raises his club and proceeds to break the baby goat's legs one by one. A sickening *crunch* accompanies each blow, along with the goat's cries of pain. Movies are pretend—Mommy and Daddy have told me this a lot—but what's happening on the screen now looks real.

Once all four of the goat's legs are broken, I fear that the chief/priest will bash it on the head with his club and kill it. But what happens is much worse. The man puts his club on the ground, picks up the baby goat, steps to the edge of the fire, and throws it in—alive. Now I understand why they broke the animal's legs. So it can't escape the flames.

The animal shrieks in agony, and I take my hands from my eyes and cover my ears. It doesn't help. I can still hear the goat scream. It thrashes wildly as it burns, body wreathed in flame, flesh turning black. Soon its screams become whimpers and then the goat falls silent and stops moving. The villagers have watched the goat's death without reaction so far, but now the chief/priest raises his hands above his head and shouts something, and they all jump up and down and cheer.

I feel sick. *Pretend,* I think. *Pretend, pretend, pretend. . .*

"Can you believe *that* shit?" Tara says. "They really killed that poor goat when they made the movie. I read an article where the director said he wanted *absolute realism,* whatever the hell that means."

I take my hands from my ears.

THE LAST CANNIBAL MOVIE

"I have to pee."

I get up from the couch without waiting for Tara to reply. I walk numbly to the hall bathroom, flip on the light and the fan, close the door, and kneel in from of the toilet. I try to vomit, try to expel the ugly savagery I've just witnessed. But nothing comes up.

"It's a short script and there's only one location, so we're going to shoot everything in sequence."

Everyone is gathered in a semicircle around me as I talk. Becky is wearing her zebra-print top, and while it doesn't reveal any cleavage, her arms and shoulders are bare, as is her stomach. I imagine lightly running the tips of my fingers across her smooth skin. I start to get an erection, and I hope no one notices.

"It's too long," Justin says. Becky has passed out scripts to everyone, and he's looking down at his, flipping through the pages. They've seen earlier versions of the script, but this is the first time they've gotten the final version.

"No it isn't. It's exactly the right length."

"It's twenty-one pages," Randy says. "A page is equal to one minute of screentime, so your script should be fifteen pages."

"He's right," Stephanie says. "Mercedes was real clear that she'll take off points if our films run long."

Not Mercedes—Professor Buchanan! Christ, have some respect!

"I've written out the action scenes in detail," I say. "They'll go faster when we film. Besides, I'll make sure the final edit is no longer than fifteen minutes. Let's just get started, okay?"

I'm beginning to think we should've started earlier in the day, but this was the only time I could get everyone together. As the afternoon wears on, the light in the clearing will get dimmer faster because of the tree cover, and I might not be able to shoot as many takes of each scene as I'd like. I. . .

She's standing by the tree where I placed the rock, wearing a long white daisy-print dress, the fabric torn in numerous places, chest and abdomen areas soaked with dark red blood. Her lower jaw skews to the right, as if partially detached, and her left eye is gone, destroyed when her killer plunged his knife into the socket.

I recognize her from pictures posted on the true-crime websites I visited. It's Cathleen Halloway, the murdered student who's become a campus icon. Her long brown hair is tangled and matted with blood, and her remaining eye is fixed on me, and I can feel the intensity of emotion coming off her, but I can't name it. Is she angry? Curious? Or is she feeling some unnamed emotion that only the dead can experience?

My annotated shooting script is tucked beneath my left arm, and my phone is in my right hand. *I should take a picture,* I think. *Better yet, I should video record her.* But I can't move, can only watch. Fucking stupid found-footage movies where someone keeps shooting no matter what happens. . .What bullshit. I can barely fucking breathe.

"Toby?" Becky says. "You okay?"

Cathy stares at me a moment longer, then she turns, steps behind the tree, and she's gone. I feel an impulse to run over and look behind the tree to see if she's hiding there, but I know she's not.

"Did you guys. . ."

I trail off. There's no point in asking if they saw her. She was behind them, and they were all looking at me. I force myself to smile.

"Never mind. Too many late nights studying for finals."

I'm a double major in both film production and business. I want to start my own indie film company someday, and I don't intend to leave the business side of things to someone else. I don't want to take forever to graduate, though, so I'm taking twenty-one credit hours this semester. Fifteen is considered a full schedule, and most students take even fewer so they can do better in their classes. I thought I could handle the work load, but I took on too much. When I'm not in class or making films, or helping someone else make films, I'm studying. I also tutor at the campus Writing Center to make a little extra money. What I *don't* do much is sleep. Right now I'm exhausted and irritable and I'm running solely on coffee and energy drinks. I just hope I can get through finals before the inevitable crash comes. I wouldn't be surprised if I end up sleeping most of the summer.

I sigh.

"Places for Scene One, please."

I direct the explorers—Stephanie, Alan, and Justin—to step

several feet into the woods so I can film them entering the clearing. I tell the Cannibals—Becky, Celia, Randy—to stand behind me and stay as quiet as possible. I do one last check of the clearing. The boxes are all out of the way, and the light looks good. There's a slight breeze blowing, making the leaves rustle softly, but the sound isn't loud enough to interfere with recording—I hope. I glance one more time at the tree where Cathleen's body was found so many years ago. She's not there, of course. Maybe she never was. I was thinking about her a few minutes ago, I'm overtired and stressed, and I imagined her, that's all.

But those eyes. . .

I can't afford to think about her anymore. I have a film to shoot. I set my phone so it's ready to record, lift it to my face, center my shot, and shout, "Action!"

"A. Cannibal. Film."

The words are flat, toneless, without intonation or meaning, as if Professor Buchanan is repeating a phrase in a foreign language she doesn't understand. We're in her office on campus, she behind her desk, me in a chair in front of it, feeling like a little kid who's been called to the principal's office. In a way, I guess I am. Professor Buchanan is the chair of the film department, as well as the instructor for the Intro to Film Production II class. She has to personally approve all her students' film projects, and if I can't sell her on my cannibal idea, I'll have to come up with something else.

"Yes."

I decide the less I say, the less likely I am to screw this up.

Professor Buchanan is in her early forties, with straight red hair pulled back into a ponytail, and large, black-framed glasses. She's wearing a long-sleeved black top, a short yellow skirt, black leggings, and what look like black ballet shoes. She always sits slouched in her chair, legs crossed, hands folded over her stomach. She rarely smiles, and when she does, the corners of her mouth tick up only the slightest bit. It's as if she purposefully keeps all her movements to a minimum so she can reserve the bulk of her energy for her mind.

I don't like Professor Buchanan. She might see herself as an avant-garde artist, but I find her views on filmmaking to be simplistic and outdated. Plus, she's kind of a bitch. But she's the most dominant member of the film faculty, and it's important that I get *her* to like *me*. Not only so I can get into the second year, but so she'll write me a glowing recommendation when I apply to graduate schools. It's how the game is played.

Her office is much smaller than you'd expect for someone who's department chair at a university. It's only slightly larger than a utility closet. Her desk is clean—just a laptop computer, an office phone, and a small lamp she uses to light the place instead of the fluorescent bulbs installed above. She has a couple filing cabinets against one wall, and a shelf filled with books on film, film theory, film production, published scripts. . .There are only two pictures on the walls, both of them framed movie posters. One is *Gone with the Wind*, except all the letters are Japanese. The other is for an arthouse indie called *A Question of Magnetism*. It's her film—she wrote, produced, and directed it twenty years ago. It got decent reviews, won a couple minor festival awards, but I watched it last fall on YouTube, and while it was good, it's clearly the work of a still-developing young artist. I'd never tell her this, of course, but between you and me, I think she made the right choice to go into teaching.

"Like the Italian movies of the 1970s," she says. She purses her lips, as if she has a bad taste in her mouth.

"You've seen them?"

She looks toward the *Gone with the Wind* poster.

"No. Horror doesn't interest me, either as a filmmaker or a viewer. It's so. . .artificial, and primarily intended for mass consumption, yes?"

I'm getting a sinking feeling in my gut. She's going to say no to my idea if I can't find a way to sell it—fast.

"I want to use the cannibal film as a lens through which to critique the subgenre of extreme horror, as well as to comment on social issues. Like Jordan Peele does—not that I'd ever compare myself to him."

Professor Buchanan continues looking at Clark Gable and Vivien Leigh, but she smiles.

"Of course you wouldn't."

Is she making fun of me? I can't tell.

"I know all those things," she says. "They're in your proposal."

THE LAST CANNIBAL MOVIE

She turns back to look at me. "What I want to know is why *you* want to make this film." She pauses, then says. "Why you *must* make this film."

I lower my gaze to her laptop. It's closed right now, and I wonder if she ever watches films on it or if she's a purist who will only watch films on the big screen. I have a good idea which she is. It takes one to know one.

I start to answer, but then I realize I'm really not sure. I haven't finished the script yet, but what I have is a collection of scattered ideas and themes, with a bare bones story—sorry about the pun— about nameless ciphers, some of whom kill the others in brutal, graphic ways.

"I noticed that in your proposal, you describe one of the scenes as *standard horror shit.*"

Oh god—she's going to lecture me on using unprofessional language in my proposal.

"That was more a note to myself than—"

She makes a languid motion with one hand to stop me, and I immediately shut up, as if I'm a pet trained to obey her commands.

"Your use of the word *shit* isn't a problem. It's the other word I find obscene."

"You mean *standard?*"

She nods, the movement almost imperceptible.

"You should never create *anything* that's standard. You should strive for originality, for true *vision*, every time. Every word in your script, every frame of your film, should astonish us. Do you understand?"

And in this moment, for the first time in my life, I do.

When I get back to my dorm room, the first thing I do is open my laptop and delete the script I was working on. I haven't gotten far and it isn't very good, so this is more of a symbolic act than anything else. Then I open a new file and begin typing.

SETTING

A clearing in an Amazonian jungle. This is

a place of primal power—ancient, eternal, unforgiving. . .

And *hungry*.

I'm back on the couch with Tara now. I brushed my teeth with extra toothpaste and scrubbed really hard, and I hope my breath isn't too bad. She's started the movie again, and I sit so close to her that our legs touch. What I really want to do is press myself tight against her, like I used to do with Mommy whenever we watched something that scared me. But I'm too old for that, and besides, Tara isn't Mommy. But then Tara surprises me by putting an arm around my shoulders and pulling me gently toward her. I don't resist, and soon I'm resting against her side, and I let out a deep, contented sigh. I don't feel safe, exactly, but I do feel *safer*, and right now that means everything to me. Tara is soft and warm, and I feel something I've never felt before—a tingly sensation down *there*. I don't know what it is, but I like it.

Tara starts the movie again.

The natives have captured one of the explorers—a thin man with white hair and a beard—and they lay him on the ground, spread-eagled, then use leathery strips to bind his wrists and ankles to wooden stakes driven into the earth.

Tara puts her mouth close to my ear. "I think those strips are dried human skin," she says softly. The feeling of her warm breath on my skin makes me shudder.

There are women among the natives in this scene, all of them topless. I've never seen bare breasts before—unless you count the one time when I was four and walked into the bathroom while Mommy was taking a shower. But I was too young to have any idea what I was seeing. I know now, though, and my face burns with embarrassment.

"Maybe we should fast forward," I say.

"No way, not when things are finally about to get *good*."

She pulls me closer until my head is resting on her left breast. I'm super embarrassed now, but I don't want to pull away from her. I'm afraid she'll think I don't like her. And I do like her. A *lot*.

THE LAST CANNIBAL MOVIE

The chief/priest steps through the crowd and stops next to the captured explorer. He gazes down at the man, face unreadable, as if his features are carved in stone. I expect the explorer to try and talk to the chief, to make some sort of deal for his freedom, or maybe just beg for his life. But instead, he raises his head as far as he can—only a few inches, given his restraints—and he spits at the man. The saliva hits the chief on the left cheek, and while the man doesn't blink, his eyes fill with fury. The explorer's defiant courage takes my breath away, and I wonder if I could ever be so brave. I expect the chief to order someone to give him a knife or a spear so he can kill the explorer for this insult, but instead the chief raises both his hands in the air and shouts a single word. He then turns his back on the explorer and slowly walks away—without wiping the explorer's spit off his face. How badass is that? I don't understand what's happening, though. Are the natives going to let the explorer die a slow death by leaving him out in the sunlight with nothing to eat or drink? I think that would be one of the worst ways to die.

A few seconds later, I realize that there are far more terrible ways to die than baking in the sun for a few days.

The natives shout and start running toward the bound explorer. The men's loincloths move with their motions, and I catch glimpses of penises. The women's breasts bounce and jiggle, and this fascinates me. All the women I've ever been around have worn bras, and I never realized how squishy breasts are. I wonder what it would feel like to touch one. Like holding a warm water balloon, maybe.

The explorer—so defiant only a moment ago—now screams and shakes his head in denial, but there's nothing he can do to save himself. The natives fall upon him and tear at his clothes, stripping him within seconds, and then they begin ripping into his flesh with their bare hands. The man's screams become high-pitched shrieks, and his body bucks and thrashes, but the restraints hold. Blood gushes from his abdomen and mouth, thick and ultra-red.

"They used paint for the blood," Tara whispers, even though we're the only two in the house right now. "Can you imagine what that must've tasted like?"

Some of the natives stick their hands inside the explorer's body cavity, while others bend down and gnaw at the ragged flaps of skin with their teeth. They pull handfuls of long, thin rubbery things out of the man's body, wet and glistening.

"Those are actually pig intestines," Tara said.

Several of the natives jump to their feet and hold the intestines over their heads, whooping in victory. Their faces, hands, forearms, and chests are covered with blood—fake, according to Tara, but it sure looks real to me. The cannibals pull the intestines tight between their two hands and bite down. More blood gushes, and the natives begin chewing vigorously, eyes wild, teeth red.

The explorer's screams give way to pained gasps of breath, and his exertions lessen. A native woman carrying a rock walks up to him, kneels beside his head, and goes to work cracking open his skull. It takes three blows for her to break it open. She pries back the top of his skull as if it was the shell of a soft-boiled egg to reveal the explorer's brain. She tosses the rock aside, digs her fingers into the red, wet meat and brings forth a small chunk. She pops it into her mouth, closes her eyes as if in ecstasy, and chews. Other natives gather around the open head and begin scooping out handfuls of brains and jamming the crimson mush into their mouths.

Nausea roils in my gut, and I think I'm going to throw up again, but I refuse to let that happen—not in front of Tara. I clamp my jaw tight and try to calm myself. It's just red paint and pig intestines, I tell myself. Not real, not *real!*

Then Tara does something that astonishes me.

She starts laughing.

"God, that's so *fake*! Look at the guy's face—they used a dummy head and filled it with strawberry jam. And the face doesn't even look much like the actor!"

I lean forward, narrow my eyes, examine the man's face. Yes, the skin color is too pale and the eyes look painted on. The beard hair is stiff and juts out at weird angles, and his lips are gray and look hard as rocks.

Tara's right. It *is* so fake.

I start to laugh too, and that's when Tara kisses me.

(The Three Explorers enter the clearing. They are hot, tired, and very lost. The clearing is deserted except for a human skull lying on the ground, and when the Explorers see it, they freeze.)

EXPLORER ONE
It appears that someone has
been here before us.

EXPLORER TWO
You mean someone's *head* has.
Who knows about the rest of
the body?

EXPLORER THREE
(Explorer Three lightly punches
Explorer Two on the upper arm.)
Don't say things like that!

EXPLORER ONE
(Walks over to the skull, hesitates for
a moment, then picks it up and studies
it.)
This is an ill omen indeed.
Do you see these marks?
(The other three Explorers gather round.
Explorer Four shows them scratches on
the top of the skull.)
They were made by human
teeth!

(The other three Explorers are stunned by
this revelation.)

EXPLORER THREE
Cannibals? I thought those
stories were just a myth,
scary fairy tales to make
outsiders like us stay away.

> EXPLORER TWO
> (Indicating the skull.)
>   Yorick there didn't stay
>   away, did he?
> (Three Cannibals burst into the
> clearing, holding knives and spears.
> They are silent and menacing. For a long
> moment, no one moves as the Explorers and
> Cannibals size up each other.)
>
> EXPLORER TWO
>   Fuck!
>
> (Explorer ONE drops the skull. The
> Explorers scatter in different directions
> and disappear into the forest. The
> Cannibals shriek a battle-cry and give
> chase.)

"This is so fake," Alan says.

He's lying on the ground, hands and feet loosely bound with gauzy scarves to four dowel rods shoved into the soil. The knots are not tight, and the dowel rods are so thin he could easily break them.

I sigh. We're about to shoot Scene Three. Scene One was the Explorers first encountering the Cannibals. Scene Two was Explorer Two—played by Alan—getting captured. Scene Three is Explorer Two's Terrible Fate.

"We've been over this. It's *supposed* to look fake. I want the audience to know it's fake and wish that it looked more realistic. That will make them *complicit*. Audiences are the ultimate cannibals, mindlessly devouring whatever meat we put in front of them."

Alan shakes his head.

"You know you're making this film solely to impress Mercedes, right? No one else is going to get your symbolism and layers of meaning."

"So? Ultimately, Professor Buchanan is the only viewer who

matters. The other faculty will follow her lead when it comes to which students get into year two and which don't."

"He's got a point," Becky says.

I look at Becky in her cannibal outfit, my gaze lingering on her exposed skin, and I remember what she tastes like.

"Can we just get on with it?" Justin says. "It's starting to get hot."

He draws the back of his hand across his forehead to wipe away a light sheen of sweat. He's not in this scene—neither is Stephanie—and he gets bored quickly if he isn't kept busy.

He's right, though. It *is* warmer. More humid, too. Like they say, if you don't like the weather in Ohio, just wait a minute.

"Okay, places."

Stephanie and Justin move off to the side, while the cannibals—Becky, Celia, and Randy—take up positions around Alan, who is scowling and muttering to himself. He's a pain in the ass, and the shoot would go a lot smoother if he wasn't here, but I can't afford to lose any of my actors, so I have to keep putting up with him. I want to start this scene with a long shot and then move in closer as the action gets more intense. I hold up my phone sideways and keep my eyes on the screen as I slowly walk backward and watch as Alan and the cannibals get smaller. . .smaller. . .

I bump into a tree, startling myself. Alan laughs, shakes his head. I imagine running over to him and stomping on his face over and over until it looks like the strawberry jam that comes out of the fake dummy head in *Flesh-Eaters of the Amazon*. The image makes me smile until I realize which tree I've backed into. It's *hers*.

Catherine's.

I start to step away, but I stop. I look at my phone screen again and see that I've reached the perfect distance for the scene's opening shot. But I'll have to keep my back pressed up against the trunk of Catherine's tree as I start filming. The idea is grotesque, but it has a transgressive appeal. No one else will know that I stood in the exact spot where Catherine was murdered when I begin to shoot Scene Three. My cast/crew have no idea, so it's not like they'll tell anyone. It'll be

Our secret, Tara says.

My secret.

A shiver runs up and down my spine at the thought of what I'm about to do, and my cock stiffens.

"Action!"

"I'm not really into horror films."

Becky and I are sitting at a small table at a coffee shop in the student union called Coffé. She's sipping cold brew, but I can't stand the taste of cold coffee. Mine's black and hot, the way God intended it. It's the week before Finals, and most of the other students are working on laptops, doing research and writing essays, although some are clearly surfing the web or watching YouTube videos. A few people are chatting, and one couple is holding hands across the table as they talk. I wonder what Becky would do if I reached across the table. Would she take my hand? Would she laugh at me? Would she wrinkle her face in disgust, get up, and leave?

"You don't have to love the genre to help me out," I say.

She smiles. "I know that. But I don't understand why you're attracted to it."

I'm attracted to you, I think.

"Horror can be so many things—entertainment, catharsis, social commentary. . .It can bypass the conscious mind and burrow straight into the subconscious more effectively than any other art form."

Becky's laugh is light and happy.

"You sound like Mercedes when you talk like that. Are you going to be a film professor too someday?"

I try to act nonchalant about her comment, but inside I'm thrilled. She thinks I'm smart!

I shrug. "I wouldn't mind teaching a few classes somewhere along the line, but mostly I just want to make films."

"Horror?"

"Sure, but I don't want to confine myself to one genre. I'm a student of film—all kinds—and the best way to understand something is to make it."

"Huh. I never thought of it like that. You want to go back to your dorm room and fuck?"

At first, I'm not sure I hear her right.

"Uh, what?"

"You know, have sex. You and me."

THE LAST CANNIBAL MOVIE

Her tone is casual. She might as well be asking me what I plan to do over summer break, what kind of music I like, or whether I'm a cat person or a dog person.

I have no idea how to respond.

Say yes, you idiot!

"Yes?"

She smiles, reaches across the table, and takes my hand.

I wake from a dream I can't remember. Sunlight filters through the narrow space between the curtains over the single window in my dorm room, and I look away. I'm not ready to face the morning just yet. I hear a rustling sound, and I turn over to see Becky standing next to the bed. I watch as she retrieves her panties from the floor and slips them on, then picks up her sports bra and dons it as well. It's weird, but watching her dress is just as sexy as watching her undress. Plus, there's a pleasant intimacy to it as well. I've had sex before—not a lot, I'll admit—but I've never woken up next to a lover, never watched as she got ready for the day. It's nice, like we're already a part of each other's lives.

"Sorry, but I've got to go," she says. "I promised Justin that I'd help him storyboard his movie this morning."

Justin's gay, but I still feel a twinge of jealousy. I'm not worried the two of them are going to hook up—it's more primal than that. I'm jealous because he's going to get to spend time with her, and I'm not.

I prop myself up, elbow on the mattress, chin on my hand.

"Want to do lunch later?" I ask.

She puts her hands on her hips, cocks her head to the side, considers. She looks so goddamned cute in this moment that all I want to do is grab hold of her and pull her onto the bed with me.

"I'd *like* to," she says, "but I don't want to give you the wrong impression."

I don't like the sound of this. I sit up, cross my legs.

"What do you mean?"

"Last night was great, but I don't want to jump straight to being boyfriend and girlfriend right away. I think it's better to start off slow and see what happens, you know?"

On the surface, what she's saying sounds reasonable and very adult, but what if this is just her way of letting me down easy? I read an article once that if a woman tells a man that two of you will "stay in touch," it really means she doesn't want to see you again. Is this Becky's version of that?

"Okay."

She smiles, steps forward, touches my cheek briefly, then turns away and finishes getting dressed. She doesn't say anything more before she leaves. She doesn't even look at me.

Flesh-Eaters of the Amazon keeps playing, but we're not watching the movie anymore. I'm not sure what we're doing. We're naked, our clothes in a pile on the floor, and Tara is lying on the couch. She's been moving me like a puppet, putting my hands and mouth on various parts of her body and telling me what she wants me to do. My heart is beating so hard that I can no longer hear the movie, which on one level is good—by this point the plot (what little of it there is) has degenerated into explorers screaming as cannibals kill them in a variety of nasty ways then feast on their flesh. But on another level, this is bad. If I could hear the movie, then I would have something to concentrate on other than what Tara is doing to me. I'd have a place to put my Self so that I wouldn't have to stay in my body and *feel* what's happening to me.

I'm sucking on one of her nipples, and she writhes beneath me in a way that makes me think of an undulating snake. I want to pull away, but her hand is on the back of my head, keeping me where she wants me. She moans and bites her lip.

"Use your teeth. Gently—don't bite."

Tears stream down the sides of my face, but if she notices, she doesn't care. Or worse, she likes it. I do what she wants, hoping that whatever this is will be over soon. After a few minutes, her breathing quickens, and she squirms underneath me. Then she lets out a cry, and her body becomes rock hard, all her muscles tightening, tightening. . .and then releasing. She wraps her arms around me and hugs me. I lay motionless and wait.

"Love a good nipple orgasm," she says.

What we're doing is wrong, I know it is, but I also know that

THE LAST CANNIBAL MOVIE

Tara likes it *because* it's wrong. I don't know the word yet, but this is my first experience of someone who gets off on transgression.

Another minute passes, and then she takes hold of my shoulders and pushes me up and arranges me so I'm straddling her abdomen. Her cheeks are flushed, her lips slightly swollen. She smiles.

"Your little dick is so *cute!* It'll get bigger as you grow. But it's just fine for right now. Let's go for number two."

She puts a hand on my chest and pushes me backwards. I scoot backwards and she spreads her legs to make room for me. When she gets me just where she wants me, she says, "Okay, now start pushing."

I don't know what she means, so she puts both hands on my butt and shows me. She keeps her hands there as I start pushing, and soon she's moaning and wiggling again. My wiener mushes against her soft, wet thing, and the hair around it is scratchy. I'm crying harder now, sobbing openly, but that only urges her to make me push faster. I'm surprised that it feels kind of good, but this makes me feel ashamed. Nothing about this is good.

She breathes faster again, keeps pushing-pushing-pushing, thrusts her pelvis up and down, up and down, and then her muscles tighten again, and she yells, "Fuck me, fuck me, fuck!" This is followed by a cry that's nearly a scream, and it scares me so much—Did I hurt her?—that I pee a little, right onto her *thing*. She feels it and cries out again, louder this time, and she shakes beneath me, and I'm terrified that she's going to die. Part of me wishes she would.

When her body relaxes, she lets out a shuddering breath.

"Damn, that was good."

She pulls me down onto her, presses my wet cheek to one of her breasts, and strokes my hair as she softly hums to herself. My face is turned toward the TV, and I can see the credits are rolling. The movie's over.

(The Cannibals gather round Explorer Two. They kneel and begin clawing at his shirt. They soon tear it open and then thrust their hands inside his abdomen. Explorer Two screams and writhes as the Cannibals eviscerate him. But instead of intestines, they pull out masses of red crepe streamers which they fling over their shoulders, draping themselves in the "organs." Cannibal Three reaches deep into Explorer Two's abdominal cavity and withdraws a fast-food bag. As Explorer Two's life rapidly fades, he watches with horror as the Cannibals remove hamburgers from the bag, unwrap them, and start devouring them ravenously. Explorer Two dies and the Cannibals continue eating.)

"Cut!"

I lower my phone and take a step, intending to go over to the group and congratulate them on getting the scene finished in one take. I'm *not* going to tell them we had to do it in one take because I didn't have enough money to buy more than one burger apiece for my Cannibals.

But before I can take a second step, my T-shirt snags on something—a branch?—and I can't move forward. I try to turn so I can see what I'm caught on and free myself, but I can only get a quarter of the way around. My shirt pulls tight to my body, and I can feel something hard between my shoulder blades.

I turn my head and stretch my neck, and I'm able to see what's got me—it's a fist, and it's attached to an arm that protrudes from the tree trunk. The arm hasn't broken through the wood, though. The bark around it is smooth, as if the arm emerged from the tree's interior without doing any damage. It's a woman's arm, of course, and then two small sections of bark open to reveal blue human eyes.

I can't stop myself from screaming. I drop my phone, take hold of my shirt with both hands, and pull with every ounce of strength I can muster. Catherine's grip is like iron, and then a thought occurs to me: what if she starts pulling me *into* the tree? What if I slide through the bark as easily as if it were mist and Catherine wraps her arms around me and never lets me go?

I put all my strength into one last pull. I hear my shirt tear, and then I stumble forward, twist an ankle, fall, and smack my head against the ground—hard. I could tell you I see stars or a flash of bright light, but I can't see a damn thing.

Not even darkness.

It's the night before our final film proposals are due to Professor Buchanan. I'm sitting alone in Coffé, staring at my laptop screen, hating myself, the world, and everyone and everything in it. I have a killer idea for my film, but I can't think of how to explain it in a proposal. How can I summarize something I haven't created yet? I'm on my second large cup of black coffee, my blood pressure feels sky-high, and my nerves are jangling like a fire alarm. I may have had a little too much caffeine.

Alan walks into the place, and I look away before he can see me. I *really* don't want to deal with this asshole right now. I'm sure the fucker has already turned in his proposal, probably did it a day or two early.

"Hey, Toby! I've been looking all over campus for you!"

I sigh, put on a fake smile, and turn to look at Alan as he approaches my table, wearing the half-mocking grin that always makes me want to punch him. He pulls out the empty chair at my table, sits, picks up my coffee cup, and takes a quick sip. His mouth puckers in disgust.

"What the hell *is* that shit?"

"Just coffee."

"Fuck me, that was *rancid!* Try putting some sugar and cream in next time, okay?" He nods to my laptop. "Working on your proposal? How's it going?"

I know it's childish, but I close the computer so he can't see that I haven't written anything yet. I admit the truth anyway.

"Slow."

"Keep at it. You'll get there. The reason I've been looking for you is that I want you to be one of the crew when I shoot my movie."

"Assuming Professor Buchanan approves your idea."

"She will. And I'm going to give you story credit at the end since you gave me the idea."

I don't know what the fuck Alan means.

"I. . .gave. . ."

"Yeah, don't you remember? It was last Saturday, when we were at the Rat-Hole?"

The Rat-Hole is a bar near campus. Its real name is Smitty's, but students have called it the Rat-Hole since before I was born, and honestly, that name fits better. It's the kind of place where the air smells like urine cake and stupid graffiti is carved into the tabletops. *Organic Chem can suck my round bottom flask! Thank Christ my parents are paying for my worthless degree! Want to know how to get into a college girl's pants? Me too!*

"Honestly, I don't remember a lot about that night. I was pretty drunk."

"You sure were! We practically had to carry you back to your room. Well, at one point in the evening we all started talking about our final film ideas."

We were Alan, Becky, Celia, Justin, and me.

"They were mostly decent. Of course, I had a few suggestions for improvement on them."

Of course.

"But compared to everyone else's, mine was shit. I'm really good with other people's ideas—seeing what works, what doesn't, what could be made better—but when it comes to my own creativity, I well and truly suck. But your idea—a man walks into his home office one day to find another man who *claims* to be him already sitting at the desk working—was genius. It was high concept but at the same time simple, and it only required one location. I said as much, and then I told you the only thing that would improve it was if the characters were played by identical twins. You said their looking different but having the same name added to the absurdism of the situation—which I get—but I said using twins would make it more surreal and disturbing. And since my brother James and I are twins, I said we could be your actors. You thought about it for a moment, then you said, 'You know what? Your version is better. You make it.' I asked if you were sure, and you said yes. At that point I didn't think you were too wasted to know what you were doing, so I thanked you and we all moved on to another topic. I turned my proposal in yesterday, and Mercedes has already approved my idea. I mean, *your* idea."

We fall into an uncomfortable silence for a few moments.

"Look," Alan says, "I'll tell Mercedes what happened, that it was a misunderstanding, and I'll ask for an extension to write up a new proposal. You can keep your idea and use it for your film. Sound good?"

It sounds fucking fantastic to me. I have no memory whatsoever of the conversation Alan says we had—and even if we *did* have it, it didn't necessarily go the way he said it did. I must've told him about my idea—I was going to call my film *Two's a Crowd*—otherwise, how would he know about it? But he could've conned me into giving the idea to him, especially as drunk as I was. Or he could've just stolen it and written his proposal early, so he'd beat me to the punch with Professor Buchanan. If I turned in my proposal after his, it would look like *I* stole the idea from *him*. I could explain the situation to Professor Buchanan, and she might believe me. But even if she did, there would always be a kernel of doubt in her mind that maybe *I* was the plagiarist instead of Alan, and I can't have that. I plan to get my MFA in screenwriting at the University of Southern California after I graduate, and I'll need a glowing recommendation from Professor Buchanan to even have a shot at getting into such a competitive program.

Besides, if I'd loved the idea, I wouldn't have given it away, drunk or sober, and I wouldn't have procrastinated this long on writing my proposal. Maybe my subconscious was trying to tell me that I needed to make another, better film. Too bad it hadn't delivered the message a few days ago. Still, part of me—a petty part—was angry at Alan for taking my idea. He was like a fucking parasite feeding on me. No, he was like a goddamned cannibal, eating one of his own.

A cannibal. . .

"That's all right," I say. "What's done is done. Like you said, your proposal's been approved, and I've just started writing mine—" If you call a blank screen a start—" I've got a lot more ideas. All I have to do is pick one and start writing." This time, my smile is more like a grimace, but I guess it's good enough to pass because Alan smiles.

"Whatever you say, man. Thanks."

I have to fight the urge to grind my teeth.

"No problem."

I stay up all night writing my script, and I submit it to the course drop box around 6 a.m. I'm terrible at titles, so right now the film is called *Untitled Cannibal Movie*. Who knows? Maybe I'll leave it like that.

The next time my parents want to go out—this time to a grown-up party with some of their friends—I ask if Tara is going to babysit me. When they say yes, I throw myself to the floor, start screaming, and shit myself.

My parents don't go to the party.

They never ask Tara to babysit me again either.

I open my eyes.

At first, my vision is blurry, and I can't make out anything. My ankle hurts like hell, and my head is pounding like a motherfucker. I hear sounds—the wet smacking of lips, soft grunts of pleasure—and I push myself up into a sitting position. The world spins around me, I fight to hold onto consciousness, and within seconds the vertigo subsides, but it doesn't entirely leave me. My vision clears, and as it does, I remember Catherine grabbing hold of my shirt, her arm protruding from the tree where her body was found, her eyes opening in the bark. . .I look to the tree, sure I'll see Catherine emerge and start walking toward me, hands outstretched, dead eyes burning with anger and hate. But I see only the tree.

I turn to look in the direction of the sounds I heard, and I see Becky, Celia, and Randy—my three Cannibals—crouched over Alan. Didn't they notice that I fell? Didn't they hear me scream before that? I can't believe they're so into the scene they're performing that they're no longer aware of their surroundings.

THE LAST CANNIBAL MOVIE

"Guys. . ."

They stop what they're doing and turn to look at me. Their mouths are smeared with blood—*real* blood, not fucking paper streamers—and their hands and forearms are slathered with it. They hold gobbets of meat, lengths of intestine, flaps of skin, dark-colored organs I can't identify. Alan's unblinking eyes stare up at the sky, his abdomen an open, crimson cavity.

I start laughing.

"Oh my god, when did you guys plan this? And where'd you get the fake blood and guts? I didn't see them in the stuff we brought. Hey, where's my phone? I've got to get some video of this!"

This joke is going to become legendary in the film department, and who knows? I might be able to use the footage in my film, intercut the stylized imagery with what looks like the real thing. Yeah, that would kick ass!

I look around me, searching for my phone, but I don't see it. I'm still sitting, so I turn at the waist to look at the tree once more, and I see Catherine standing there, holding my phone horizontally in front of her face. She's filming me. Funny, I hadn't realized how much she looks like Tara.

"If I were you," she says, mouth stretching into a cold smile, "I'd start running."

I turn to look at my friends, and the blood on their mouths and hands no longer seems as fake as it did a moment ago. They're staring at me, teeth bared, and Becky licks crimson off her lips. The three of them stand, and start walking toward me slowly, in no hurry, eyes sizing me up as if they're trying to decide which parts of me to eat first. I lurch to my feet, and—half-running, half-hobbling because of my ankle—head for the trees.

I run—if you can call it running—without any thought of destination, unless *away* counts as one. The underbrush is thick here, which makes forward movement hard, and my throbbing ankle and pounding head don't make it any easier. If I wasn't full of adrenaline, I doubt I'd be able to keep going.

The parking lot, get to the parking lot. . .

Once I'm out in the open, I can call for help, maybe find a

campus security officer. If nothing else, at least I'll be able to see them—the people I thought were my friends—coming. I can't see shit right now, just branches and leaves slapping me in the face as I run, and I know they could be anywhere—behind me, ahead of me, on either side of me. And I'm making so much goddamned noise thrashing through the foliage that I won't be able to hear any of them approach before they attack.

Where the hell *is* the parking lot? Am I even running in the right direction?

I don't know, I don't know. . .

Why did they kill Alan? Why do they want to kill *me*? Possibilities race through my mind. Catherine's spirit—offended that I intended to use the location of her last, nightmarish moments on Earth to shoot a student film—has possessed my friends and turned them into the characters they were portraying. She's using my own film against me, see? Poetic justice, real *Tales From the Crypt* stuff. Or maybe my friends have been infected with a virus that escaped from one of the campus labs, and it's turned them into cannibalistic monsters. Or maybe these aren't *my* friends, maybe they've been replaced by shape-changing aliens or duplicates grown from oversized seed pods. Something went wrong during their transformation/growth and now they lust for human flesh.

These ideas are drawn from horror movies I've watched over the years, and I know they're all bullshit. I remember hitting my head when I fell. Maybe I injured myself worse than I thought and I'm hallucinating all this. Or maybe I'm still lying in the grass unconscious, and this is some kind of fucked-up dream.

If this isn't real, then I can't be hurt, can I? All I have to do to prove it is stop running and let them catch up with me.

Fuck *that*.

The air seems to get hotter and heavier the more I run. Sweat pours off me, and I feel as if I'm breathing through a mouth filled with wet cotton. The woods change, tree leaves becoming large, thick fronds, underbrush becoming exotic plants with bright, colorful flowers. Monkeys leap from branch to branch, and flocks of blue-feathered macaws perch in the trees, watching me with their intelligent eyes as I run.

Welcome to the jungle, Toby.

A figure steps out of the green and blocks my way. I'm moving too fast to avoid it, and I crash into whoever it is, and we both go down. The pain in my head and ankle flares bright, but I barely notice. I have a more immediate problem to deal with—I've just fallen on top of a cannibal, and if I don't do something fast, I'm going to feel teeth bite into my flesh. I push myself onto my knees, wrap my hands around the cannibal's throat, and tighten my grip. I've never committed an act of violence—*real* violence—against anyone before, but this is the jungle. It's kill or be killed, eat or be eaten.

I squeeze harder, and the cannibal's eyes bulge. She kicks and twists beneath me, grabs my wrists, tries to pull my hands off her throat, claws at my forearms, scratching the skin, drawing blood. I clench my jaw, bear down harder, concentrate all my strength into my hands. . .

Then I truly see the face of the person I'm strangling. It's not one of the cannibals—it's an Explorer, Stephanie to be precise.

I yank my hands away from her throat, horrified.

"Oh my god, Stephanie! Are you all right? I'm so sorry, I thought you were one of them!"

I help pull her to her feet, and she coughs and gasps, trying to breathe. When she speaks, her voice is a halting rasp.

"Who. . .the fuck. . .are. . .you?"

"It's me—Toby. Don't you recognize me?"

She shakes her head, winces at the pain this motion causes.

"Never. . .seen you. . .before."

A thought occurs to me. Maybe she thinks she's the character she plays in the script, just like the Cannibals do.

"You're one of the Explorers."

"Yes. Our. . .company sent us here. . .to look for oil deposits." As she speaks, her voice gradually becomes more normal. "Or maybe we're from a pharmaceutical company. . .and came searching for plants that might result in new medicines. I can't really remember. But who cares? We're being hunted. . .by savages who want to eat us!"

The voice is Stephanie's, but the rhythm and cadence of her words are off.

"What's your name?"

"Explorer One."

Right. I didn't bother naming the explorers in the script—a comment on the anonymity of the characters in Italian cannibal films. They aren't really people; they're just meat.

Without realizing it, I take a step toward her.

"Look, Stephanie, I think—"

She steps back and her hand falls to her holster. She's wearing a gun on her hip, and the weapon looks much more real than the prop ones I brought.

I hold my hands palms up and take a step back.

"It's okay, I'm not going—"

Her body stiffens and a spearpoint juts outward from her mouth, accompanied by a spray of blood. She stands there, body spasming, her eyes fixed on me, pleading with me to do something to stop the pain. For an instant, her face resembles Cathleen's, then Tara's, then Professor Buchanan's, the faces changing fast, as if each was a single frame spliced into a film of Stephanie's death, the kind of gimmick that might've been used in an old William Castle horror movie from the sixties.

Randy is standing behind her, holding the other end of the spear, a look of maniacal satisfaction on his face. I walk forward calmly, remove the pistol from Stephanie's holster, and switch off the safety. Randy plants a foot on Stephanie's back—her eyes are wide and staring now, all life gone—and shoves her off the spear. I step to the side so her body doesn't hit me, and as she falls, I point the barrel at Randy's head and squeeze the trigger.

I hear rushing water, and I head toward the sound. I didn't know there was a stream in the woods, but it's not like I've spent much time exploring here. I'm just grateful there is one. My throat is sandpaper-dry, and I've sweated so much I feel there's no moisture left in my body. I desperately need a drink, and I don't care how clean the water is. If I get a gutful of intestinal parasites and end up with explosive diarrhea for a week, it'll be worth it, just so long as I don't collapse from heat exhaustion now. If I pass out, odds are I'll end up like Alan and Stephanie, dead and on the menu. Supposedly, Charles Bukowski said *Find what you love and let it kill you.* I love movies—especially horror movies—so mission accomplished, I guess.

The sound of flowing water grows louder the closer I get to it, much louder, and when I break through the trees and see a huge, fast-flowing river, I'm not surprised. My movie does take place in the Amazon, after all.

I step on the bank, close my eyes, spread my arms, tilt my head back, and luxuriate in the river's cool, misty spray for several moments. I open my mouth and stick out my tongue to catch whatever moisture I can. It's not much, but it tastes like life itself. My head and ankle still hurt, but I don't feel as dizzy or nauseated, so I open my eyes and look at the river once more. The bank here is too steep for me to get close enough to the water to take a drink, and while I'd love to jump in and cool off, the current is too strong and swift. I'm a decent swimmer, but this river would kill—would *devour* me—within minutes. Maybe if I walk along the bank for a while, I'll find a place where the slope's more gradual and it's safer to get to the water's edge.

I still have Stephanie's gun. It's heavy in my hand, and part of me would like to let it drop to the ground and walk away, but another, larger part is terrified of being without it, as if it's a charm to ward off evil. I never fired a gun before today, let alone killed someone. Andy's blood is spattered on my clothes, face, neck, and hands, and while I should be disgusted by this—and more to the point, horrified I murdered one of my friends, I don't feel much of anything. Maybe I'm in shock. Or maybe everything's become so unreal that I'm unable to believe in it. Kill one person, kill a thousand. It's all the same here in the land of dreams.

I rub a spot of Randy's blood off my face with an index finger, touch it to my tongue, contemplate the taste. I don't get the attraction. It's like sucking on a penny. Evidently, cannibalism is an acquired taste. Hey, that would make a good bumper sticker slogan, wouldn't it?

It feels like I've been walking for a long time, but the bank is still as steep as ever, keeping me from the water I so desperately need. I'm contemplating throwing myself into the river and letting it do with me what it will, so long as I can get one good drink before I die. But the river curves here, and when I go around the bend, I see Celia crouched in the grass, machete gripped in her right hand. I almost don't recognize her at first, since she's wearing Justin's skin like a cape, the boneless arms tied around her neck, his head—minus the jaw—perched on top of hers like a grisly hat. Four squirming balls of spotted fur surround her, and I realize they're jaguar cubs, so young their eyes aren't open yet.

Celia glances up at me as I approach.

"You forgot to include one of the most important elements of an Italian cannibal film in in your movie: animal cruelty."

Out of reflex, I almost start lecturing her that animal cruelty—real animals getting hurt and killed—only appears in a couple classic cannibal films. Sure, it was included as an additional transgressive thrill for the audience, but it's not like it's completely gratuitous, reprehensible though it is. The animal deaths were used to illustrate the innate eat-or-be-eaten nature of the jungle, the setting used a metaphor for existence itself. On the commentary track for the Blue-ray release of *Flesh-Eaters of the Amazon*, the director—Stefano Gallo—said *Animals living in the wild often lead short, brutal lives—and I wanted to show it's no different for humans.*

Her empty hand darts out lightning-fast and catches of one the jaguar cubs around the middle. She presses it against the ground, and while it's squirming, she raises her machete and chops off its tiny head. Blood comes out, more than I expect for such a little animal, but the bleeding quickly stops.

"One," she says, a ghost of a smile playing on her lips. She grabs hold of another, repeats the process. The first died silently, but this one lets out a tiny cry of pain before its head is separated from its body. "Two."

Her smile widens. She reaches for a third, and I raise the gun. "Don't."

She looks at me, hand motionless, machete only inches from the third cub.

"Is a human life worth less to you than a fucking animal's?" she asks.

"Don't talk to me about the sanctity of human life. You're wearing Justin for a goddamned sweater."

"Fair point. I'm still going to behead the last two cubs, and you're going to stand there and watch me do it, just like you watched me kill the first two. You're a *watcher*, Toby, not a *doer*. At least I'm acting in your movie. You're not doing shit."

I raise the gun, fire, hit Celia right between the tits. Her sternum shatters, blood fountains into the air, and she falls backward. She loses her grip on the machete, and it falls, the blade *chuck*ing into the ground. She gets shaking hands beneath her, tries to rise, but her left hand slips out from under her, and she tumbles down the steep bank, Justin's skin still tied to her. She splashes into the water and is carried away by the river's current. I wonder what will kill her first: the gunshot wound or the river. Either way, Becky is now the last cannibal standing.

Wherever she is.

I look at the two remaining cubs. They're only a few days old, and there's no sign of their mother around—which is bad for them, but good for me. After avoiding getting eaten by cannibals that look like my friends, the last thing I want to do is get killed by a momma jaguar. It would be a real letdown of an ending. Without nourishment the cubs won't last long. I think of the Intro to Psych class I had in fall semester. When the professor was introducing Maslow's Hierarchy of Needs to us, he said that instead of the five traditional levels, there is only one: the things we need to sustain life—air, water, food. Anything else is extraneous bullshit.

I can't leave these babies to lie here and die painful, lingering deaths, but I can't take them with me. I have no way to care for them. If I leave them here, predators might get them before they die of thirst or starvation, but there's no guarantee that'll happen. Such a death would be a natural, although hardly painless. My gaze falls on the machete sticking upward from the ground only a few feet away.

"Fuck."

I walk toward the machete, pull it from the earth like some demented version of Excalibur, and I do what's necessary.

I walk for hours, following the course of the river. The sun remains high overhead, never moving, its oppressive light and heat hammering down on me without mercy or pity. My skin stings, and I wish I'd been smart enough to put on sunscreen before heading into the woods. Hell, I'd settle for having a fucking hat to wear, along with a pair of sunglasses. I'm not sweating as much as before, and at first I wonder if I'm starting to adjust to the climate, but then I realize I'm sweating less because I'm dehydrated. My mouth feels like it's filled with hot sand, my head feels like it's going to explode any second, and sharp pain shoots through my twisted ankle every time I put weight on it.

Good times, good times.

My vision is blurry—that, or the world around me has lost all definition—and I navigate primarily by sound, keeping the rushing river on my right. Eventually shapes loom in the distance, and I struggle to make them out. They seem familiar, but. . .

My vision sharpens, and I realize that what I'm seeing are buildings. *Campus* buildings. I have literally made it out of the woods. I feel no elation, no relief. Instead, I feel a bone-deep weariness, and all I want to do is get to my dorm, drink several gallons of water, take a cold shower, and then sleep for a month. Maybe forever.

I continue trudging onward until I reach the quad. Every university has one, an open area surrounded by the campus' four main buildings. Ours is paved with red brick, and in the center is a large, raised rectangle enclosing grass-covered earth and a couple trees. Sometimes students toss around a frisbee here, or they sit and have lunch with friends, or sit alone and pretend to study. Other students sit on the edge of the short wall that surrounds the small field, talking with friends, looking at their phones, or staring off into the distance, bored. There's usually a half dozen guys—sometimes with a girl or two in the mix—playing hacky sack, and you might see faculty hurrying across the quad, late to teach their next class. All of these things are present now, only they're different in one important aspect: everyone is eating—and what they're eating is *meat*, raw and bloody. They bite into it with the savage desperation of starving predators, or they slowly gnaw on it, a look of dreamy contentment on their faces, mouths and hands slick with blood, clothes stained red.

I don't have to guess what kind of meat they're eating. Human bodies are strewn around the quad, lying on the ground, hanging from tree branches, all naked and in various states of mutilation. Abdomens torn open, limbs missing, swaths of skin ripped away, tops of skulls sawed off and brains exposed, eyes and sex organs gone. . .The hacky-sack kids are kicking around what looks like a child's heart, and the students reading aren't studying textbooks but rather cookbooks. A couple sits at the base of one of the trees. At first I think they're kissing, but then I realize they're chewing off each other's lips.

I stop, stare, and then the ridiculousness of it all hits me, and I start to laugh, the sound loud, wild, and mad. Everyone stops feasting and looks at me. They lick blood from their fingers as they regard me, gazes intense and probing. They're trying to decide if I'm one of them or if I'm food.

"Hello, Toby."

Her voice comes from behind me, and I turn around to see Professor Buchanan standing there. She's holding a Styrofoam box, and I know she's just come from the cafeteria. I'm surprised she's still here so late on a Saturday afternoon. I know she's dedicated to film and to the students she teaches, but come on, it's the *weekend*. No professor works on a weekend if they can help it.

"Not to put too fine a point on it," she says, "but you look like hammered shit. Did you have a rough shoot?"

I glance around. Everyone in the quad is still staring at me.

"You could say that—and I don't think it's over yet."

"We all must suffer for our art. Are you hungry? I just came from the cafeteria. They're having a special on fingers."

She opens the Styrofoam container and reveals a mass of human fingers—male, female, adult, children, White, Black, Asian. . .

After everything that's happened today, I'm not surprised.

"No thanks. I've recently become a vegetarian."

She laughs, plucks an infant's finger from the box, pops the whole thing in her mouth, starts chewing.

"People say they're vegetarians because it's socially acceptable, but no one really means it. The body needs what it needs, and what it needs most is meat."

She swallows, sighs in contentment. Then she looks at him, eyes narrowing, gaze growing cold.

"You can eat or be eaten, Toby. Which do you choose?" She takes another morsel from the box, this one a woman's index finger with cherry-red nail polish. She holds it out to me. "Think of this as your final exam."

The people in the quad are all standing now, watching me intently, muscles tensed, waiting to see what I'll do next. I imagine them salivating.

I reach out, but instead of taking the finger, I grab the entire Styrofoam box, and fling its contents into the air.

"Come and get it!" I shout.

I throw the box aside and start running. My ankle screams, but I ignore it. Professor Buchanan cries out "No!" falls to her knees, scrambles to collect her meal. Her fellow cannibals rush forward like a pack of hungry dogs, intending to claim the fingers for themselves. Within seconds they're fighting and snarling, clawing and biting, and they've forgotten all about me—for the moment anyway. I keep running, and I hear Professor Buchanan scream behind me.

"F! You hear that, you pretentious little prick? F, F, F!"

My broken, dehydrated body will only let me run for a few moments, and soon I'm walking—hobbling, really—chest heaving as I desperately gulp air and fight to hold onto consciousness. I know that if I pass out now, I'll wake to feel someone's teeth tearing into my flesh. I may not want to eat human flesh, but I sure as shit don't want to be eaten.

I should head to my dorm, lock myself in my room, and wait for this nightmare to end, assuming it ever will. But instead, my feet carry me toward the student union, and since I'm too exhausted to argue with them, I decide to let them take me where they will. Maybe they know something I don't.

It takes me three tries to push open the glass doors and enter. The air conditioning is on inside, and the sudden cold shocks my overheated body. The pain in my head becomes so intense my vision goes white, and nausea hits my gut like a sledgehammer. I stumble, almost go down, but I manage to stay on my feet. The pain in my head and gut lessens, my vision clears, and I see something that, if I had any moisture left in me, would cause me to weep like a baby.

A water fountain.

It's positioned against the far wall, beneath a flatscreen monitor displaying campus news, one image giving way to another every few seconds. An announcement of the tennis team's next game. A reminder that puppies will be available to play with for stress relief during finals week. A picture of me with the subheading HAVE YOU SEEN THIS FOOD? IF SO, EAT ON SIGHT in blood-red capital letters. It barely registers with me. All I can think about is the water.

I want to run to the fountain, but all I can manage is a weak shuffle. It feels like it takes an eternity to cross the floor, but at last I get there. Go slow, I tell myself. Drink too fast and you'll vomit it back up. I reach a trembling hand to the spout, depress the button with my thumb, and watch in almost holy rapture as a stream of water bubbles forth. I lower my mouth, and at first I sip slowly, but my body quickly takes control, and I start gulping as fast as I can. The sensation of cool water filling me is orgasmic, and I wish that I could freeze this moment and dwell in it for eternity.

My stomach cramps painfully then, and I turn my head just in time to expel a gush of water onto the floor. Except it's not water—it's blood.

Holy Christ, what's wrong with me? Is the blood from my dry throat? From my stomach? Did something break inside of me? Am I bleeding internally? Am I dying? Given what's been happening to me since that moment in the woods, it might be a blessing if I am dying. The faster, the better. My thumb is still depressing the button on the spout and liquid is still coming out. Only it's not water now. It's thick, red, and smells like copper. I fall to my hands and knees and vomit again.

Coffé is located in the student union, and my feet take me there of their own accord. Fucking feet, taking me places I don't want to go. Maybe I'd be better off if someone ate them.

The place is crowded as usual, but it's completely silent, except for light jazz playing through the ceiling speakers. The customers sit upright and unmoving, naked and very dead. They're missing limbs, and what's left of their bodies is covered with tooth marks. Their wounds look fresh, and blood drips to the floor, pools around chair legs. I recognize some of the dead as students and faculty I've seen around, but I don't know them personally, couldn't tell you their names. Stephanie, Alan, Celia, Justin, and Randy are here, as is Professor Buchanan, Cathleen Halloway, and Becky. I'm surprised to see Becky—I thought she would be the one waiting for me here at the end. But of course, she isn't. That role belongs to someone else and always has.

Tara sits alone at a table in the center of the room, looking very much alive and exactly as she did on the night we watched *Flesh-*

Eaters of the Amazon. In fact, the DVD of the film sits on the table, along with a pair of drinks, one for her, one for me. There's a plate of cookies in the center of the table, and at first I think they're animal crackers, but I see that they're in the shape of people. People crackers. Tara smiles warmly and waves me over. I don't want to sit with her, but I'm so fucking tired that I can't stay on my feet anymore, so since I have to sit somewhere, I suppose it might as well be with her. It's better than sitting next to eviscerated corpses, though not much.

I fall into the chair opposite Tara and nearly fall right out again. I grip the edge of the table with both hands and manage to remain seated. She pushes one of the cups toward me.

"It's black and hot, just the way God intended," she says.

I don't reach for the cup. After my hellish trek through the jungle, I never want to drink anything hot again.

She shrugs. "Suit yourself." She takes a sip of her drink. I don't know what it is, and I don't give a shit. It could be battery acid for all I care.

"Been a long time," she says.

"Not long enough." My voice is raspy, and it hurts to talk, but my words are clear.

"Your movie is almost over."

"I know."

"It's a piece of shit. Did you know that too?"

I don't answer.

"It's childish, slapdash, shallow, and worst of all, *derivative.*"

I start to get angry now.

"It's a commentary—"

"The only commentary in your film is what a bad writer and director you are. If you'd finished the film the way you intended and showed it to the class, Mercedes would have recommended that you *not* move on to the second year. She'd would've told you that you aren't without some small measure of talent, however, and that if you wanted to take the first-year classes over, she and the other faculty would reconsider next spring—providing your second thesis film was good enough."

Her words hit me like a punch to the gut.

"You're lying."

"You know I'm not. You can feel it."

It's true. I refuse to acknowledge it, though.

THE LAST CANNIBAL MOVIE

"The cannibal is a powerful metaphor for—"

"You know what metaphor the director of this film—" she taps the case of *Flesh-Eaters of the Amazon*—"was going for? Violence and gore equal money. He copied other, better cannibal films, none of which were all that good to begin with, crapped out this turd in less than three weeks, delivered it to the studio, got his check, and moved onto the next piece of shit he was hired to make. He died of a heart attack before he could start shooting that picture, though, which was a blessing for the world of cinema."

"But *my* film—"

"Is about how people use one another, symbolically devouring both themselves and others. It's not a difficult concept. Nor is it a particularly original one, and you used Cathleen Halloway's murder to add an extra level of transgression to your film."

She takes a cookie from the plate and holds it out for me to see. It's shaped like a woman, a very *specific* woman. Cathleen.

"The man who killed her used her, too. He spent the next twenty years using other women the same way before he finally died of pancreatic cancer. You could've made a serious film about Cathleen, and even if you fictionalized her story, it would've been more real, more *honest*, than the shit you came up with."

She pops the Cathleen cookie into her mouth, bites down, chews, swallows. When she's finished, the real Cathleen—or at least her corpse—disappears from the table where she was sitting, leaving an empty space.

"You used Mercedes, or at least you hoped to. You didn't care about what she could teach you, so much as you cared about what she could do for your academic career."

Tara selects another cookie, this one resembling Professor Buchanan. She puts into her mouth, chews, swallows, and the professor's corpse vanishes.

"You used your classmates to help you make your movie, but you wouldn't help them with theirs."

She chooses six cookies this time, each resembling one of my friends. She examines the cookie that resembles Becky and puts it back on the plate. She eats the other five, with the same results as before, and the wounded, unmoving bodies of my friends fade from existence. But not Becky. Her cookie is still intact, and so is her corpse. Tara picks up the Becky cookie again.

"This one used *you*. She was horny and you were available. She liked you enough to fuck you at least once, but she had no intention of starting a relationship with you. As far as she was concerned, the two of you were friends with benefits, and *friends* was stretching it."

She takes her time chewing the Becky cookie, and because of this, the Becky corpse takes a while to discorporate. Pieces of her disappear, bit by bit, until finally there's nothing left but lonely, empty space. I feel a pang when she's gone. Maybe she *was* using me, but that was okay. Sometimes it's nice to be used. I look at Tara.

Sometimes it isn't.

"You used me more than anyone," I say.

She nods, lifts her cookie doppelganger from the plate, holds it out to me. I take it, hold it gently between my thumb and forefinger.

"I sure did. My parents neglected me emotionally from the day I was born. Alcohol was their first, true love, and while they fed and clothed me, they spent most of their money on booze. Is it any wonder that I was craving some affection, and that I didn't care what I had to do to get it, or how many people got hurt in the process? Did you know my parents died in a drunk-driving accident less than three weeks from when your mother forbade me from seeing you anymore? After that, I was sent to live with an aunt in Connecticut, and I never saw you again."

"Lucky me," I say.

"What you really wanted to do was make a movie about what happened between us. But you were too scared to dig that deeply into yourself, too worried how other people would see you once they found out your secret. But that's what an artist—a *true* artist— is supposed to do. Go deep, deep as you can, find your pain, rip it out, and serve it for others to feast upon. Take, eat; this is my soul. I know what I did to you is beyond forgiveness, but I hope in time you'll—"

I make a fist around the Tara cookie and crush it. The real Tara collapses into fragments of flesh and bone, which splatter to the floor like cast-off pieces of meat in a slaughterhouse.

"Fuck you" I mutter, then I wipe my hand on the edge of the table to remove the cookie residue from my palm.

The dead bodies that remain in Coffé come to life then, or at least a version of it. They stand stiffly and begin awkwardly advancing toward me with hungry moans, hands outstretched, mouths wide.

I realize this has now become a zombie movie. Fuck, Tara was right. This *is* a clichéd piece of shit.

Some cookies remain on the plate, and one of them looks very much like me. I take it, hold it up to my eyes, inspect it. Yes, it is me. Cookie-me is sitting down at a table, looking at something he's holding in his hand. Another cookie, no doubt. Cute.

The zombies have almost reached me, and I'm too tired to try to fight them off. Hell, I'm not sure I can stand up right now. I look at cookie-me who's looking at yet another cookie-me, and so on, perhaps ad infinitum. If an artist's career goes on long enough, they eventually start repeating themselves, don't they? Cannibalizing their earlier selves. Maybe I should go ahead and get it over with now.

I open my mouth, place cookie-me on my sandpaper-dry tongue, and start to chew.

I AM THE RAINBRINGER

ANDREW NADOLNY

PART I

I

AT THE END of John Woo's *The Killer*, Ah Jong and Jennie, so pitifully in their ill-fated love, crawl toward each other, both blind, as Ah Jong is bleeding to death. They crawl past each other, just missing one another, as Ah Jong's last few moments of life pass by in that cruel desperation. It's incredibly sad, and as I watched it late at night on VHS, I remembered how hard I cried at that ending scene, only to peer up and see my dad—never "father"—staring at me from the door of my bedroom. I sat on the mattress with my knees pulled up, wearing my flannel pajamas, gazing up at him sniffling, reaching for a tissue without saying anything.

The credits were just starting to roll and even as I seemed to lose vision, I could hear him say angrily, "If you loved me, you'd be crying for me instead of that movie."

And then he left.

I swallowed without saying anything to his slowly retreating back. Because I'd said it so many *many* times more than I ever had since finding out he was sick. It didn't mean anything, though. Words were only words, and it was my actions that belied those words said so many times in response to him telling me blackly, coldly, that I secretly hated him.

If you loved me. . .

The nice thing about working at the video store in the mall was that my boss let me use the store as my own personal rental library, as long as I got the guy at the game store by the food court to shrink-wrap the tapes so he could resell them. I returned *The Killer* the next Saturday I worked, swapping it out for something else Dad and I could watch together that evening.

Dad's horror movie standards were always higher than mine. Before he got sick, he would sift through stack after stack of "stupid, stupid, boring, stupid" at the Movie Lobby until hitting on a gem he would declare satisfactory. This Saturday, left on my own to decide, I picked *Wes Craven's New Nightmare* since it was on sale, and it had been a while since we had seen it. I recalled he had actually liked it, and I didn't think I would be as scared this time around.

It was the scene with the dinosaur that had done it. The kid finds the stuffed toy ripped to pieces because it had kept him safe from Freddy, and I actually felt myself almost crying as Dad and I watched it because it reminded me of him and how he still made me feel safe from the monsters even as sick as he was.

It was that momentary terror of losing him, waking up and seeing him ripped to shreds at the foot of my bed that made me close my eyes and turn away and tell myself not to cry because I didn't want to make him mad at my crying; I made sure I never cried at another movie no matter what.

I used to cry easily when I was a kid, and Dad would tell this story about me being in kindergarten and bursting into tears every time this one kid would hit me—or so the teacher said—and it's hard to imagine now because I can still remember in middle school my dad standing with me out back, showing me how to make a fist, telling me about some kid on the bus who was putting lipstick on all the freshmen when he was starting high school sometime back in '61 or thereabouts.

Dad, who was a giant even then, picked him up and slammed him against the ceiling and dropped him; no one messed with him after that. I thought I wanted to be just like that, so I made sure to pay attention when Dad told me how to throw a punch and how to get in someone's face and how to pick them up and toss them. I would do it because I'd give anything to be like him. He would nod smiling, ruffle my hair and say, "That's my girl," as if he'd never had a doubt in his mind that I could do anything he believed I could.

It was his heart that turned against him. That's how I think of it, anyway. It was his damn stupid heart that seemed to beat just fine until one day it didn't. He went to the doctor because he kept swelling up bigger and bigger and couldn't breathe and his skin would split like a hot dog on the grill and ooze water. He told me he'd have nightmares about suffocating to death and the doctor said it was his heart.

I AM THE RAINBRINGER

Congestive heart failure was what they said, except it wasn't that simple because Dad said nothing in his life could ever be that simple. He was also in a car accident in '72 and he technically died. My mom had cried because it was mostly her fault. So she said she'd marry him, after all. The engine had ended up in his lap, the steering wheel had split his face wide open, and they thought that's what killed most of his heart, leaving the rest to keep getting bigger and bigger; but it could only get so big, so there you have it.

Mom had turned against him, too, although that was before he had ever gotten sick. He'd said she probably only married him because she felt bad, and she wanted to get out of the house because my grandfather was a sonofabitch. It was also my grandfather who kept them together because he didn't believe in divorce, which didn't keep Mom from sleeping with the principal at the school where she taught. But Dad just shrugged in the end and said that was a lesson I should learn in life: everyone you ever love will turn against you and that's just how it goes. . .except for one person, one exceptional person who you can trust to love you unconditionally and never betray you and that's what matters more than words.

Words never meant much to Dad. I learned it *never* mattered much what I said once he got a notion about something. Once he got sick, the notion was that I didn't love him, and I wanted him to die. Some nights I would lay awake and look at the little popcorn stalactites on the ceiling and wonder if that were true. Sometimes I thought about him dying and it would make my heart seize in the same way it would if I saw a spider skitter across the floor, or if I thought I would fail a test, or if I thought I was about to trip and fall down the stairs

It feels like your heart stops, only you know it's still beating except you're cold and nauseous. You start to shake and you try to talk but your teeth chatter and you can't control it; nothing really makes it stop until it just does.

The thing I've always loved about movies is those scenes where you have this fantastic gesture a character makes, and the movie makes it better than a book because the words can't bring the music with the soft piano or the violins, the crescendo or the dim fluttering light, the pan of the camera, or the filters letting just the right color palette set the mood.

Books and words and the pictures they paint are limited to

everything you've experienced in your life, but if your life is short and pointless and stupid like mine has been, that only takes you so far. But when you watch that scene on the screen, especially in a theater, when the salt from a hot dog and pretzel bites hits your tongue, just as the salt from your tears creeps into the corner of your mouth, it's kind of a magical amalgamation of experience. At least it was back when I still cried at movies, anyway.

So I thought of the scene. I do that sometimes: visualize something I'm going to do like it's a scene from a cinematic masterpiece. I think of the gestures, the dialogue, the inflection, the lighting, right down to my hand's movements—what would be the most dramatic, the best way to convey exactly what I'd like the audience to feel and see.

I sat at my desk and thought about something that would make dad happy and know that I loved him and didn't hate him. I drew little doodles of "S S S" in my notebook like I used to in fourth grade, looking at the pens and other art supplies. The long-handled metal scissors glinted sharp and heavy in a soft, warm spotlight. I swallowed because it would be touching. It would be beautiful. I only hoped it wouldn't hurt too much if I really had to do it.

He was at the kitchen table, talking on the phone, and I paused before I got to the doorway, standing just out of his line of vision because I wasn't quite sure this was right; the phone hadn't really factored into the scenario, and these were the sorts of moments where you expect the audience to put their full attention on you. I swallowed, and my hands shook.

I stepped into the kitchen, in my pajamas on a Friday afternoon, and I asked him if that was the doctor and if that meant he would have to have a heart transplant. It was, and he would. So there went the scissors in my hand and I told him through tears— these ones were good and genuine I think—that he could have my heart.

In retrospect, I'm not even sure where I was going with that one because I would've had to stab myself, and the heart would've been most logical except he needed the heart. Thankfully, I didn't have to work out that detail because he was already wrestling the scissors from my hand as I raised them.

Both of us cried, and it was rather nice. That was worth a few weeks of goodwill as he told all his friends on the phone how much I cared about him before he remembered I hated him and wanted him dead—that was because I had let my clothes pile up too much in my room. I'm not really sure why I even let things get cluttered like that when I actually prefer my space to be neat and tidy.

It seemed to me New Jersey got an inordinate amount of rain in relation to the popular conceptions about its weather. Sometimes I liked it and sometimes I hated it. I either love or hate the rain, depending on who I'm talking to and what seems like it would be the most impactful and interesting thing to say at the time. I'm not really sure whether I like it or not, actually, but if there's one thing I am utterly, unflinchingly uncompromised in, it's my thought that rain is lazy, cinematic symbolism and I wish people would do away with it entirely.

It doesn't mean anything, and any time you either see it on screen or read about it in a story, the creator is trying to convey a *mood* or tell you something; you're supposed to glean some deeper meaning and understanding. It was raining on the day my dad died, and it didn't mean anything except that it was harder to carry his coffin through the cemetery and my hair got wet and a few people skipped out on the funeral who might have otherwise showed up. The sun was shining when my mom died, if I recall, and I wasn't invited to the funeral, anyway, so who the hell cares that the weather was nice.

There's a great scene in this anime called *Rurouni Kenshin* where one of the antagonists, a young man named Soujiro, is relating the story of killing his (adoptive) family—ostensibly in self-defense, the story implies—and they had abused him, anyway, so they really had it coming. But it was raining as he looked up to the night sky, and the fugitive Shishio, whom he had been secretly hiding, came upon him and asked if he was crying. He turned with the most brilliant, beaming smile, and replied through that wet expression, no he wasn't.

Then there's this *brilliant* scene later where he suffers a mental break and the words flash across the screen in a moment of revelation that, in fact, he wasn't laughing in the rain but was crying. I've heard that in songs as well. It sounds deep and poetic the first one or two times you encounter that trope, until you become cynical and realize that "crying in the rain" is a tired, overused metaphor that passed cliché and now borders on self-parody.

It was raining that Saturday night when Dad and I finished

watching *New Nightmare*—a steady, drenching rain, not the type that produces lightning or thunder or good drama, just rain beating steadily on the roof, just me watching it through the drapes Dad and I had bought last year, and I drifted for a while. I remember watching *Poison Ivy* with Drew Barrymore when I was like thirteen or fourteen and thinking how absolutely thrilling it must be to fuck on the hood of a car in that sort of steady cool, rain on a day when it's just warm enough to be perfect on feverish skin.

I didn't see Dad get up and go out back until he came storming back in, yelling for me. Our house shared a driveway with the neighbors behind us, and as I threw on my shoes and jacket, I could see he had the driveway gate open. He shoved his truck keys into my hand as he thundered onto the deck. His hand crept up to his chest with every step—to his heart—and my head echoed the doctor's ever-present diagnosis "at high risk for sudden death." It was the most hideous metronome ticking that *anything could kill him, anything could kill him, eh-nee-thing-cood-kill-him.*

I swallowed. I asked what was going on. He looked grim. He was shaking. *He could die tonight. He could die. . .now.* Not worries, worries gnawed, they didn't bite like these thoughts bit, took hold, sank teeth deeper and deeper, drawing blood spilling from my heart to flood my body, same as his. *He could die tonight. He's going to die tonight.*

He was yet again having an argument with the neighbors, because he was always at odds with one of them for some reason or another. I could feel that cold gripping heart stop, that ice that made me commiserate in cardiac suffering before bursting in a flood that made it hurt to breathe. My own blood pounded in my ears as he ripped the truck door open and told me to get in, start it up, this is it, *be ready.* I turned over the engine and he took the lead, headed to the edge of the driveway where there were several people. He told me I needed to watch out for him. I needed to be the one protecting him, now. He told me if he was in trouble. . .if he called for me. . .if he raised his hand and gave the signal, that I had to go.

If you love me. . .

I'd have to kill them all.

I AM THE RAINBRINGER

Reading *Wizard's First Rule,* it always stuck out to me the way in which Confessors were selected: Prospective young female candidates' families were attacked, and should they be unwilling to raise a sword or knife or whatever the hell else to try and defend their families, they were deemed the ideal candidates because "the greatest cruelty comes from the greatest kindness," or some bullshit like that.

I never understood how it could be that anyone, even a child, could be unwilling to defend their family no matter who it was that stood in front of them. That night, I sat in the truck as it ran, deep breath, deep breath, watching for that signal because it didn't matter that I never wanted to hurt anyone, it didn't matter if the law or the Bible or God or Godot or who the fuck ever said killing is wrong because, if killing for him was what he wanted me to do, then there was no room for hesitation.

I stared at them, hearing their voices as a large woman wearing a *McDonald's* manager uniform stared at me with an expression I didn't understand. I only glanced back at her long enough to see her transform before my eyes into a Lovecraftian monster that wanted nothing more than to draw every last bit of the life force out of Dad.

She was pointing at me, one tentacle rippling in the dark night streetlight, reflecting off its suckers as another tentacle reached for Dad. It struck me as the most preposterous thing anyone, even a little girl, could cower and tremble and watch her dad be murdered in front of her because there is no life—*no life*—more important than his, and I owed him my everything and he was my everything. I turned on the headlights.

My hands were steady on the wheel.

My foot was steady on the gas.

The neighbors scattered—an angry murder of crows into the bushes, into the street. They were screaming. It had to be them screaming, and I only slammed on the brakes to avoid hitting the houses across the street. I twisted around in the driver's seat. They were gone. Dad was there. And he knew I loved him again. I smiled at him in the rain.

There were cops, but only because Dad called them. They took a report; they talked to Dad, they talked to the neighbors, *McDonald's* Woman was bellowing like an old iron freighter, they talked to her, too. One cop laconically took notes telling us all to keep to ourselves. Dad said, "attempted murder." *McDonald's* Woman said, "attempted murder." The Keystone Kops told us all to keep on our own property as they piled back into their old paddy wagon and sped off to some jaunty old instrumental.

It was late, so Dad took us out to get *McDonald's* where he complained when they didn't toast the bun on his Quarter Pounder, then drove his new F-150 fast down the highway playing "Weird" Al Yankovic's *Dare to be Stupid*. I remembered I had to work a few hours the next day, still had to study for midterms, remembered he was still dying, remembered life would just stop, a film reel with the tape snipped right in the center, and then just black screen, the sound of popcorn being crunched amidst some disgruntled grumbles.

2

The best thing about being adopted is you never worry about being unwanted by your parents—at least not the ones who actually count. You can also live the rest of your life never having to think about them having sex. I once got into a fight with a kid at school who called the people who provided my DNA my "real" parents. Dad always told a story I faithfully repeated, even after I was old enough to understand adoption doesn't actually work that way. He and my mom went looking for a baby to adopt and took me home because I looked like a little monkey, and he thought that was cute.

I used to have nightmares about my "other" parents coming for me. Dad was always the one who would hold me, tell me it was okay, and how that was never going to happen. I saw an episode of *20/20* one day when I was older. It was about a girl who found out her parents weren't her real parents—she was actually kidnapped and "something something" trauma. I didn't understand that, because I had already decided if someone had said that to me, I didn't care, it wouldn't matter, and I would do anything I could to get back to Dad; Mom, maybe not so much. I didn't see her much after she ran off with that principal—who never was and never would be my "pal"—so she didn't factor into the equation.

I AM THE RAINBRINGER

(Dad liked to say God kept him alive during that car crash so he could be my dad, although my aunt Agnes said God was the reason he got sick—because he was an arrogant and loudmouth piece of shit—but so was she, which was why they never got along. She also never got over being cut out of Grandmom's will because she walked out of the room when the doctor at the nursing home told her and Dad that someone would need to move in with Grandmom in order for her to go home.)

I never told him I stopped believing in God some time right around Christmas in '93 when I caught him wrapping my Christmas presents and found out *he* was really Santa Claus. It stood to reason that in my world, Dad was the closest thing to God I was ever going to get. Sometimes I wonder if his getting sick wasn't really just God punishing me for thinking those sorts of things, but my friend Louis would definitely tell me that's just narcissism on my part. That's probably true because Dad liked to tell me I was selfish and it was a good thing I had never wanted children because I was too self-centered to be a good mother, anyway.

Dad was always a good judge of character.

I remember when I was ten, walking into his room one night after watching TV, recounting to him with some confusion that thinking about April O'Neil topless gave me a "funny feeling down there." He just shrugged, said it was normal, and went back to watching Howard Stern. I suppose that was as close to a "coming out" story as I'll ever have, but it was just a silent understanding after that: I liked girls just like I did boys, and I would tell him about different classmates I had crushes on over the years. That lasted until I realized I was too ugly/weird by whatever esoteric standard my peers decided these things on and decided to focus my energy on eating junk food, watching TV, and reading books instead.

I saw the counselor who heard me talk about my anxiety with maybe having to kill someone; I guess I was a little more bothered at first than I thought. She looked like she was talking to Hannibal Lector himself, so I realized my problems were probably too weird and unique to be talked about in that sort of forum, so I just needed to man the fuck up and deal with them.

ANDREW NADOLNY

This brings the circle back to 1999 when I got my job working at the video store where I proceeded to turn around and deposit each paycheck back to buy movies. That was when Dad got sick. We got that news on a sunny day, too, so I guess that's the universe keeping the balance or some shit. We also got the Internet, and I found people to talk to. It was nice being able to chat on the computer late at night, but it was also kind of lonely because the people I talked to were words on the screen and not words in my ear, words from a voice in a throat, words from a face that looked me in the eyes, words from a body who held my hands—a body with arms that hugged me. I didn't like the phone much, either. Sometimes I just wanted to talk about silly stuff without Dad there, but he always thought I was talking about him or telling people weird lies like Mom used to. I never understood that; but he would say it was because I was a "woman in training" which was a phrase I always hated because I'd have rather been more like him than anyone else.

I *did* ask once my freshman year of college if I could go to a queer meetup after classes, because up until then my vaunted college career consisted entirely of driving to class, messing around on my laptop, then coming home without talking to anyone, but he thought that was a stupid waste of time, so I didn't bother. We *did* go out to see *Jeepers Creepers* which was fantastically scary until they actually showed the monster and then I stopped caring. Things that you can't see are always a lot scarier until you get a good look at them.

Unless it's bugs, then all bets are off.

I've been terrified of insects ever since I was four years old. I lifted a wooden pallet in our yard, and it seemed like every pill bug on Earth swarmed out to kill me; it didn't help that Dad had always called them "trilobites" where my peers had always called them the innocuous "rolly pollies." But Dad always protected me from all the crawly things, and even after he got sick, he was the first one I ran to if there was a spider or a centipede. Finding one under my dresser one night, I went to his room and knocked. All of eighteen years old, I stood there asking in a small voice if he could help because I was scared.

He told me how stupid it was even as he was getting up, his face screwed up in pain because sometimes sudden exertion hurt his heart; I tried not to cry because if he died it would definitely be my fault when getting up and down on the floor was something he shouldn't be doing. I stepped back with my sleeves over my face because I didn't want to cry over something so stupid when it hadn't happened. I needed to be able to handle these things because (as he'd gotten fond of saying) it wouldn't be long until he was gone and I'd have to do this myself, have to do that myself, and I swore, I *swore* I wouldn't live a day past him. I reaffirmed this to myself every time he talked about insurance policies or bank accounts or anything useful because you don't need that sort of thing when your world ends.

The first time I saw *The Sixth Sense,* I conceived of this notion that maybe Dad and I weren't really alive anymore just like Bruce Willis's character. The way it played out for me, Dad had died in '73 and I had died in '93. When I was ten, I had hopped on a public bus instead of going to school because I overheard Dad telling Grandmom he'd heard Mom was sick. She was at a hospital in Philly, but she didn't want to see him. I thought maybe she would want to see me. When I asked Dad if I could see her, he said it wasn't a good idea before reminding me all the negative feelings she had, had nothing to do with me.

I've never understood the whole idea of kids blaming themselves when their parents have trouble or get divorced or whatever, because as long as I could remember, Mom and Dad never argued about *me* and every time I heard her on the phone complaining to a friend, it was always about "that bald headed bastard." I'm pretty sure I didn't have anything to do with that or with her screaming at him that she never loved him or that "If I loved you, I'd be upstairs fucking your brains out, right now." And then one day she was gone; I came home from school, opened the door, and all the furniture that wasn't mine was moved out. I felt terrible about that, because a lot of Dad's things were gone, too; nothing of mine had even been touched. He just stood there when he got home from work and didn't say anything at all when I asked if we'd been robbed.

If you loved me...

From the bus, I'd hopped on the train from the station in

ANDREW NADOLNY

Trenton, and once I got to Philly, I realized it was a lot harder to get to the hospital than I expected. Between transfers and eating lunch it was already nearly three by the time I got there. It turned out she really *didn't* want to see me, either. So, like pretty much everything else, Dad was right. It wasn't raining that day, but it was one of those annoying partly cloudy days where the damn sky can't decide if it's going to be warm and welcoming or overcast and threatening, *and* it turned out it cost a helluva lot of money to call home from Philly since it wasn't "local." So as much as I would've wanted to call Dad, I couldn't afford it. Accepting I was definitely going to be late and get yelled at, I decided I may as well get *McDonald's* since they had the Halloween McNuggets and I really was hoping to get the vampire (I got the Frankenstein). I also spilled hot mustard on my shirt, so I mentally added that to the list of things that would get me yelled at as I got off the bus and trotted back down the block to home.

I can't even guess at how many times I've fallen down the stairs in my life, but in most instances, Dad was usually there waiting at the bottom to catch me. I would slip, would feel the world give way, feel my arms flying in all sorts of directions, feel my hands banging the walls and railings, feel. . .weightless. That was how it felt that night as I got off the bus and crossed the street, sniffing the night air, smelling that musty, nose-curling pre-rain musk I've always hated.

I remember the revving engine. The Polish teens liked to drag race down the street late at night, and the cops never wanted to deal with it because the center line divided two districts, and the teens always acted like they didn't speak English, anyway. No one had gotten hurt by their dumb shit to that point; I don't know if I could really say I'd been hurt, either, because I don't even remember going to the hospital when the car hit me. Or didn't hit me. Because I was weightless for a moment right after hearing the engine. . .and then I wasn't weightless because I was in Dad's arms just like when I would fall down the stairs.

I think I would've remembered getting hit by the car and dying.

Dad always said dying is something you definitely remember. You remember waking up on a table, sitting up, and staring down at doctors and nurses and machines you've never seen before, wondering where you are, and realizing you're peering down at yourself. So Haley Joel Osment was full of shit when he said the

I AM THE RAINBRINGER

dead don't know they're dead, because there's only one conclusion you can draw when you're standing over your own corpse seeing it full in the face: *Jesus Christ, do I really look like that?*

I don't remember much of that weightless night, which is odd because I'm sure Dad yelled a lot and said I was just doing this sort of shit to hurt him, except that doesn't ring a bell. All I can remember are flashes in some dream world of Mom saying I wasn't *her* daughter, I was *his* daughter, and telling Dad I would never love them like a real child would or something like that, remember her playing dead sometimes I think just to test me, remember how I'd scream and cry and beg her to wake up, remember...remember...There was something missing inside me because it was a test I never seemed to pass.

Dad saved my life, and I saved his (he said), so I suppose that made us even somehow, even if it never seemed to stick for him.

I remember Grandmom yelling at Dad sometimes when they got into a fight over her not taking her meds, or him being too bossy or overbearing, or her calling him an educated idiot and—funnily enough—a bald-headed bastard, while I sat in the living room on the red recliner eating Sugar Smacks out of a box of cereal watching whatever movie of the week was playing. I remember that, "I brought you into this world and I can take you out of it,." she would scream in triumphant conclusion. I wondered if that sort of bargain ever had an expiration date or if it continued *ad infinitum* until one of them died. It made a certain logical sense to me, too: that notion of owning a life whose existence was owed entirely to you. I tended to think that like baking a cake, it was yours to do with whatever you pleased until you either ate it or threw it away or gave it to a guy you were dating who'd take one bite, make a face like he just swallowed a molded mushroom wrapped in turd bacon, and tell you it was the best thing he'd ever eaten before taking another bite—or something like that. Metaphors were never my strong point.

That sort of scene always struck me as being cinematic perfection even if it was absolutely cliche; I made sure to add it to the scenes of my life that I'd like to perform some day.

ANDREW NADOLNY

As far as I was concerned, it was the same for Dad—more so if you think about the logic of it—and me, which is why it was all the more egregious that I was the one who killed him.

Dad told me I should make sure whenever he ended up dying, I would kill all his enemies for him. He had a rather macabre sense of humor at times, so I could be forgiven for thinking he was joking; except I wasn't completely certain he was. I thought about it, though, for a long time afterward. I remember this fantastic writer sometime somewhere penning this marvelous story of the trauma and aftermath and all that muck of being the one who gives the order to pull the plug on a parent, and I wonder if that's really the way those sorts of things work.

When Dad finally ended up in the hospital—walking in under his own power when, evidently, he was supposed to already be dead, go figure—it was, well. . .boring. The floor I had to sleep on was cold and wet because they'd just shampooed the carpet for the night. That shit soaked through every thin blanket they'd lent me that I tried to sleep on. All I honestly thought about was how uncomfortable I was, and how I really just wanted to sleep until finally it was morning, and things could get moving again. The doctor explained that his heart was basically fucked, which gosh golly gee he sure needed a PhD to explain it—with all the gravity of Jupiter's center.

It was incredibly annoying, because you think of the dramatic potential that's lost when you have some generic doctor speaking like he's reading from a cue card; you compare it to the bitter and beautifully awful black humor of Zhang Yi-mao's *To Live,* when the doctor who's there to save the daughter's life ends up unable to help her because his stomach full of rice incapacitates him. But in fairness, that's the sort of thing that's difficult to capture. Dad was lying there looking like he was already dead with a tube down his throat, oxygen stuffed up his nose, I.V.s and other lines running in and out of him, and the doctor told me Dad might live if I let them do some radical procedure to reroute *something to something to something else;* I can't recall the specific terms because it seemed Dad was screwed to the wall no matter what.

I AM THE RAINBRINGER

Maybe if I hadn't been having these intrusive thoughts of how much easier and cleaner things would be if he was gone, then maybe that fruit wouldn't have been borne into the present.

There's not much an extra tube or straw down someone's throat is going to do when someone like me just spent the last four years willing something into existence. Or maybe I should've just left it alone—should have known as many times as he'd pulled himself up and back for me that if I'd let him, he'd have done it one more time. But I didn't let him, because it seems I'm always making stupid decisions; I'd be the one fucking moron in a slasher film running up the goddamn stairs, when everyone in the audience is screaming at her so loudly it's actually satisfying when the axe or knife or whatever sharp thing, stabs her thirty improbable times while she flops around on the hospital room carpet and sprays blood.

So of course the procedure didn't work, and in the interim when the doctor told me to gather up all the family, it seemed a nice opportunity to take that literally and drive my F150 all around Jersey gathering people up like a Chicken Little sky-is-falling sort of thing. It made for a happy adventure. I made sure to play some good music, popping in an Eagles CD as I pulled up the driveway to pick up the one aunt who actually gave a shit: Dad's older sister, Aunt Shirley. That was followed by CCR when I drove to retrieve a friend of his who insisted she was far too distraught to drive.

I stopped at Aunt Agnes's and surprisingly it was my Uncle Kevin who answered the door, just as scary looking as he'd ever been. I screamed through the open screen door that Dad had died. He responded with an annoyed "Jesus Christ" coupled with an irritated look off to the side, so I made sure to let Aunt Agnes know she got her wish before stalking back down the driveway without another word, because that was the *best* way to play the emotionally impactful drama of the scene. As both director and star, I was supremely satisfied, not having missed a line or a word, and I made sure not to look back as I sped out of the cul-de-sac where they lived.

Dad died while I was gone. That seemed unfair to me as I walked back through the empty hospital hallways. I didn't think he'd actually die. How could he die? He was one of the main characters of my life, there from season one all the way until the finale, or at the very least not written out of the show until the end of season six because he got a better gig on fucking *Becker* or something.

No, those sorts of things don't actually *happen* unless they're supposed to, and this didn't seem like a supposed-to-type scenario; I didn't understand why he was cold when this wasn't really what was supposed to happen. I was done with scenes, I was done with make-believe drama; I just wanted to go back home with him to watch TV and mess around on my computer in the living room while he yelled at me for ignoring him and staying up too late and there were so many things I didn't take right and things I didn't say and he didn't say and I didn't get my redemption arc and. . .and. . .and. . .

Later I realized how absolutely stupid that was, because I can't stick with anything very long: Shortly after he died, I determined it would be good, it would be profound, it would be *beautiful* to visit his grave and speak to him aloud with every emotion notched up to eleven. Except that got boring fast, and I probably haven't been to that grave in well over a decade.

Of course it rained the day of the funeral. It was cold. It was utterly cliché except for my insisting on being a pallbearer; that was new and novel, though I didn't and still don't understand why. It seems only appropriate to me that children who are physically capable should bear the weight of their parents before anyone else does. That's not a burden girls should just get to opt out of. The funeral director disagreed, also thinking it was weird when I insisted Dad be buried in a T-shirt. It wasn't like some dry rotted band T-shirt he got in the seventies. It had a picture of me on it, screen printed when that shit was expensive. But I had the money to pay cash, so she shut up smugly reveling—at least that's how it seemed—when she watched me struggling with my part. The coffin was heavy as shit and Dad was just as solid as ever.

I don't remember much of the funeral; it was unremarkable and wasn't worthy of being remembered past that. Father Urich had such a thick Polish accent you couldn't understand a goddamn word he was saying at the eulogy or any other time. I'm sure it was really profound. It was nothing like in *Heathers* with that scene of Heather Chandler's funeral. Heather's when she's speaking with Veronica, or like the brilliant scene where Kurt's dad declares through tears, "I love my dead gay son." Hell, for all I know that's exactly what Father Urich was saying. I slept for most of the gathering afterward.

It also turns out Aunt Agnes didn't come to the door, or come to see Dad in the hospital, or come to the funeral because she had rheumatoid arthritis to the point where she couldn't even touch her own face. So I guess it's like they say, there *is* a God.

3

I'm not sure why, but I started going over there a lot. I guess I'd gotten so used to taking care of sick people it was easy to pick up: that whole thing about feeling needed or whatever. Uncle Kevin was at work all day—which was really for the best considering his idea of care involved bruises and spitting—so she was alone with my cousin, Nicole, who was ten years older than me. She wasn't cut out for living on her own, so she was Aunt Agnes's primary caregiver. I use the term loosely, because if you've ever seen that *Hoarders* show, that's more or less what the house looked like.

The kitchen counters were covered in cups, crockery, and cockroaches while Aunt Agnes declared the room behind Uncle Kevin's shut door was impassable and full of bags of shit-filled underwear because. . .Well, hell if I know why an able-bodied man would shit his pants for funsies so I left that one alone. The living room was the closest to clear with a path to walk through to reach a wall of rabbit cages that stank to high heaven a few feet from where Aunt Agnes slept in her recliner. A glass cabinet that ran half the length of the front was full of Furbies. I couldn't say which was more disturbing to look at.

I took some time off school because waking up was hard. Doing anything except driving around aimlessly was hard, and I found out you can take a few semesters to get your shit straight. It made me consider if someone in your family dies every few semesters, you could just stay enrolled as a student forever but never have to go back to classes. I never did decide if that appealed to me.

I figured I'd go back at some point, but I wasn't sure what I wanted to do. I was only going because Dad told me I had to. That was how I made it through a lot of that time: I thought of all the things Dad told me to do: I paid bills, I helped neighbors, I cleaned my room, I cleaned the kitchen, I called his friends, my aunts, my cousins, I helped his friends move furniture until for a while it seemed as if I just became him.

Except I kept coming back to that thing about his enemies and that was a pretty sizable list. Aunt Agnes was on it because of the rift she'd caused between Dad and Grandmom. She was on it because of an incident at Grandmom's funeral, because she called the cops on her eldest son—the only one not crazy and trying to actually get out, and lastly because she was a pretty terrible person even *before* getting sick. I've never understood how someone being ill suddenly makes them a good person, but that seems to be a common trope in "redemption arcs," which again, is absolutely lazy writing.

But I was spending so much time over there sitting on the couch between her and Nicole, a little butt spot carved out for me, I felt conflicted. I was alone in my house and being there felt like it was a chance to keep an important connection alive to my family. Dad always said family was important; but nothing was more important than loyalty. My visiting Agnes so often conflicted with my loyalty to him, and that was becoming harder and harder to reconcile. I felt bad while she cried, while she complained about how Uncle Kevin hit her, called her names, and threw Nicole against the wall, choking her. I sometimes saw spinning Visibar lights when I pulled in. The cops were always over there not doing shit, because Uncle Kevin would say she spit in his face or something. They were all his buddies. She seemed especially pathetic now, defanged from the great hulking creature she once was when I was younger—loud, brassy, and always arguing with Dad about something or another.

There's been a big movement nowadays about not making kids hug and kiss their relatives if they truly don't want to. That missed me by a few decades, so I always had to suck it up and hug a whole bunch of people who made my skin crawl, like Uncle Kevin. *Especially* Uncle Kevin. Not because he was the "bad touch" creepy uncle but because—at the risk of being dramatic—he gave off this dark aura like Christopher Walken in *The Prophecy* and I was terrified to be anywhere near him.

He was this tall, white-haired, scarecrow looking slender man with a long hook of a nose, thick eyebrows, and a way of looking down at everyone that made you feel like he was two steps away from summoning a thousand demons from Gehenna to smite you or rend your flesh. Dad always said he looked like an evil Steve Martin and therefore refused to watch anything with Steve Martin in it because he reminded him of Uncle Kevin. In retrospect if there was any positive to come out of having to give him a hug at Christmas and Thanksgiving, it was that he seemed equally repulsed by the familial affection convention.

The problem with Uncle Kevin as a villain is that he's so obvious. It doesn't work. It's especially lazy filmmaking. You throw in some haunting music when he enters the room, adjust your lighting to accent his most severe features, and you have a villain who's comically formulaic. I suppose you could add some character-developing monologue about how my aunt treated him like shit when she was healthy, or how his parents beat him or something because ontologically evil villains in horror are old hat. But as best as I could always figure, it really did just boil down to some disassociated apathy on his part for the people around him. You could say that's worse than outright malevolence because of its banal brutality.

That's also why *Hereditary* didn't work for me, even though millions of people dick ride it for God only knows what reason. If you spend ninety minutes clicking your nails on the arm of your chair in exasperation, praying for the aggravating bitch you're supposed to be rooting for to get hers, then you have a seriously poor protagonist. Of course you have movies full of obnoxious teenagers getting picked off one by one that still get classed as "horror," though I think of those as more tongue-in-cheek; you don't have something truly horrifying unless you give a shit about the person getting gutted in a forest by some inbred hillbilly. Watching some shit bag get his isn't horrifying. It's satisfying.

Which is all a long-winded way of saying nothing bad ever happened to my Uncle Kevin. In fact, he's still alive to this day, somewhere north of a thousand years old, just as healthy and hateful as ever. He was in a car accident a few years back getting off at an exit, rolled his car, trashed it, the thing caught fire, and he walked away without so much as a scratch. Don't get me wrong, I thought about killing him, but my Aunt Agnes is a much more tragic figure and that simply works better for the story.

ANDREW NADOLNY

The killing part isn't exceptional. The scene you really want to pay attention to is the dramatic confrontation which leads up to it. Aunt Agnes liked to tout all the good deeds she had done over the years as some cosmic proof her current health condition was the byproduct of an evil and malicious god, or a curse, or something other than a loss at the genetic lottery. She also liked to share stories of her youth, and more often than not they contradicted events Dad had talked about, naturally putting her in a much better light. Dad always said the reason Grandpop gave her his old car when they were teenagers is because she was the baby, she was the *favorite* and telling her this launched her into this long-winded story about her and Dad in a field trying to drive a stick. It devolved into her talking about what a stubborn asshole Dad was, and how Mom was a saint for marrying him. I never understood why Aunt Agnes and Grandmom, seemed to like my cheating and crazy mom better than Dad. That got annoying after a while.

It was especially annoying that night. I'd already been called over at 2 AM to take Nicole to the hospital because she was "in pain" from something or another. We never found out what. We sat in the ER most of the night only to be told to go home. So seven rolled around, and once again Mom was "Saint Patty" to Dad's overbearing intolerable male offensiveness. I reminded Aunt Agnes as I picked coffee grounds out of the dirty mug I was drinking from, that despite what Mom liked to tell people, Dad never laid a hand on her. In fact, she was the one who whaled on him when he wouldn't sign the custody papers. She also had me in therapy for a year so some quack could try and convince me Dad was molesting me. I could give a good voice crescendo at that revelation because Uncle Kevin was out, so I wasn't worried about him emerging from the bedroom like the phantom. I told her with a dramatic poignancy I was exceptionally proud of, that I still had nightmares about that as a result.

You can imagine my *annoyance* when she gave this stilted shrug in response and said "Well we all wondered." Annoyance then blossomed into a white-out anger that just sort of dropped and sat in my chest like a neutron star, the density pulling everything in until it was so heavy with rage there wasn't room for anything else. And then the cup broke. Held in my hand, the handle cracked off letting it drop to the stained carpet, splashing cold tea into a dozen other dried stains.

It was cinematic perfection. I must have replayed it at least three or four times in a slow black-and-white reel in my head before I decided to get up slowly and just look at her—look *through* her. Then I left. She was on the list, after all. There wasn't anything else that needed to be said. I heard her yelling after me. I heard Nicole yelling, too. It was tempting to say something dramatic or foreshadowing, but there's a certain art to foreshadowing that's difficult to capture. I could think more about that at home.

I didn't go directly home. I stopped at the cemetery and stood at Dad's grave, reminding myself I needed to figure out how the whole headstone thing worked because he only had a footer. I thought it would be a nice scene to talk to him, especially since it had been a while. I didn't talk to him out loud. I could hear him in my head telling me how stupid that was to say the sorts of things I was going to say out loud where anyone could hear me. So I knelt, clasped my hands, and spent a good while reflecting on how lost I was without him. He was right about Aunt Agnes. He was right about everything. I was going on twenty and still a giant aimless fuck-up. I was also failing most of my classes which I could fortunately do over once I went back. I thought about Aunt Agnes saying such a disgusting thing: *"We all wondered."* Grandmom had also once said because Dad and I spent so much time together and he tended to be overprotective, that it was i*nappropriate*. To love a daughter as I was loved to them was a sickness or maybe something I didn't deserve in their eyes. I'll never know. That day I prayed I didn't have another nightmare about it. Those sorts of dreams were especially awful.

It's always the same dream: some nowhere dreamscape where it's just me and Dad and we're on the way to fucking and in the dream it's something I want and long for and luckily I always wake up before it happens, sticky, aroused, crying, whimpering, dry heaving over the side of my bed and then I spend the rest of the day wondering what the fuck was wrong with me. It was worse once he was gone because, every once in a while, I found myself thinking that if it would bring him back. . .then that would be okay. . .if he was like *that*. . .if he was the monster mom tried to paint him out to be, that was okay if it would mean he was alive again. But that comes back around to my not knowing that I'd feel that way if he *had* been that sort of man. But then again, I remember he was my dad, and I owe him everything and—

If you love me. . .

That night, I set the house on fire.

Uncle Kevin was the only one who survived.

PART II

4

IT FELT LIKE magic the night I met Jonathan. Or should I say, "It was magic the night I met Jonathan." I think the latter. The scene opens with a voiceover. If the movie weren't already in motion, it would be a fantastic opening scene. It starts with a dramatic shot of the parking lot of the mall that night, before Amazon and online shopping, or the economy, or millennials, or sunspots, or whatever-the-fuck put most of them out of business. It's just after a rain in autumn, and the blacktop glitters from the yellow lights of the tall lamps, shimmering the puddles with oil rainbows. If you were foreshadowing, there would be a low bass—the type that reverberates in your chest—but I'd use a soft piano instead, maybe strings. There would have to be a trace of melancholy to it, something akin to that scene in *Titanic* with the old woman. It was bittersweet like that. I heard my own voice in my head saying that line right after I met him, right after he left.

That night, I was dressed up behind the counter in some retro-rockabilly-red-cherry dress from *Hot Topic*. He (yes, this first one absolutely has to be capitalized, because the sight of him *felt* so overwhelming) came to the counter in a black button-down shirt with the sleeves rolled up, tight around his biceps. I smiled at him as I picked up the *Key Largo* DVD and scanned it. I noticed his forearms first, the Japanese characters drawing my attention because of how much I loved anime, Japanese culture, and my kanji reading had gotten decent enough—notwithstanding my failing Intermediate Japanese II grade—that I could read the word for "Loyalty." As soon as the translation clicked, an even wider smile stayed glued to my face as I scanned up an open shirt collar to a dark brown beard, to a wild mop of hair that had been left

73

thoroughly untamed, and a small pair of silver glasses. I was still holding the DVD. I couldn't let it go because he smiled back.

He smiled back.

"Is there anything else I can get for you?" My voice came out sounding normal, which is wild, because the way these scenes go there's always a flicker or a falter, but no matter how hyper-aware you are of your changes in demeanor and posture and tone, they barely register. I've seen enough high school drama bullshit to know that, in real life, none of this crap actually shows on your face—unless it's directed with an accompanying score. Right then, the ambient music was the same episode of *Mystery Science Theater 3000* that had played several dozen times before. I was never so glad I was alone in the front of the store.

I hated looking people in the eyes. It made me irrationally nervous. Most days the best I could manage was a slight off cast glance to a cheek or a nose, but once my eyes tracked from that man's mouth to his eyes, I got caught. "Deer in the headlights" is such an overused simile that people will be bleating it out a thousand years from now when there are no more deer or cars or people, and whatever octo-jelly things we become swinging from trees with three eyes and a beak will still be burbling that same bullshit at each other. In the present though, meeting his eyes cued the soft strings to rise just a little bit, followed by the occasional painful piano break because of any come-on I'd gotten from middle-aged customers—and I'd put him at forty probably— nothing was like what he answered with, unscripted and so, *so* heavy.

"What if I wanted your soul?"

I licked my lips, peered down, looked to the side—left then right—and felt my heart race faster than it ever had in my life. I finally put the stupid DVD down; my mind was actually blank. Hand to God it wasn't just my heart; as my pulse raced, I felt *hot*. Like arousal dialed all the way to the max. I felt my face fill with blood at those words, at that look. I don't think it would have mattered if he looked like Clint Howard when he said those words to me. They held an intensity I'd never felt from another human being. It's crazy when you feel a rush like that, because it's like your dumb animal brain can't even process it right; you want to laugh, cry, swallow, and a bunch of other things all at once. The wheel spins and picks something to land on. The wheel spun for me, forcing some idling electric pulse to fire back up and birth a thought out of that short-circuited darkness. It was the overwhelming imperative *I want to be yours.* I leaned in, my arms purposefully crossed on the counter. That dress was cut kinda low, I had some decent sized tits, and sure as hell wasn't above using them.

Dad used to tell me I was a good-looking girl. If I stepped back and tried to look at myself like a casual observer I could see the appeal. But when you spend the better part of your life being called things like a dog, "Hairy Mary"—thank you childhood mustache—"Dandruff Girl," and all sorts of other flattering little nicknames, you tend to start viewing yourself out of that lens. You don't realize you're actually a fairly solid Fellini fuckable 8½ and not a "dying unloved with ten cats" 2. Working in the video store had been good in that regard. I had enough guys paying attention that it didn't seem so inconceivable that one would want to date me. Which was good because I was a horny little shit back in those days.

"And what would you do with it?" I asked him softly, spellbound, tilting my head like some twenty-degree coquettish thing. He leaned in to match me which did wonders for my panties. He smelled like warm vanilla. I was starting to wonder what he sounded like when he came.

"Anything I wanted," he whispered back, and I wanted to bite his lower lip just a bit. Love at first sight may be a stretch, but really love and lust and all that are just chemical reactions, and there were definitely chemicals doing their reaction thing. In that moment I utterly believed in everything he made me feel.

"Then it's yours." I tried a sultry whisper. For all I know it sounded stupid as shit, but the scene was so good, so right, the light on his face had just a hint of shadow; a mesmerizing image I could replay forever. I couldn't have scripted it better when he spider-walked his fingers over the counter and right to mine. His hand was warm. Mine was warm and a little sweaty.

"Is it really?" a drop in pitch, a little bass—commanding, like Dad could be—and I melted into him, watching his eyes flick from a pale brown into some golden vermillion sea. If I'd been directing this scene, I'd have insisted the whisper be kept. I'd have turned the rain back on so the steady beat of it could be heard on the roof. I thought what a beautiful backdrop the rain could've been if it wasn't a tired and overused trope. I even thought of the foreshadowing lightning strike, except that didn't happen until the night I went to his house.

"Yes."

The thunder and lightning didn't foreshadow anything; they just made it hard to get to his house and the power went out when I finally got there. There's this brilliant bittersweetness at the end of *Suzhou River*. Meimei's farewell note simply reads *"If you love me, come find me."* He had found me even though I didn't know I was missing. No, that's not correct. *Everything* had been missing, and everything was what he had found. That night, he put his hand to the side of my face—without a smile or care for some lady who decided to line up behind him with a stack of *Spongebob* DVDs—and ordered me like my goddamn God, *"If you're mine, then come to me and be mine."* He was God with the cinematic spotlights ringing around him like he was about to ascend, in this case the dusty focused register lights on the ceiling that were always hot. I went without hesitation.

He lived down south—down south like the Pine Barrens, New Jersey type of south, where everything looks the same, and there are deer, ticks, and second cousins who are probably fucking in the shacks hidden where there are more trees than grains of sand on the beach. There aren't any roads. There are only places to drive a car that aren't lit, places there may be potholes, places that may lead off into monsters and swampy lakes to drown if you're not careful. He gave me the address and wrote the directions down. I followed them in the darkness until I'm sure I missed a street named after a state, turned down Missouri instead of Montana and found myself parked by a lake. I remembered driving around it earlier, looking out on the water as the rain turned to a little drizzle. I thought of the artistic wavering shots of the river in *Suzhou River*, and thought what a lovely picture it would be if there were a violin accompanied by a haunting Hungarian Rhapsody. I played it in my head. I heard Jan A. P. Kaczmarek's *The Death* wafting faintly in the air. Long notes were drawn out when I sat in the grass right before the muddy bank and looked out over to the other side.

The moon was the only light, and it was still cold enough in

I AM THE RAINBRINGER

March that there were no crickets or cicadas. The world was still frosted over death outside. My fishnet stockings had ripped. I adjusted the knee-high boots I thought were sexy but weren't really because they weren't heels. I stared at my fat tits and fatter stomach wrapped in a faux-vinyl dress from *Hot Topic* that was the only 2x they had in the store. I started chewing on my too long—too thick—split ends, wanting to skip a stone across the lake and wish that I could be better than I was. My glasses slipped on my face. I pushed them back up, then pulled the folded directions out from my purse, reading them again, out loud this time, with only that moon, for light, whispering softly, desperately—and very prettily, I thought—*"I will find you. I will find you."*

I turned just in time to see the headlights of an old Chevy Celebrity crossing the single lane bridge and I smiled. If I was behind the camera, I would've filmed the shot in black and white. It would've been stylized and in a slower frame when the car pulled next to mine, and then him stepping out of it. I would've started to pan up from his muddied, dirty boots that were knee-high like mine, wrapped around his calves, thick thighs in tight dark gray denim, the camera-eye moving slowly up to a vest that stopped low enough to invite the eye to linger at his crotch—the camera would linger just a beat longer—then to a rumpled tie that looked like it had bleeding lines or bloody tears, rising to a shirt with the sleeves rolled up, and then, finally, to the tattoo.

There would be absolutely no color until the camera reached the end of his dimly flaring cigarette—American Spirits, he told me later—and a pair of small glasses that would be mirrored like Elijah Wood's playing that psycho Kevin in *Sin City*. There was a similar sense of understated danger that made me shiver in the cold as I brushed myself off and found myself whispering, *"You came for me. . ."* because it was the perfect line to say. He caught it like a precious butterfly landing on the tip of his finger.

There are so many cliche lines that irritate you in film. "I thought you weren't coming" takes the lead, being not just one of the most inane, pessimistic, and self-deprecating things to say, but also one of the most dishonest. In reality, most people will sit there for two goddamn hours while a waiter refills the water and brings another free basket of chips, before shuffling back to whisper pityingly about your plight to his coworkers, while you sit there with your head turning at every ding of the bells jangling above the door—and you keep up with this pointless exercise until the place closes and they gently escort you to the door, praying that whatever social malaise you must obviously possess isn't contagious. It's only real when you show that hope wilting over the course of those hours: not having some Conventionally Attractive Asshole with perfect white teeth telling Generically Aesthetic Blonde #2—after waiting a whopping five minutes—he thought "she wasn't coming." Fuck that noise.

Jonathan didn't just hold out his hand, but bent down in front of me, dropping that cigarette in the dirt with a soft brush of lips to my forehead, before taking my hand in his like a child. He told me he was too impatient, it had been so long, he needed me, he couldn't wait, I was beautiful, I was everything he had ever dreamed of or wanted in a woman. I stood up equally impatient, put my arms around his neck, peered up, tilted my head, and prayed silently for the rain to fall again—it had to be here where this night, this scene made it *perfect.* I thought of a brilliant line to say when I looked over my glasses, catching sight of the moon in his. That picture made me tremble because I could feel the mist it reflected, could feel the fog as I told him *he* was everything *I* had ever dreamed of in a man, threading my fingers through his thick mane of hair, watching him swallow and shake and tell me *"you have to get in the car now, please."*

I got in his car, abandoning mine where it was parked.

He went from 10 to 20 to 30 on those dark wooded roads, faster and faster until it seemed as if there were faces in the trees. Not just the trees but faces in the darkness as the rain started up again. I watched the faces of the woods mold into these wide eyeless grins that stretched across pine. I watched the rain batter them, and it made me think of the last song of *Fantasia*—of Czernebog pulling the souls of the dead into the sky—and I swear I saw them flickering as he put his hand on my knee and told me he needed to fuck me as soon as we got to the house. I'd forgotten the scene, swept away in the illusions of the forest, as I put my hand over his hand and squeezed it tightly, asking him if he'd ever seen *Night on Bald Mountain.*

"I was thirteen when Dad took us up to see it in New York. In Flushing specifically, back when Laces was still there, and you could still roller disco. Never did; don't ask. My Uncle Bob still lived there with my cousins. Only family on their block who you'd

I AM THE RAINBRINGER

catch eating a pastrami sandwich on white bread with mayo, if you get my drift. Dad and him both wanted to show us all something from their childhoods. Let me tell you, it scared the shit out of me. Aunt Hen—what we called my Aunt Henrietta—already took my youngest cousin Matt home because he was bored and wouldn't shut up, and when shushing him didn't work, he threw up his popcorn all over. . .Fan-fucking-tastic film. The original and the one I saw all used the Rimsky-Korsokov arrangement, but then in 1982 Irwin Kostal did the re-record which was fucking brilliant. I have it. He was an amazing composer—just died a few years ago. Okay I'm going to shut up because you *don't* care about any of this, do you?"

It was a door that had opened. I realized we had stopped. We were in a driveway, and I didn't know when the car had stopped moving, or when his hand slipped out from under mine, because we just sat there in silence when I saw the lightning flash over the top of the trees. I expected the thunder, but I didn't hear any; there was a door that had opened, and he walked into the mouth of Hell—or (as he would later tell me) into the darkest edges of the north side of the Third Heaven (the *actual* location of Hell)—as the Dark Prince himself, and there he lingered. The door seemed to swing back and forth like a flip book, flickering to the image of a shy bookish boy who I imagined him once to be. I saw lines, like the scene in *Robot Carnival,* the short film *Presence,* the female robot once beloved of the man, broken and quiet in the corner, covered in cobwebs.

The door shut, breaking that trance, and I peered up to see him crawling toward me on the bench seat slowly, inexorably like the tide lapping up over my feet. He pushed my skirt up and looked me in the eyes, his bright—burning Tyger bright—with the drizzle outside steadily increasing. I saw myself back on my hands, trembling, his face a blur as I thought of every screaming slutty horror girl slaughtered by the killer, devoured by the monster—by the Conqueror Worm, the inevitable death of the mimes onstage— as he told me he was going to rip my stockings off. His fingers squirmed between knitted loops, pulling like a speculum, like Devastator in the original '86 *Transformers* movie tearing the Autobot's base wide open, and my eyes adjusted just enough to see his shadowed face in black and white once more.

I let myself fall back on that plush cushioned seat. The shadows fell even over the gleam of his eyes. He fucked me. "Fuck" was a verb, a noun, an adjective, a goddamn *prayer* in that car with my hands banging the dash, the window. Then grabbing his hair, grabbing anything I could reach and try and rend from his body deeper into mine. He snarled like a goddamn werewolf when I grabbed his ass and dug my nails in; they never show that shit in those over-sanitized pretty bedroom scenes, we were Cronenberg crashing, that's what we were. I made him bleed and he made me bleed and I'm pretty sure we ruined the goddamn upholstery as I turned my head toward the windows of his darkened house where a dozen ghosts were watching me, welcoming me home.

Dad never believed in locked doors, closed doors, or anything that would mean I was *trying to hide something*. I came to take it for granted that anything I ever wrote down—anything I kept a record of—was done so with the intent of it being read. When you love someone, you don't keep secrets from them. You tell them everything: every little ugly dirty thought that passes from your soul to the electrons firing off impulses in your little ugly dirty brain. I told Jonathan everything I needed in that moment, dirty, sinful, pure, innocent, beyond provocative prose and into the delirious dreams my very soul cried out for.

I loved Jonathan from the moment I kissed him in the darkness. I loved him the same way Aunt Agnes told me Dad had loved when he loved a girl—with this intensity that bordered on madness. He proposed to every girl he dated on the second or third date, and that was the sort of conviction I admired about him. It's the sort of thing they call "toxic" nowadays, the sort of thing people tweet about, and the sort of possessive madness that had Patrick Bergen chasing Julia Roberts across the country when she left him in *Sleeping with the Enemy*. That's the beautiful thing about being on the receiving end of someone else's madness; you become a damn *god* in their world. Then you learn there's nothing humans love more than defiling and desecrating their gods.

And when you have the eyes of a zealot fixed on you with shaking hands that fumble for the zipper of his pants, that tremble as they pull out his cock—sweat on his brow as he tells you he *needs*

I AM THE RAINBRINGER

to fuck you *now*—and you feel that devotion, you feel that insanity, you swallow down fear. No, you don't swallow it because you're drowning in that mania. That fear gives way to the same glorious madness as a car crash. That's one of those things about *Crash* that Cronenberg gets utterly, stupidly wrong—the idea of meaningless disaffected sex, of a lack of intimacy, of dragging the holy down to something desultory and rote no matter how beatific it is. The shots are washed and dreamy to make you feel like these people are grasping for meaning and finding none. The real meaning is to find someone who'd sooner kill you than see anyone else so much as touch you—because if your love isn't "toxic" then you're not fucking doing it right. That's what I adored about Jonathan. And part of that unconditional adoration was the condition that I never hide anything from him. So I didn't.

We sat in the dark that night, disheveled and reeking of sex with the rain beating down steadier and harder, with our sticky communion bleeding onto the kitchen chair where I sat, watching him smoke a cigarette. The power had gone out, but we'd stumbled up the stairs of the darkened split-level house after a fumbling curse to an ineffective light. But we didn't need light to fuck and fuck some more—scare the cats—and make the whole goddamn place reek. That was when he told me he loved me, he wanted to be my one and only, and in the shadows, his eyes were bright, wide, demanding, but most of all *wanting*. That's the sort of thing the fat bookish loser only dreams of. But I looked for that sign from God, and I got it.

They go out of their way nowadays to tell you how unattractive smoking is. You only have to watch Bogey in *To Have and to Have Not* with the cigarette dangling lazily from his lips, to know what an utter crock of happy horseshit that is. The shot of Jonathan in the darkness, lighting that American Spirit and bringing it to his lips—his hands never steadier than when he raised it up and took a long deep drag—was intoxicating. It made him look composed, powerful, and nothing like the begging creature who told me he wanted me to be his. I could see the illumination of his chest, of the dark hair, of the large pecs he would often call "moobs" in self-deprecation. I could see the swell of his stomach—my eyes and my mind already flashing back to his cock before I brought them back to those sensual lips. I saw the sharpened lines of a man who I would learn seemed to spend every second of his life in torment.

ANDREW NADOLNY

That was also when I saw the roosters. Seriously—*roosters*.

They were all over the kitchen. In the dim light from the cigarette-turned-candle, they were distorted into fantastical shapes. There were statues on the microwave lined up like sentry gargoyles. A shelf that was placed above the cabinets held a massive angry bird peering down with a wavering wattle, comically large eyes that watched my every move. They decorated the dish towels, marched like soldiers across the curtains covering the kitchen sink window, and pranced and preened along the border wallpaper into the dining room. From there, they gazed out from the hutch, those glass doors the only sacred prison holding them back. I could hear faint clucking followed by the faint flapping of wings that couldn't fly; I imagined them cawing and crowing, circling like demons the more I stared at them, the cacophony growing louder until it was so deafening I had to turn away. That was when I glanced across the table and saw the bright flare of his cigarette before he pulled it slowly, deliberately from his lips; he stared at me so intensely I drew my legs back together until my knees touched. I sat that way, unmoving, staring at the placemats..

"Tell me all your secrets," he said, slowly tapping the cherry into an old glass ashtray. I stared long and hard at the rooster on the placemat—some abstract cubist something-or-other with its harsh lines and big bulging eyes that flew out into opposite directions, its tongue prominent, wavering long until in my head I could hear it screaming.

It didn't crow.

It screamed.

I saw the shift of color to black and white—that rooster, the only color in the world—and heard that scream morph into the violent glissandos of the violin in Bernard Herrmann's classic score when Janet Leigh is being stabbed in *Psycho*. It was right as I stared back up into his eyes, asking him with a pitiable softness in my voice after a hard swallow, "Can I ask you a question first?"

It was good. The artifice was practiced to perfect deference, and I saw the slight flare of his nostrils just like Lauren Bacall's in *The Big Sleep* when Humphrey Bogart arouses that certain something inside her. I could feel the scene in my mind shift to a pointed question, building that dramatic tension, thinking how I wanted to know as much about him as he did about me. My eyes floated up, from the queen of the roosters, to a sad, Bette Daviseyed woman in black and white, framed amidst those birds with a *Mona Lisa* smile.

Jonathan's eyebrows raised. I took a sip of iced tea from a Tupperware tumbler older than I was—sweet, too sweet—and moved my gaze from that sad, spirit-broken woman to a picture of a man next to her, just as grayscale, just as sad, with a short, neat parted haircut, and thin severe lips, but with a hardness behind his eyes, glaring over thick military-issued glasses . Then I asked him—still soft, stuttering just enough he had to lean in, "Do you love your dad?"

He smiled.

"Yes." Just "yes." No "of course." Nothing else was spoken, and for a moment I thought I saw a flash of red off to the side of the microwave behind him. It was a little red dot, like a sniper's sight on me, that made me curl in just a bit, peer over my smudged and dirty glasses, and take a piece of hair, chewing on it like I used to when I was a little girl. I thought now, as then, that it better affected innocence, and I thought I saw a flash of lightning through the curtain, though the thunder was silent. I wish I was wearing a shirt of his or something else that would make a better image than the flopped-over rolls I hid by crossing my arms over my stomach self-consciously.

"I couldn't help but notice you looking at all the roosters; at all our little friends here. Why do you think we have so many?" he asked suddenly, and I was annoyed at the moment breaking. But I felt like there was a beautiful monologue hanging in the air, so I just shook my head as I looked at them again, watching me like those little orchestral demons. I spoke a little softer, a little higher in pitch, a little more innocent.

"I guess I thought you really liked roosters."

"No. I hate the goddamned things." Jonathan took a long drag, looking off to the side. I could imagine him rehearsing that artful pose in front of a mirror just like I would, and I made sure my memory greedily captured every moment. Then came the monologue, glorious villainous, piteous, perfect thing that it was.

"When my dad came back from World War II—and by the way, he came back really fucked up, couldn't get any help from anyone, some terrible shit happened to him during the war—anyway, when he came back, he wanted to raise chickens. He wanted to be a chicken farmer. And you can't have chickens and be a chicken farmer unless you've got roosters to ah. . .you know, perform certain duties. So when Mom and Dad were trying to save up money for it, he started working these factory jobs. And you know every so often, life came along and he'd have to empty the 'farm account'. So Mom kept buying him roosters; statues, placemats, more roosters every time something went wrong, every time he'd have to empty the chicken account, the farm account, whatever the fuck they were calling it that year.

"I always used to wish they'd get rid of the goddamn things because every time he would look at them, it only reminded him of a dream that was never going to see fruition. It just made him seem like more of a failure in his own eyes. That's all he could ever see most days, his failures. He had a lot of failures," Jonathan put the cigarette out hard in the ashtray, and the lights came back on. "A lot of failures," he repeated, looking at me with a sad little smile.

I don't know why, but the first thing I said to him after that was, "I loved my dad more than anything in this world. And I killed him." His smile only grew wider, sensual and soft; I looked at it rather than into his eyes as I saw the red dot blink again behind the microwave.

"Let's hear it, baby," those red little lips commanded.

5

I told him all my secrets that night. And he told me his. Jonathan killed his dad, too. Then he told me he was also going to die. Not in the "after age thirty, your cells are decaying at a faster rate than they're able to replenish themselves" sort of way, but in the *Love Story* "What can you say about a twenty-five-year-old girl who died?" kind of way. There was a scar on his thigh from where doctors went in to place a stent in his heart. They let him know it opened him back up; he should be fine, they said.

But the ghosts were coming for him. He pulled the plug on his mom. He pulled the plug on his dad. I remembered the cold hospital floor when he said that. I remembered Dad saying he loved me before he went in. He said it would be okay. Except it wasn't okay. Jonathan said no one holds a grudge like the dead.

"Please. . .please. . .that's what Mom said. She tried to shake her head, but she was too weak by then. Dad couldn't do it because his brain was fucking soup at that point, so he just sat there in the wheelchair when I told them to do it. You know what he said? The only thing he said to me that day? 'Please. . .Please. . .' Like a fucking parrot." Jonathan laughed, looked at the picture above the cabinet over the stove, and lit another cigarette whispering "please" before he laughed louder and started crying. His dad looked at both of us and I could see the lips of the picture move "please. . .please. . ." I crossed myself because Jonathan wasn't the only one they talked to.

Their pictures lined the living room, faces I never saw that first night in the dark as they watched us fuck on the floor. But I saw them when I sat to read a book, when I dusted them. I thought of the old *Scooby Doo* show, and how the eyes of the paintings would follow the gang around. That was what they did. The house was his parents'. The bad, bad heart was his father's. *"It'll get you too, Johnny. Mark my words, boy, and eat the goddamn steak already. The cow's already dead and you're not a fairy, are you?"*

"No sir, no sir." Because Jonathan wasn't a fairy, and Jonathan wasn't a failure. He got to go to college and "get educated." He got to make movies like some big Hollywood hotshot. That's how the story should have gone in a Horatio Alger sort of way. Except he didn't make big movies. He didn't make money. He worked as a janitor at a library, and as a bartender at some country club in Medford, kissing rich ass for scraps as his dad would say. His dad called him shit like "Dead Wood," a reference to Johnny—I started calling him "Johnny," too, after moving in—didn't have to explain to me, because I already knew who Ed Wood was. That was when he told me he knew he was right in picking me.

He picked a girl before—a *woman*, I should say. She was the type like my mom who wore sensible shoes and tasteful pantyhose, mustard yellow blazers with shoulder pads, and insisted on being referred to as "Mz." She was a woman with a *career,* who made money, drove a Lexus, but still believed he "hung the moon," as his mom would say. And because she believed in him, she went to work, and he went to work. She made the money, and he spent the money. She doted on him like a little pet and doled out money and pussy like he was a prize poodle. In the early days, every film he made had some sort of tribute to her, whether it was a character named after one of her old stuffed animals, or an actress whose face and body type favored her.

ANDREW NADOLNY

She didn't cook for him like I did, or rub his shoulders and his feet, or ride him till his eyes rolled back into his head or suck his cock like it had the fucking antidote in it, but she loved him like a proper equal woman did. That's all well and good nowadays, except she wasn't his the way he needed her to be.

I go back to *Kenshin* because it was such an incredible show, only it wasn't Soujiro I thought of, but Yumi. She couldn't fight for Shishio like Soujiro or Kamatari could. In the end, all she could do was sacrifice herself so he could run his sword through her in order to kill Kenshin—she died happy, knowing she could serve him at last in a way she never could before, a way no one else could. Jonathan had never seen it, but he cried, and I cried when I described it to him and told him—as he held my hands and made love to me and made me his woman over and over—that I wanted to be his unconditional sword and shield. The rain fell outside that day, beating steadily on the roof as he asked if I'd ever remarry if he were to die. I told him I could only pray to die with him so I would never have to live a single second without him. He whispered to me Ya'aburnee which means something in Arabic like "you bury me," and that was when I realized it was the most wonderful, terrible, beautiful thing in the world to be loved by him.

"That was the worst fight we ever had. Can you believe that? We didn't fight about money. Not about kids, even though she didn't want any and I did. We didn't fight about Mom or Dad, or how her mom hated me. Did I ever tell you that? The first time I met her, Jill and I went to their house for dinner. It was a lovely dinner. She was a lovely woman the entire time. We had a *good time*, and then a month before we got married, her mom wrote her this long letter telling her why she shouldn't get married to me. She listed everything I'd ever done wrong—though she stopped just short of calling Ma 'a whore and a white woman' and believe me, I had a few things to say to that woman about *that*—and sent it in the mail like it was a fucking birthday card.

"But even that was fine, that is 'til we got to planning the wedding and talking about the vows. We wanted to write our own. She didn't like 'love, honor and obey' and I didn't like 'until death do us part.' You know Teddy Roosevelt thought that was a weakness of character—to remarry after a spouse died; I mean, he was a hypocrite just like every other politician, but can you just imagine it? Your spouse is waiting for you at the pearly gates, and

I AM THE RAINBRINGER

you show up with the newer model on your arm. Worst goddamn argument we ever had."

He laughed. I could see his face redden and bead with that post-coital sweat. He was on his way to getting worked up, so I put a hand on his forehead and kissed his eyebrows. I worried so much about his heart, his blood pressure. . .I worried about him having a stroke or a heart attack when his hands got to shaking and his eyes glazed over, faraway, mumble stutter mumble if it didn't go to rage. Rage was easier to deal with because it reminded me of dad. I was glad the rain had tapered—it would be cliché for thunder in that quiet, although some might call it cinematic.

A thunderclap would have been poignant when he was thrusting into me, demanding I look into his eyes as he took my hands and squeezed and squeezed in pleasure pain while he called me his wife. It was a sort of beautiful madness that swirled in that look. I loved it. I loved it because it allowed me to be just as free and reckless as him. It allowed me to beg him to tell me again how he'd kill anyone who touched me. It allowed me to revel in the building, choking pressure when he put his hands on my throat as he came and promised and promised *"mine mine"*, which was more than someone like me—"Hey, you're pretty; pretty ugly haha"—could ever hope for.

When I had finally gone back to finish school—Jonathan insisted I graduate because it was *necessary* even though I hated being away from him—I had taken a film class. It didn't have much to do with the major I had started and ostensibly intended to finish. I didn't give a shit. I didn't have anything better to do with my time. It was on Chinese Cinema specifically, and the only thing I remember about it was watching this movie called *Yellow Earth*. It was directed by Chen Kaige, and everything was yellow because color was important. It was symbolic. That's why *Red Sorghum* is so lush and vibrant in contrast, I learned. The color is supposed to set a mood or speak to some inner eye or some-such shit.

That's how Jonathan's house was. Everything was yellow like the 70s. The cupboards were full of old Tupperware and thick amber glasses. The ashtray he used in the living room was the same, with the couch being this yellow and brown tint of flowers. Coppercraft hung along the walls, reminding me how my mom supposedly sold it years before I was born. Coming home through the front door made me think of the basement in my house where my grandmother had kept tins of buttons stacked in stupid fucking Danish cookie containers. The old Kirby next to the kitchen doorway had a home sewn rooster in an apron draped over it, his beak seeming to pull nearer and nearer to me each time I passed by; his anatomically impossible grin drawing wider and wider. I thought one day he might peck my eyes out; I would wake next to Jonathan to find the blood streaming down my cheeks, seeing nothing but his face grinning at me, a long strand of nerves hanging bloody from the tip.

The lights were all soft yellow lamps, and they all turned on with little clicks at the sides. The overhead lights hurt Johnny's head, so those were the only lights we used. They all had dust—the damn things attracted dust so easily, especially with Johnny's smoking—that it seemed I'd spend hours dusting every little dust attracting nook and cranny while the house and its yellow tint fell and hung around me like shitty technicolor.

The bedroom had an olive-green carpet that had once been thick and plush but was now flat, dull, and nearly threadbare where his parents woke every morning and slid their tired old slippered feet in the same spot until it wore through carpet and pad, to the aged wood below, now covered with cheap woven mats. It was his parents' room, so it was preserved with the flowery duvet, the dark wooden furniture, his mother's perfume bottles and lotions on a little silver tray in front of the mirror on the dresser, doilies, and old pictures with that retro tint to them. It wasn't until you opened the closet, did you see Johnny's clothes, see his underwear in the dresser drawers. He had a lot of clothes and a lot of shoes, though he only wore the same rotation around the house.

He loved talking about the colors of film; he was the consummate celluloid pedagogue in his classroom, in the main basement theater where we would often sit and watch movies. The other rooms down there branched off of a small hallway on the opposite side. One was a room full of nothing but tapes and reels, and the other room at the end of that hall was Johnny's office. He spent most of his days down in that dark when he wasn't with me, coming out to sit and have me next to him while he put something on the flatscreen that cost a fortune at the time. At first, in spite of my love of film, I couldn't tell Peckinpah from Pasolini, but I could not allow that ignorance to stand. I wanted to know all of it. I wanted to know as much as he did.

IRIS OUT:
INT. BASEMENT NIGHT

The basement is a cavern of brown carpet and brick walls—a stovepipe furnace in the corner, long sitting unused. JONATHAN and I sit on a large worn sofa, back from a TV that is the newest thing in the house. It is a flat screen with surround speakers—old but powerful JBLs—and various media players for everything from reels to betamax, to film, and a DVD player.

> JONATHAN
> Useless knowledge, all of it's useless. You see where it's gotten me, my darling wife to be.

> ME
> Oh c'mon, Johnny. I bet it's gotten you all the girls. Didn't you say you've been with like sixty women? I don't even *know* sixty women.

> JONATHAN
> Only forty. Christ, you add another five every time you mention it. And I didn't seduce them by talking about <u>Bring Me the Head of Alfredo Garcia</u>.

ANDREW NADOLNY

ME
What about <u>120 Days of Sodom</u>?

JONATHAN
Maybe. Some people think it's frightening, all the useless shit I have instant recall about. Did I ever tell you I traded my spleen for all this shit? Yeah. Right as rain, I was eight years old and sick as hell one night. Running a fever high enough that it probably killed a good several thousand brain cells I'll never get back. Maybe I could've been a Rhoades Scholar. I was seeing little cowboys and Indians coming out of the radiator pipes. Mom told me to stop making shit up 'cause they couldn't afford to take me to the hospital, anyway. And that night, I swear I saw Old Scratch himself, standing at the foot of my bed while I was praying to God to let me go this time, because Mom and Dad didn't have the money to bury me, either. Funny how many prayers that sonofabitch answers cause the Big Guy upstairs can't be bothered. Anyway, he told me right then and there I wasn't gonna die. I asked him then if he had come for my soul instead, and he laughed—honest to God *laughed*—and told me he

had plenty of souls, but boy howdy could he sure use a spleen. I thought he was fucking with me. Had to be, but I asked him anyway if that meant I could make a deal with him for my spleen, I mean, c'mon, what the hell did an eight-year-old kid know about lymphocytes or monocytes? Now if that fucker had come when I was eighteen instead of eight, I might've asked for a ten-inch pecker, so maybe it was better that all I wanted was to know everything I ever wanted about movies. So *bang-zow-pow*—to quote those lovely onomatopoeia phrases from *Batman*—that's what he gave me. I never forget anything I learn about them.

ME
So even if I mention like, this obscure Japanese silent film we learned about in class they say gets compared to *The Cabinet of Dr Caligari* all the time—

JONATHAN
A Page of Madness. I have it downstairs. We should watch it sometime.

ME
How about now?

ANDREW NADOLNY

```
          JONATHAN
Now? Now, I have something far
different in mind.
```

IRIS IN: END SCENE.

The first thing I asked him when we finished watching *Man Bites Dog* was if he ever killed anyone. I mean, like *really* killed someone. He didn't answer me, and it was really dark; the curtains to the basement window were drawn, coupled with the clouds being in full Jersey bloom. I played with the rim of the plastic Tupperware bowl we'd put the popcorn in, waiting for him because I'd passed that ball to him, after all. But it was me who continued talking—even though we both hated being interrupted—because the question reminded me of something I hadn't so much forgotten but hadn't thought about in a long while. The silence was good because somehow it had morphed from this ominous oppressive thing into a confessional silence. It added an extra layer to the intensity of what I was going to say, so I made sure I delivered it very pointedly and without too many additional verbal flourishes and descriptors. It needed to be bald, stark, raw.

"I always thought Dad probably killed someone. One day we were driving along the canal going up to Flemington, and he'd normally point out the street where he and Mom used to live before I was born, but instead he started telling me out of the blue the best way to kill someone and never get caught. Do you know what that is?"

A pause. No answer. Johnny knew exactly how *the pause* worked, and I loved him so dearly for it. I could see the shadow of him staring straight ahead, listening, contemplating like he always did.

"You go somewhere small, remote, where no one knows you and no one's ever seen you, a place where you've never been and will never go again. You pay cash. You don't drive your own car, but you don't rent one either. Pay cash for a bus ticket or hitch a ride and walk. Go there, do the thing, don't linger, don't stay overnight, don't even miss work, and then you come back and never speak of it ever again to anyone." I always wondered about that. Did he do that? Was that him? Some unsolved murder in the middle of nowhere, in a town where shit like that just doesn't happen, except for that one time. . .

"The Town Where No One Got Off." Johnny said suddenly, poignantly, and then he laughed and shook his head. And laughed and laughed and kept right on laughing.

"I don't get what's so funny?" Because that wasn't how scenes like these are supposed to go.

But somehow his performance made it all the better.

FADE IN:
INT. BASEMENT—NIGHT
The credits to *Man Bites Dog* roll silently on the television screen. A Tupperware bowl, empty except for a few unpopped kernels of popcorn, sits on the floor in front of the sofa. Seated on the sofa, JONATHAN takes MY hands.

> JONATHAN
> When did your dad tell you that story?

> ME
> When I was ten, I think. Why?

JONATHAN whispers with a kiss to MY cheek

> JONATHAN
> Twelve years. Twelve years. That beautiful, brilliant bastard.

The wisp of his beard makes ME shiver as his lips brush MY neck

> JONATHAN
> That's okay, baby. We'll do it even better.

PART III

6

ME
So I have a question. How are
you going to shoot the video?
I mean like the confessional
style? Or even like. . .me
just riffing on stuff like—
stuff about you or me or about
anything else that's around?

JONATHAN (O.S.)
Well with the camera, of
course.

ME
Funny. Johnny, I can't. . .I
wouldn't want to. . .I
mean. . .I mean sometimes I
might say something that'll
upset you, y'know?

JONATHAN (O.S.)
Babe, you can say anything you
want in the film. It's not
gonna work if you don't talk,
or if I have to keep editing
around awkward pauses. I don't
know what you think would
upset me or why you think I'd
get mad. And even if I did get

mad, you know I'd never hurt
you.

                    ME
I know that. Honestly, I
almost wish you did. You know
'cause of your heart. . .You
know how much it scares me
when you let things upset
you. . .You know it reminds me
of Dad, and you know I'm
terrified one day you're gonna
overdo it, or something's
going to upset you or—

           JONATHAN (O.S.)
Babe. You're overthinking
things again. Let me worry
about the movie. Okay, how
about this: when I'm holding
the camera—when this little
light here is on, I'm not
Johnny. I'm the director. I'm
not watching this thinking
about what you say, or if you
joke about my snoring or bitch
about my smoking—

                    ME
You know I still think your
smoking is kinda hot—

           JONATHAN (O.S.)
My *point*. . .is that it's
okay.

                    ME
But what if there are things I
don't want you to know? Things
I don't want to talk about?

JONATHAN (O.S.)
Is there anything you haven't
told me?

ME
I've never lied to you,
Johnny.

JONATHAN (O.S.)
But things have happened that
you don't tell me about?

ME
It's. . .it's not you. It's my
head, I think. I think it's in
my head. Or maybe it's not in
my head. Maybe it's really the
ghosts.

JONATHAN (O.S.)
The ghosts?

ME
Yeah. . .You don't see them
here now?

JONATHAN (O.S.)
No. It's just you and me, Mrs.
H.

ME
I love when you call me that.
I love it so much. I'll never
get tired of hearing it. I'm
so happy. . .so *so* happy I get
to be your wife, Johnny.

JONATHAN (O.S.)
Then tell you what, Mrs. H.

You just be honest for the
camera. You just say what's on
your mind, and I'll take care
of the rest.

> ME
> Okay, Johnny.

CROSSFADE:
INT. KITCHEN—DAY

> ME
> Well first thing, you weren't
> the first one to tell me I
> needed to finish the list. I
> guess that was something I was
> keeping from you. Because I
> didn't know how to tell you—

I take a DEEP BREATH.

> ME
> He talks to me. Both of them
> talk to me.

I stop kneading the dough on the floured
countertop and look at it.

> ME
> Does that sound crazy to you?

I look PAST the camera. JONATHAN raises a
hand to his lips and shakes his head. I
frown and go back to kneading

> ME
> It was your—

JONATHAN passes his fingertips in front of
his throat and holds up three fingers.

ANDREW NADOLNY

ME

Three?. . .Oh! Right, right. *His* mom. *Johnny's* mom. So, I like to collect old magazines, and I like to sit in the living room to read them. It was right before we got married. I looked over and saw her sitting on the couch. And you'd think most people would jump up and scream but I'm kinda used to ghosts. My old house, the house I grew up in, was full of them. A lot of times I'd see Dad watching me from the hallway or see Grandmom downstairs in the basement washing clothes in this old tub she used to have. So it wasn't all that weird when I saw her sitting next to me. I didn't think anyone had broken in or anything, because if you've ever been like. . .really close to a ghost, they're kinda translucent. You wouldn't mistake them for anything else, and they kinda unsettle the air. Like that noise you hear when the TV turns on—it's like that. She looks so sad in all the pictures around here, like my mom used to. Johnny says that's why he never smiles in pictures. Well, he says he gets that from both of them. So I was surprised when she smiled. She sat right

I AM THE RAINBRINGER

there on the couch with me,
and she kept on smiling.

I turn around and point to the sofa. The
camera follows. The window is open a
little. A breeze blows the curtains. The
north facing window doesn't let in
sunbeams. Instead, it casts a *shadow*. The
faint outline of a woman can be seen for a
moment.

                    ME
          I was afraid she was angry. He
          said she never liked his first
          wife, but she just told me she
          was happy he had found me. And
          she made me promise to look
          after her boy. . .look after
          her Johnny. It's funny 'cause
          you'd think that translucent
          thing would just pass through,
          but I guess if a spirit can
          sit they can hold things, too.
          So she just smiled when I said
          of course I would, and she
          took my hand and squeezed it
          and actually it um. . .it
          kinda hurt but I don't think
          she meant it. I don't think
          she meant it, it was
          just. . .just cold. The sort
          of dry ice cold they say
          breaks down and destroys the
          cells in your body, and I was
          actually afraid for a little
          bit that my hands were gonna
          turn black and fall off but
          see—

I smile and hold up MY hands, wiggling MY

fingers. JONATHAN makes a face behind the
camera. MY eyes drop.

> ME
> See, my hands are fine, and I
> always put my wedding band on
> the counter right here so you—
> so *Johnny* doesn't have to
> worry about me losing it
> again. I put it right here in
> this little dish and I never
> forget it. So it won't be like
> that scene in *Rolling Thunder*
> where William Devane gets his
> arm mutilated in the garbage
> disposal. Nope, no one needs
> to put their hand down there
> cause my dumb ass dropped a
> ring. Right, I was talking
> about Johnny's dad. I see his
> dad a lot. Sometimes he talks
> to me. Sometimes he kinda
> talks to himself. He's just
> sort of around, really. He'll
> be sitting here smoking—Pall
> Malls which fucking reek—

I look up at the picture on the soffit
above the stove and smile fondly. There is
a closeup of the picture. The man in the
photograph is dour, but almost seems to
grin a little Mona Lisa smile. I speak to
the picture.

> ME
> Sorry, Jimmy, but it's true.

I look at the camera with MY own shy smile.
MY hands continue to form the rolls and put
them in a round cake pan spaced out neatly.

I AM THE RAINBRINGER

          ME
     They'll come together when
     they rise.

I wipe my hands on the apron. When I turn,
there is a closeup on the watercolor
rooster printed on the front.

          ME
     I talk to him a lot about Dad.
     They were a lot alike I think,
     and for some reason I don't
     see Dad here, so it's nice.
     It's nice to have someone to
     talk to when Johnny's working
     in the basement downstairs—

The camera shifts and shakes a little and I
look past it with a frown.

          ME
     Johnny does *really* important
     work, and he works *hard,* and I
     love him for it, so he
     shouldn't blame himself, or
     say mean things about himself,
     or hit himself.

I clear MY throat and turn away, covering
the rolls back up.

          ME
     He blames himself for a lot,
     but I guess I'm just as bad.
     Helluva pair, we are. But
     anyway, Jimmy—he said I can
     call him that. . .pretty girls
     always call him Jimmy—Jimmy
     asked me. . .he asked me if I

loved Dad so much why. . .why
wasn't the list finished?

The camera shows the kitchen window. It's
on the south side of the house and the sun
comes in prettily with the little motes of
dust, carried along like stardust forming
at the beginning of the universe into a new
galaxy.

> ME (O.S.)
> He said. . ."If you loved him,
> honey, if you really wanted to
> make up for being a bad
> daughter, if you really felt
> bad about killing your old
> man, honey, you'd finish the
> list, wouldn't you? Make him
> proud of you." If you love
> me. . .if you love me.

I laugh softly. The camera remains light
beaming into the old linoleum.

> ME (O.S.)
> Dad always used to say "Love
> is patient. Love is kind. But
> love is not just." Johnny said
> the same thing to me.
> Cause. . .cause we wrote our
> own vows and I thought that
> was so perfect.

The camera goes back to MY face as I wipe
MY eyes. Traces of flour smudge MY cheeks
in little tracks vertical beneath like
drying tears.
ME

> And if I must, I'll kill every

last one of them.   Just like
he asked me to.

BLACKOUT.

SLOW FADE-IN:
INT. BEDROOM—DAY

I sit in front of the vanity and its large
spotless mirror, on a small, cushioned
ottoman. The silver tray sits there as
well, with bottles shiny as if they were
new. The shirt-waist dress I wear is black
with red cherries on it. They seem to dance
with the camera. There's a steady beat of
rain outside. I slowly rub a faint amount
of blush on MY cheeks myopically, sitting
closer to the mirror than necessary.

>   ME
>   You'd think the guy at the top
>   of the list would be the ugly
>   old fucker Mom was having an
>   affair with when she and Dad
>   were still married. And I
>   mean, he's still *on there,* but
>   he's not at the top. See, they
>   were divorced, but Dad still
>   cared so much about Mom, that
>   the person he couldn't forgive
>   was her sister Annette.

I roll MY eyes.

>   ME
>   He could forgive Mom for
>   anything. Anyway, we spent our

holidays at Aunt Annette's house when Mom and Dad were still together, and she made the most amazing turkey. She always had this pinched sort of expression on her face, but we played board games, and it was always fun: me, Mom, Dad, Aunt Annie, Uncle Dan, and my cousin, Doug. I remember our team beating theirs in Trivial Pursuit when I was only seven, and I won the whole game for us 'cause I just learned Hans Christian Anderson wrote *The Ugly Duckling* that week in school. Doug nearly had apoplexy.

I put the brush down, and sort through various palettes of eyeshadow.

                    ME
Dad always said Mom never loved him, that she just wanted to get out of the house, and I guess things were different back then because, I'm pretty sure if you're *that* desperate to get out, you can always enlist. That's what my cousin did—my cousin Mark, not my cousin Doug—and even with the hump on his back, and being all of five foot nothing, the Navy still took him. But Mom wasn't what you'd call "a strong woman" as much as she liked to pretend to be all "I don't need a man blah

blah" after they got divorced.
That's probably why she died.
At least that's what all those
breast cancer cultists will
have you believe with their "I
kicked cancer's ass" bullshit.
But even if she hadn't died,
she wasn't a strong woman. She
was weak, and she always did
what everyone else told her to
do, and honestly if she was
gonna to be *that* useless, she
might as well have stayed
married to Dad instead of
trying to play this
independent feminist bullshit
when she clearly wasn't cut
out to be alone. She left
everything to Aunt Annie. Or
is that the pretzel place? No,
that's Auntie Anne's. I called
Annette Annie 'cause mom did.
Aunt Annie took me there once
when I was a kid. It was the
only time I ever had a garlic
pretzel, too.

I talk as I continue putting makeup on. MY
own toiletries are contained in a large
case that rests on the vanity. I pack it
back up and then take a bottle of perfume—
White Linen—from the tray, then give it a
little spritz.

                    ME
Ma—that's what I call Johnny's
mom, Ma—said I could use her
perfume. Says Johnny really
likes it and ahh. . .

I trail off and look down shyly. I turn and twirl a lock of MY long hair around MY finger before chewing on it. I sigh.

> ME
> He really likes it, if you get what I mean.

I look directly at the camera as I put MY glasses back on. I keep staring over the dark, thick, cat's eye frames and smile.

> ME
> I think it excites him more when I wear it. Maybe that's some Freudian thing. . .

There's a laugh from behind the camera, a soft titter from JONATHAN.

> ME
> You should've seen him when I bought these red heels with the pointed toe.

I look meaningfully beyond the camera.

> ME
> (whispering)
> Maybe. . .maybe we could. . .I really need it, Johnny.

The camera is set down on the bed. It flops lazily to the side. There's a gasp, followed by a moan. A male voice—presumably JONATHAN'S—murmurs something unintelligible. Suddenly MY face is in front of the camera. The camera is sideways and so am I. The angle makes ME appear upright on the bed as it shakes. It gives the impression of an earthquake. Or possibly a kaiju attack. MY eyes screw shut. MY face is now damp with sweat.

> ME
> Yeah. . .yeah. . .please. . .g
> ood. . .so good. . .I love
> you. . .more God more
> more. . .

The rocking continues until the rain stops. I bury MY face in the duvet just as a tear forms in the corner of MY eye and begins to fall. The camera cuts before it reaches MY cheek.

7

EXT. FRONT SEAT OF CAR—NIGHT

I am in the driver's seat. In the distance, the bright lights of the TRENTON MAKES bridge lights up behind ME. I glance down for just a moment before peering back up. Occasionally, a car passes by. When it does, the bright lights blind the lens and make it fuzz out as it struggles to adjust back.

> ME
> I keep meaning to ask Johnny
> if he thinks it's better for a
> killing to be neat and tidy or
> brutal. There's a certain
> artistry in brutality. Like I
> remember watching Kill Bill
> with Johnny when it came out
> and I was struck with the
> beauty of The Bride fighting

O-Ren Ishi in the snow.
There's this perfect elegance
in that splash of blood on the
pure white and it's kind
of. . .

I trail off and look briefly out the
window. I finger a chain around MY neck. MY
other hand remains on the wheel.

                    ME
        After Dad died, before I met
        Johnny, I would go for long
        drives at night like this.
        Sometimes I'd drive all night
        and find my way somewhere up
        in like Connecticut or some
        shit. Y'know, even at 3 AM,
        driving through New York City
        sucks fucking balls. But it's
        like hypnotic when it's dark
        and all the lights are gone
        and you just drive and drive,
        and you think what it would be
        like to close your eyes for
        just a moment, and just float.
        Like I know intellectually
        you'd end up dead or in a
        wheelchair, but there's this
        moment I think, where you let
        go, where you feel like you
        could do anything. . .like you
        could fucking fly.

MY hand reaches for the radio but stops. It
hovers in midair with a little shake before
gripping the wheel again.

                    ME
        Right, copyright shit. I'll

settle in a moment. Dad always used to say this is how women drive: choking the steering wheel. I usually drive with one hand like he does. I should talk about it, shouldn't I? I feel like Benoit was a natural. I mean obviously since that was a movie and not a real documentary, so he was an actor who knows how to act like the camera isn't there. Actually, that reminds me how when I was a kid, I used to end the day with a little theme song:

(SINGSONG)

Doo doo doo doo doo, doo doo, doo doo doo doo, doo doo doo doo doo doo, the M show. "M" for "Me." Pretty lame but, anyway. . .I kinda don't know what to say. I mean like, there's the how I did it but that's the sort of thing you see on all sorts of cheap crime drama shit. Or like *Columbo* where you could just watch it unfold and watch some rich asshole get caught at the end. I'm kinda mad it didn't rain today too because I think that would've made a nice backdrop. A little fall of rain. Like that *Les Miz* song. Mom and Aunt Annie went to see that when I was seven. I couldn't go because I was too little. But we still sang the songs in the car. I think rain is pretty for death. It's that whole "washing away the blood" type of symbolism. So I guess that makes it overdone? It was a nice night tonight. I'd open the window if the camera wasn't rolling. I don't know if I feel happy or sad or whatever. With my Aunt Agnes it was kinda like setting a mousetrap that someone else has to get rid of. You don't really think about it. You don't see it. A pig spends its whole miserable life not able to stand up, tortured and forced to live in its own shit, and fed and fed and fed, scared and miserable, until something cuts its throat or however they do it. And in the abstract, it's sort of awful, but I still eat bacon. Johnny still eats bacon. Johnny cries at the end of *Charlotte's Web* and almost cried at the end of *Babe*, but he still eats bacon.

The camera cuts away from ME to the dim cityscape of Trenton, New Jersey at night, bleak and broken, a remnant of a city that once made things people wanted and had people that other people cared about. The car drives slowly by a disheveled woman walking on the street.

                    ME (O.S.)
She shouldn't have let me in tonight. It was awkward.

I AM THE RAINBRINGER

Actually, it was kind of horrible. I know it's been a long time but—

I sniffle. The camera pans back to MY face, MY lower lip quivering, both hands clutching the wheel tightly as I stop at a light before the ramp to 95 south.

                    ME
But I missed her. I realized that when I saw her standing there. I haven't seen her since before Mom died. I haven't seen her since I was a kid. I. . .I spent time there in the summer. But even with that face and that stern look and that teacher's voice, she let me "do chemistry" in the kitchen sink. I made this green slime that bubbled everywhere, and she didn't even yell like Mom would've. I thought she was gonna be pissed, but she laughed. She *laughed*, and I missed her so much. I miss my family. I don't know why so many of them have to be dead or hate me 'cause of shit Dad did; I mean. . .no no, it wasn't his fault either, but like. . .I don't understand why she held out her fucking hand like I was a stranger when I told her who I was, and introduced herself like she never met me, like I never ate oatmeal at her kitchen table or came over

and went with Mom and Dad and them to see fireworks, and didn't love them, and didn't miss them, and fuck her, and fuck her. I hope it fucking hurt when I pushed her off the fucking balcony because this hurts, and it's not supposed to hurt, it's supposed to feel good, and it's supposed to make you feel powerful and godlike and give you a g-glorious fucking erection and we're supposed to go home and drink and fuck and I—

A car honks the horn. The light has turned. It has been green for several seconds. The sound of the tires squealing as it tears around the stopped vehicle can be heard loudly. MY head is pressed against the steering wheel, soft dying animal noises catching in MY throat before they're swallowed down.

                ME
I'm not crying. I just have a headache.

If I cry, the camera doesn't see it. It sees only a curtain of hair hiding everything, but the hands curled tightly over the steering wheel. The mic catches a soft whisper.

              JONATHAN
Good babe, that's so good.

INT. LIVING ROOM—DAY

I AM THE RAINBRINGER

The camera is static. It sits unmanned on a
tripod, catching only the soda that sits in
front of the bay window behind it. Behind
ME, a tree can be seen through the window.
The leaves are falling off every so often.
The sky is gray, making the room inside
appear even darker. The curtains are drawn
open to let in the natural light. It leaves
MY face in the shadows.

> ME
> In a Vaulted clock tower
> somewhere sits my soul whole
> and pure, lighting the dark of
> his innocent evil heart.

I pause to consider the words, staring down
introspectively. There is a small self-
satisfied smirk the shadow does not
entirely obscure.

> ME
> (whispers)
> That's good.

I look at the camera, stoic now.

> ME
> I gave him my soul. It's over
> there.

My head gestures right at those words. I
get up and come closer to the camera until
the paisley print of MY dress goes out of
focus. The camera swivels to the right, to
a wall that holds a large copper plate.
There is a wooden dry sink underneath the
plate, and a small silver Jesus crucified
on the cross hanging between the two. There
are two carefully polished urns buttressed

by pictures of JONATHAN'S MOTHER and JONATHAN'S FATHER. They are older in the pictures. Their faces are drawn, neither smiling as they stare ahead like the pupil-less dead. The angle and light make their features harsh. The sclera of their eyes appear nearly black. In the center is a small wooden box with a cracked and faded picture of a Victorian woman on it.

> ME
> That was Grandmom's jewelry box. It was probably one of the nicest things she owned. Her wedding ring is in it. Dad's is in it. He still kept it after all those years. That's all that's in there now. I mean except for my soul, that is. I promised it to Johnny when we first met, and the Devil may have enough souls and not need any more but Johnny isn't the Devil. He takes care of my soul, and I take care of his body. As for *Johnny's* soul. . .

I laugh.

> ME
> Well all the angels and saints never did shit for mine, but maybe they can save his.

I move the camera back to face the couch before sitting down again, smoothing MY skirt underneath ME, fixing MY hair as if I'M in front of a mirror.

I AM THE RAINBRINGER

ME

I promised I would take care
of him. I promised his
mother. . .Mother Margaret. It
sounds like a nun's name when
I say it like that, which is
the other reason I just call
her "Ma." And the damndest
thing is, she was all set to
become a nun and give it all
up for the big man upstairs,
but then she met Johnny's dad
after the war, and suddenly a
life spent cloistered away in
a convent didn't seem like so
much of a calling after all. I
think it's a noble calling. I
think taking care of Johnny is
a noble calling. I guess I'm
kinda like a nun that
way. . .called to serve my
lord and all. 'Cept the big
guy who *I* spread 'em for
spends all his time downstairs
and not upstairs.

I stop *suddenly* as if someone is speaking,
and turn MY head shyly to the left,
speaking half into MY shoulder.

ME

Okay, yeah, I guess I could've
said it a little more
ladylike, Ma. But I. . .I
think there's something
especially romantic—especially
exciting, even freeing—about
your body, your entire being
belonging so thoroughly to
someone else. I like that his

ownership of my body is like a *fait accompli*; Johnny taught me that phrase and I love the sound of it. But anyway, I don't see that it makes much difference whether your God is in Heaven or on Earth. Yeah, I'll stop with the blasphemy for today, Ma. I know it makes you—

I jump at the sound of a loud bang. For a moment, MY eyes roll briefly heavenward. MY head turns left with a slow breath out.

> ME
> It's really not that bad, it's just that the living room here is right above his—

The *BANG* is so loud this time there's a faint tremor in the camera.
ME

> I promise it's not an earthquake.

I smile. The smile looks like it hurts.

BANGBANGBANG

> ME
> Ladies and gentlemen, please remain in your seats, we're just experiencing a little turbulence, but the captain has it under control.

The laugh looks even more painful. It sounds like a scream. MY fingers rest at MY throat and I speak louder. My words become singsong toward the end.

                    ME
          The captain has it under
          control and I asked the
          captain for a collar because I
          wanted to feel that pull
          around my throat and know and
          know that's why I can't get up
          and go to him right now
          because he doesn't want to
          hurt me—

BANGBANGBANGBANG

                    ME
          So instead, he's hurting
          himself and he can't hurt
          Ma. . .he can't hurt Ma.
          Please, Ma, please please. I
          know he can't see you but
          pleasepleaseplease can't you
          help him? I know this is just
          a thing he does; he's done it
          since he was a kid. Jimmy
          would get drunk and flip his
          shit if something set him off,
          or if he was in a lot of pain
          that night. Johnny would kneel
          on the laundry room floor and
          BANGBANGBANG his fucking head
          on the wall. He told me I
          can't go down there. That's
          why I need a collar, because I
          don't need it there to feel
          it, to *feel* it around my neck
          pulling tighter and tighter
          and choking me right there
          with him and—

ANDREW NADOLNY

BANGBANGBANGASCREAMAHOWLAFUCKINGSHRIEKBANG
BANGBANG

                          ME
    (through tears)
            It's holding me here and I
            can't move and it's kind of
            awful really actually really
            really awful when he was a kid
            beating his head against the
            wall against the wall right in
            time with Jimmy here beating
            on Ma and Jimmy got better but
            Johnny didn't and Ma says
            that's why his big head is so
            hard and if you really forgave
            him for killing you you'd help
            him you'd help him, you'd make
            him stop and I. . .I beg him
            to hit me. I b-beg him to hit
            me   instead.   Hit   me
            instead. . .

It stops. I stop, too. I stop shaking. MY
arms are folded tight against MY body. I
peer down silently. I take one deep breath
and then another until I am steady.
Footsteps can be heard coming up the
stairs. I wipe at MY eyes and smile at
them.

EXT. FOREST—NIGHT

It is raining hard. There is only moonlight
and the lamplight of a car's driver's side
headlight illuminating the faint clearing.
I am standing, holding an umbrella. I am
wearing a long plaid cape, black boots,
black tights. The camera closes in on a car

just behind ME. It is a red '99 Mercury
Mystique. Its right front end is smashed in
against a tree.

> ME
> I had a dream the other night
> that everyone else on Earth
> died and it was only the two
> of us, only me and Johnny left
> in the silence. Or maybe I had
> killed everyone on Earth for
> him. . .for Dad. And it
> was. . .it was the most
> glorious, beautiful silence
> I'd ever experienced in my
> life. It was like being
> reborn. . .reborn from the
> blackened Earth for him. And
> then Johnny woke me up with
> his screaming. . .with his
> crying and. . .and then it was
> gone.

The camera pans back to ME. I slowly
approach the car. My boots sink into the
mud.

> ME
> I hope you understand you're
> rooting for a bad person. I
> wonder if I was rooting for
> Benoit? No, I think I was
> rooting for Remy. Benoit was
> too arrogant, too much like
> Icarus. Now there's an analogy
> that's been done to death.

I stop suddenly and turn around.

> ME

I already looked once. I
already checked once and no
one's coming. It's fucking
Tabernacle, no one's fucking
coming. You could set off a
goddamn bomb here.

I take a few steps away and then stop
again, holding the umbrella more tightly.
I swallow. I smile a stretched out smile
that for a moment makes MY face look like a
Muppet.

                    ME
It's like the easiest,
stupidest thing in the world
to say one of those tired,
overused lines like "Who hurt
you? Tell me who hurt you and
I'll make them pay." Or
something like that. And then
they tell you, and you know
what, you're not doing shit
about it. You're holding them
and letting them cry on your
shoulder, and your mind is
wandering to who's winning the
game Monday night or wondering
if this is gonna make you
tired for work the next day,
or if you'd look like a
fucking asshole if you told
them you really had to take a
shit. That's it. You're not
even gonna sit there and shit
your pants for them so they
can keep crying without a
fucking interruption. I'm not
crying. It's the lens. It's
the rain.

I AM THE RAINBRINGER

I lower the umbrella and drop it to the ground.

                    ME
        It's always the rain.

I tilt my head back and let the rain wet MY face. I hold that pose a few beats, then lower my head and continue speaking.

                    ME
          You know. . .it would've been
          better if there was a fire.
          There's probably too much
          darkness for the camera
          but. . .No? But a fire
          would've been nice. It
          would've added something to
          the scene. It would've been
          far more dramatic of a
          backdrop. Or even if I'd stood
          over him with a bottle of
          nitroglycerin that he couldn't
          reach; that would've been
          especially poetic. I could've
          done it, too. I still have all
          of dad's old pills, though I
          think some of them are coming
          close to dust. But he was
          always on me not to throw
          anything like that out, just
          in case. I still have his
          Xanax. Once in a while, I'll
          slip one when Johnny's
          downstairs and I get worried
          about him. Yeah, the
          nitroglycerin would've been
          poetic, but I didn't think of
          it. And that wasn't the point.

Maybe there should be some deeper moralizing like *Saw*, but I really hated that movie. . .And it's not like he didn't already know all the shit he's ever done wrong in life. Uncle Charles. . . heh. . .wow. . .didn't mean to call him that. . .I'm not crying, it's this rain. Shouldn't have done that but I just felt like I needed to.

I wipe my face off with my sleeve.

                    ME
Before I knew he and Mom were fucking, he was just Mom's friend from work. He'd come over sometimes when Dad wasn't home, but not always. He'd come over when Dad was home too, and he and Mom both liked art and wine tasting and shit like that. He'd always bring me a bottle of "wine" that was that sparkling apple cider or sparkling grape, and seeing him always put Mom in a good mood so she wasn't screaming at Dad or at me. One year he bought me this giant stuffed lion that was big enough for me to sit on, and I called him Uncle Chuck, and he was always nice to me and didn't baby talk me, and sometimes when mom was in a mood, he'd sit in the living room with me and let me read to him from one of

I AM THE RAINBRINGER

my Dr. Seuss books, and he watched *Dumbo* with me when Mom and Dad were sick to death of it, and I. . .I had forgotten until tonight that he once said to me there'd be a place for me and Mom if Dad got too bad. After it all "came out" that dad was an abusive asshole and he was hitting mom—except Charles and the rest of them didn't fucking live there and didn't know how she'd scream at him or me or throw things because **no one** did, because poor delicate mom wouldn't lie, or serve him divorce papers on his birthday, and *I was there. I WAS THERE* and I don't know why I'm remembering all of this now, and I'm glad he's dead, and I'm not crying it's just hard to breathe with the rain and the cold and—

I shiver and walk slowly back to the car. There hasn't been another car to come by the entire time the camera is on. There is faint light from the moon and the camera light that both reflect off the window. The headlight has since flickered out. I stop in front of the car door and turn back to where I had dropped the umbrella. I speak to it.

                    ME
Imagine you're me. Imagine you're the Rainbringer. Imagine you're the vengeful

arm of God sent to be his sword. And then imagine you say to him, "Who hurt you?" But you already know; all he has to do is say a name, say a word. . .and then they're gone. Destroyed. Dust. A never-was. A "wasn't" like Dr. Suess would say. And then imagine they tell you the name of that person—the name of the person who causes them to wake up screaming, to be sitting in the middle of the happiest fucking movie in the world, sitting through *Xanadu* or some shit and start crying—not because it's a shit movie but just because the name of the person who makes them bang their head against the wall until something cracks or breaks, they finally tell you in a small quiet voice, that person is them. Then tell me, just what the fuck are you supposed to do about that? Nope, still not crying. It's just the fucking rain.

I go to retrieve the umbrella but stop. I kick it. I walk to where it lands, and I stomp on it. I keep stomping on it. The mud flicks onto the camera lens. I walk away and leave it there.

I AM THE RAINBRINGER

INT. GROCERY STORE—DAY

I push a cart slowly. MY hair is done up in pin curls that are already starting to straighten out. I wear a flared pink dress and black patent leather heels. They are out of place amidst other customers' more casual dress.

> ME
> I asked Johnny why he keeps his parents on the hutch like that. If it's like a religious thing or a weird penance thing.

For a moment MY eyes flick slyly past the camera, just a touch past the lens to JONATHAN.

> ME
> But no, it's because the house is where they belong—the house they both loved and worked their whole lives for, and roosters or not, I like to think they had everything they truly wanted. Sometimes I wonder if that's why they're still there, but I'm glad for the company.

I grab a box of crackers, making a small click of MY tongue. I mumble about the sodium before putting them back, then find a box of saltines that are salt free.

> ME
> People use that phrase "house full of ghosts" or spirits or

whatever and it's usually in the context of some overused horror trope. I don't think that ghosts are some intrinsically malevolent force. Well, obviously!

The camera wanders as I walk, lingering long on boxes of cookies, on Devil Dogs and Tastykake, remaining fixed on the bakery. MY voice alternates between loud and soft while I walk around the bell peppers and zucchini. It's as if the camera doesn't want to listen to what I'M saying.

ME

They don't talk to Johnny. It's not because they don't *want* to talk to Johnny. They just. . .can't. I know Johnny wishes he could talk to them but. . .I guess that's the sort of thing you have to be ready for. I know he knows they're there. He doesn't think I'm delusional or anything like that. I know he smells the Pall Malls sometimes, or smells Ma's *White Linen*, but he just gets this faraway look and sometimes he cries like that time watching *Xanadu* cause like. . ."How can you put Gene Kelly in a movie and not let him dance?" That was what he was saying when it started, but I know that's not really what it was. He gets those though—the moles, the little

I AM THE RAINBRINGER

tunnels dug around underground until you step on the dirt and fall down deep deep and break your leg. No, Johnny doesn't talk to them or ask me to say anything to them, either. Every now and then I'll see him in the kitchen with a cigarette whispering "please please" though.

The camera follows ME again when I finish.

                    ME
Sometimes I imagine another universe exists where I was a girl who people wanted to be around.   .   .or   even just. . .had friends. Like *Clueless* or *The Sisterhood of the Travelling Pants* that came out last year or even just. . .just a best friend who I didn't fuck over cause Dad told me to. I guess Louis is kinda like that, but we never lived that close. We only saw each other a couple times a year. I mean people like those guys you grew up with, like Ben who helped you make your first film with that old 8mm or Carl who got you busted for stealing records. Johnny, I mean Johnny. But like people who would come to your birthday parties, people who you'd have sleepovers with or go to the movies with. Like. . .people who you call

on the phone in the middle of
the night cause some boy
dumped you. . .people who
cared that you were alive.
(sigh)
What a world that would be.
But that's a world that never
existed and so for me, there's
Johnny, and there's the
ghosts.

I stand in front of the meat and pick up a
package of liver.

                    ME
Johnny loves liver but I can't
make it for him 'cause of his
heart. Maybe for his birthday
but. . .but not now.

I look at it for a long time.

                 JONATHAN
(whispering so softly it may just be a
digital artifact)
Love you babe. . .

                    ME
There was this anime called
Giant Robo, and the style was
super retro and way cool and
there was this character,
Fabulous Fitzkarald who was
one of "The Magnificent Ten",
part of the Big Fire
organization and he had this
power where he could just snap
his fingers and slice people
apart. But not like some
pornographically violent way,

I AM THE RAINBRINGER

they just like. . .sorta atom-
blasted away. Like dust
really. Just a snap of his
fingers.

I punctuate that sentence with a snap of MY
own fingers. Then I pick up a pack of
chicken breasts, followed by a pack of
boneless pork chops. I drop the chicken
into the cart.

> ME
> Sausage is so fucking salty
> but this'll grind up and I can
> season it myself. Everything
> has so much sodium, it's
> disgusting. Sodium and sugar.
> It's ridiculous. And then
> every now and then some genius
> talks about taxing soda. How
> about they just stop putting
> so much goddamn sugar in
> everything? We finished
> watching *Death Note* the other
> night and that was especially
> nice. Well, not the end, but
> imagine being able to write
> someone's name in a notebook
> and they drop dead of a heart
> attack. That would be simple.
> Clean. And does that really
> make you a killer? How
> directly do you have to cause
> someone's death to be
> considered a murderer?

I'M still holding the pork chops and tap
them for emphasis.

                        ME

Like eating this pork; you
stop eating it, they stop
killing pigs. Does that make
us all murderers? Probably. I
guess that's why some people
stop eating it. But it's not
like we get some sort of
enjoyment from the killing—the
act itself I mean, not the
shit wrapped up and sanitized
in this package. I mean some
people probably would. But
what kinds of people would
those be, anyway?

I sigh then finally drop the pork chops
into the cart and resume pushing it.

                        ME

In *Man Bites Dog*, Benoit is
surrounded by friends, family,
love, support, all that shit
you need to turn out "well
adjusted." And it's not like
he's going around torturing
rabbits to get his rocks off,
but there's still a zeal to
his killing as calculated as
some of them are. Hell, don't
a lot of serial killers have
those types of setup? Maybe
that's what you need to really
enjoy it. I don't know. But I
think it makes for a sort of
sad documentary that you have
to follow me to the grocery
store to get any real change
in scenery. But it gets us out
of the house. We should get

out of the house more. Find a
movie theater that hasn't
banned Johnny yet for being
disruptive and catch a double
feature. Christ, do they even
still do those?

I stop and stare ahead, drumming my fingers
on the cart thoughtfully.

I wonder if I would be more fulfilled as a
killer of men, as a bringer of rain, if I
had some big family support system like
that. Heh, I wouldn't even know what to do
with it all. Neither would Johnny, come to
think of it.

8

INT. LIVING ROOM—NIGHT

There are no lights on. The only light
comes from the large window behind the
couch. Flashing lights can be seen, but not
any vehicles. There is a spotting of rain
on the glass. I walk in front of the camera
slowly and sit. MY hair is pulled back into
a loose ponytail that's partly undone. I am
wearing a red satin nightgown. The light
reflects off of it. It is torn on one side.
MY right shoulder is raw with a large muddy
scrape. MY glasses are just as dirty. MY
eyes cannot be seen behind them. MY right
breast is partially exposed. I try to pull
the fabric up higher, but it continues to
slip down. There are deep scratches that
are bleeding. I look down at MY knees. I'M
breathing heavily. A small smile can be
seen as I shake MY head.

ANDREW NADOLNY

          ME
     Yeah, Jimmy. The old man—
     Officer Moore—said he
     remembered you and your boy
     always making trouble for Ma.
     'Cept it wasn't Johnny's fault
     this time. I told him that.

I glance up and to MY right, taking a
cigarette that's passed to ME.

          ME
     You trying to get me addicted
     to these things, Johnny? Ain't
     that partly what did Jimmy in?

MY face draws down from amusement in an
instant.

          ME
     I'm sorry. I didn't say that.
     I didn't say it. I know I
     can't unsay it, so I didn't
     say it in the first place,
     okay? Is that okay?

I droop in visible relief then smile again,
shaky for the camera before taking a long
drag from the cigarette.

          ME
     At least these are Camels. I
     had one aunt who used to smoke
     filterless Pall Malls, too.
     They're fucking vile.

I consider the cigarette, playing with a
few different ways until I settle on
holding it curiously.

I AM THE RAINBRINGER

                    ME
        Yeah, I know I know, but I
        want it to look *aesthetic*.

I giggle and take the elastic from MY hair.
I shake it out. It's wet, and a little
muddy, a few drops spatter on the camera
lens.

                    ME
        Sexy, right?
    (shrug)
        So anyway, Dad always hated
        cops. Not because they
        bothered him like on the
        criminal end, but because we
        had this one neighbor who
        always used to make noise and
        have wild parties and do all
        sorts of annoying shit. He had
        a buddy on the force, so
        calling them never did shit.
        They'd just walk off laughing
        about it, and about how touchy
        my old man was. Sometimes they
        took reports if it was on
        something else. Dad just took
        to calling them puffed up
        pencil jockeys. Then there was
        that whole thing with the
        neighbors, but I don't wanna
        think about that. The cops
        weren't much good tonight
        either, but they sure had
        their pencils at the ready.
        'Cept for good old officer
        Moore who came swaggering out
        like Buford T. Justice,
        cigarette and all and offered

one to Johnny as his two thugs held him back, spitting and cussing. And he just looked at me and asked, "Now just what were you gonna do with that mean looking stick, little lady", talking about a piece of rebar I picked up from our yard. I'll tell you what I was gonna do with that "mean looking stick", I was gonna kill him that's what. I already had to take out one of the dogs with it.

I pantomime swinging a bat, sitting back shaking, **jittery**, with nerves.

                    ME
They got these two dogs—guard dogs, like that shitty old shack's got anything worth guarding—and every now and then they get to barking their stupid heads off over a squirrel or a racoon or the goddamn Jersey Devil for all I know, and tonight was one of those nights where Johnny could tell he was gonna get one of his migraines. That fucking barking was gonna make it so much worse. So he went over there to ask the guy. . .I think his name is George or Gus or some generic G name, if he could bring them in or quiet them down a bit, and Johnny's usually a lot more polite when the halos aren't dancing

around his eyes and the earthquake from *The Mole People* isn't raging on in his skull—and don't get me started on why that dumb bitch at the end ran under the pillar like a squirrel in the middle of the road—so he probably wasn't as nice as he could've been.
(shrug)
Jimmy's told me before that Johnny always had a temper. Well, maybe not always. I don't know, but he's always been sensitive, and Jimmy used to call him a powder puff when he was a kid to toughen him up. He used to cry easily and the other kids would pick on him, but then he smashed his cousin with a guitar when he was nine and threw some other kid who called him a fairy into a lunch table. He likes to tell me in that moment he saw *Ben Hur* in his mind, the Galley scene where he frees the slaves and rises up mighty and strong, and Johnny did grow up big and strong—the strongest, bravest man I've ever known in my life next to Dad. He reminds me of Dad a lot.

I sit up straighter. MY hips give an excited wiggle, like a puppy.

                    ME
I'm proud of myself. I didn't

hesitate. It wasn't like when I was a kid. I'm better than that now and I didn't hesitate at all. That fucker took a swing at Johnny, and I was on him, in this get up and all. It was probably a sight, and he sure wasn't expecting it, either. I'm stronger than I look. He went right down, big bastard went right down screaming at his wife to let the dogs out, but I attacked. No hesitation. You'd be so proud of me, Dad. I attacked. No hesitation. I was gonna kill him, hundred percent. Kill him kill him kill him and if it wasn't for the dogs, if Johnny hadn't taken over then because he's brave and wonderful and I love him so so much, and that worthless Mrs. Bitch of *his* just hung back shrieking, because she doesn't know shit about love or loyalty like I do. I think I remember grabbing the rebar and catching one of the dogs as it bit him. I feel bad because it wasn't the poor fucking dog's fault that his asshole owner fucked with my Johnny, but that doesn't matter and I—I didn't cry about it because it was *necessary* and I'm Johnny's unconditional sword and shield and he's mine and I remember telling Johnny how much I

loved him and how I hoped he
killed that fucker for *ever*
laying a finger on him—

I'M smiling and breathing heavier when I
finish. MY body is vibrating like I'M
overly caffeinated. Suddenly, I snort and
look **annoyed**.

> ME
> I never understood that trope
> in movies, either. A man is
> wailing on a guy who fucking
> deserves it—or maybe he
> doesn't, who the fuck cares—
> and his dumb bitch is
> screaming at him to—
> (falsetto)
> —stop it, you're gonna kill
> him!
> (normal)
> Like yeah that's the whole
> fucking point. Who cares if he
> kills him? Who cares if he
> deserves it? Johnny's enemies
> are mine and mine are his, and
> there's nothing more to be
> said about it.

I peer up and can be seen watching the path
of something behind the camera. A moment
later a man, JONATHAN, stands halfway in
the camera shot in muddy, blood-stained
jeans. HIS hands are extended towards ME. I
continue looking up at HIM. MY smile gets
wider.

> ME
> Hospital later?

I reach for HIM. The room goes dark to nothing but silhouettes. The lights fade away from outside.

INT. BATHROOM—DAY

The bathroom has soft 70s lighting, the cabinets are dark wood, the toilet seat is wood, and there's a window above the equally avocado tile that's open a little ways. I sit on the edge of the bathtub—an ancient avocado colored bit of porcelain—and hold up a small plastic pregnancy test.

> ME
> "Once that strip turned blue, I could no longer do any of those things. Not anymore. Because I was going to be a mother." I think that was one of the dumbest things I ever heard in a movie, when The Bride says that in *Kill Bill 2.* I can say that now.
> (smile)
> I can say that now.

The strap of another silky nightgown—black, this time—slides off MY shoulder. MY hair is tangled. MY face is flushed. MY eyes have remnants of red. There's redness around MY mouth as well—a telltale beard burn.

> ME
> Okay, I'll be honest. It's kinda soft scripted here. The

camera wasn't on at first and we got carried away. We didn't want to stop, and I thought we could recreate it but not really. I wasn't crying, if that's what you're thinking it looks like. Sometimes. . . sometimes when I get really happy, when something is so wonderful or feels so good, my eyes water like that. One time, Johnny and I were fucking, and I even knocked my own glasses off.

I continue to look at the test in MY hands. MY legs rapidly bounce up and down.

> ME
> Dad always said when you have kids, they need to come first, they're all that you think about and live for. That's probably what The Bride was getting at too—about changing priorities—which still seems stupid as Hell given that she was there to serve him. That was a charge she willingly undertook which *nothing else* should replace. And I wasn't sure how I could do that.

I look straight ahead, but MY focus is just north of the lens.

> ME
> How could I ever put anyone above Johnny? I'm glad he promised me that's a choice

I'll never have to make. I believe him.

The camera pans up to the ceiling, past the gently blowing curtain over the small window above the tub.

> ME (O.S.)
> For love does not envy, it does not boast, but most of all, love is loyalty, to love is to obey and if I hear my king say, "If you love me—"

INT. A STRANGER'S BEDROOM—NIGHT

The only light comes in from the window where it storms violently outside. No other details can be made out. MY silhouette is visible, standing at the foot of an unknown bed. I appear to be holding a pillow. It's not very large, and abruptly vanishes, possibly underneath a long dress I'M wearing.

> ME
> The stairs aren't hard yet, but everyone keeps swearing they will be. Well, Ma does, anyway. I don't really talk to anyone else, though I read a lot of things online. Baby forums and whatnot. But they're kinda worthless since it's all one mom of the year pissing contest.

I AM THE RAINBRINGER

I look down at the carpet and shuffle my feet.

> ME
> I'm starting to feel like Laura Dern—that 30 or 40-minute monologue she delivers in David Lynch's *Inland Empire.*
> (*a short but bitter-sounding laugh.*)
> I'm not actually sure why Christine was on the list. She was one of Dad's closest friends. She helped me out with the arrangements, the wake, all those things I couldn't be bothered to do because I just slept and slept, thinking I would wake up in some magic kingdom with singing animals, or in some anime with a *bishonen* prince or some shit. She and I used to talk all the time until I married Johnny. She didn't come to the wedding because she thought I should've been marrying Louis—he's her son—and I broke his heart. She said I broke Dad's heart because I was such an ungrateful little bitch for everything everyone had ever done for me, but I'm not the one who took all my son's money when he was living here, and then threw him out of the house after he complained. I'm not the one who kept going through his mail, then calling

his work all the time. So which one of us is really the bitch, Christine?

There's a pointed crack of thunder and flash of lightning. MY voice can be heard *sotto voce,* saying how perfect it is.

                    ME
I think that's a good sign. The storm and all. Not just as a cinematic backdrop—those are overdone as hell too—but rather, the godly hand of it all. I wasn't sure how I was even going to do this one. Well, I guess you could say God and Christine did it for me with the power outage and her stupid fucking smoking, and the oxygen machine not having a plan B. That's why I stopped smoking. That's why I kinda wish Johnny would too, but then he stands there at the patio door leaned against the frame looking like 70s cinematic sex itself, and I say fuck it. What's one thing on top of everything else? And we already decided anyway, he goes, I go. I think. . .I think that's still okay.

MY head tilts down. MY hand draws down over the pillow bulge on MY abdomen thoughtfully.

                    ME
When I was in fifth grade we

had a class guinea pig named
"Oreo. During free time each
day we'd be allowed to take
him out and play with him at
our desks a little bit. I
always liked doing that.
Petting him, sometimes feeding
him hay, which in retrospect
seems kinda stupid since he
had all the hay he wanted
right there in his cage. But
something about one of us kids
hand feeding him always seemed
to make it special somehow. So
one day, I took him back to my
desk. I was petting him as he
lay there, and I don't know
why, but I just stopped and
started pushing. . .and
pushing. . .and pushing down
until he started struggling
and started squealing. I don't
even know why I did that.
(swallow)

'Cause I love animals. Johnny
will even tell you I almost
crashed the car the other day
because of a racoon running
out into the middle of the
goddam road. I always feed the
stray cats that come 'round
the back patio. I didn't *enjoy*
hearing Oreo crying, but I
still kept doing it, and I
couldn't seem to stop myself
until this one kid in class,
Jay, came over and asked what
I was doing, so I stopped. I
snapped out of it and felt
like I hadn't even been there.

I look over at the bed. MY shoulders tremble. MY hand goes up to MY mouth.

                    ME
When I was sixteen and Louis was Nineteen, Dad—out of the blue one weekend—rented a limo and invited him and Christine to come with us to Atlantic City, to see a show and get dinner. Dad gave her a ruby bracelet. I thought I should get something for Louis, too, so I got him these cheap little stones at the Hallmark store in the mall that said things like, "Believe" and "Imagine". Would you believe he still has them? We ate at this Chinese place up high. I think it was *Bally's* or somewhere that wouldn't let us walk back through the casino because Louis was under twenty-one. It's funny 'cause he was older than me, but they didn't say anything to *me*. Probably because Louis was short, and I was wearing these five-inch platform heels, but I always looked older for my age, anyway. Christine looked so pretty standing next to Dad, and it was one of the most magical nights I ever had. She was like a mom to me; I don't know why I had forgotten about that. I don't know why she was on the list,

because she shouldn't have
been on the list, and I need
to clean up and put the key
back under the rock and
I. . .I. . .I'm not crying.
I'm not crying. It's just the
rain that makes it look that
way.

INT. KITCHEN—NIGHT

The camera is static. It does not move. The
sink is piled high with dishes. A sea of
roosters, of rooster eyes look back from
the vertical plates. A breeze blows the
curtains, the twin birds sway with the
flickering fluorescent bulb above the sink,
making them seem to dance. I sit at the
kitchen table. I'M wearing white satin and
White Linen. MY arms are folded as tight as
the swell of MY stomach and breasts will
allow. MY phone—a magenta Motorola Razr—is
flipped open.

> ME
> Hey, I wanted to apologize for
> what happened last night.

A man's voice comes from the phone. It is
LOUIS. It is strained but understanding.

> LOUIS
> Yeah, um. It's okay. You don't
> have to apologize. Not your
> fault and all. That guy,
> uh. . .your husband, Johnny, I
> mean. Is he okay?

                    ME

Yeah. Don't worry about him. I
mean he's ah, a little high
strung, and sometimes he's a
little intense. But he's not
like, gonna Jack Nicholson
through the door, or leave
dead shit on your step, or
call you and ask if you like
scary movies or anything like
that. I just—I just know that
was the last thing you needed
after your mom died. I thought
seeing a movie would be nice,
and Johnny wouldn't see a
Scary Movie if you held a gun
to his head. Thinks they're an
affront to horror fans, but
don't get him started.

                  LOUIS

Well. . .him showing up like a
screaming maniac *did* take my
mind off Mom for a while.

                    ME

That was my fault. I forgot to
turn the phone back on after
the movie. Really, I'm glad it
was just a bad dream he was
having, not a stroke or a
heart attack or God knows what
else. He felt really bad about
it this morning. It was just
so real to him. He thought
something was gonna happen to
me, or to the baby. And
sometimes he gets worked up
over things and with his
health—

I AM THE RAINBRINGER

                    LOUIS
Is he really okay? You
remember I'd get like that
too, then Mom got the doctor
to put me on this Abilify
stuff a coupl'a years ago, and
now I don't feel like flying
off 'cause the car won't
start.

                    ME
Yeah, remember I was there
that morning 'cause it was
when you crashed at the house?
I thought you were gonna throw
my pan through the window.

                    LOUIS
I'm sorry for that. For
scaring you. Uh. . .Johnny
doesn't. . .scare you like
that, does he?

                    ME
Johnny? No. Not like that. Not
like—

            JONATHAN (O.S.)
Babe, have you seen my
lighter?

I peer up and scan the table. I stand and
look around the kitchen with a frown.

                    ME
        No.
    (louder)
        No! I don't see it here!

Footsteps are heard approaching. I stop, turn around, and look past the camera.

> JONATHAN (O.S.)
> You talking to someone?

I glance down at the table and pick up the phone.

> ME
> Yeah. Just Louis.

> LOUIS
> Hi.

I grip the phone tighter, continuing to look past the camera.

> ME
> Lou, I'm gonna let you go so I can give Johnny a hand. I'll talk to you later.

I end the call before he answers.

> ME
> I wanted to talk to Lou for a sec before I finished the dishes but—

JONATHAN rushes past ME. HE checks all the surfaces in the kitchen. HIS hair at one point was pulled back, but it's since come undone. HIS black shirt is partially unbuttoned. HIS face is flushed with **angry** red splotches over his cheeks and forehead.

> JONATHAN
> It's not downstairs. It's not where I left it by the couch

on the end table, and I *know* I
left it there because I was
going back over the footage
from the other night, and I
know it was there.

                    ME
It'll turn up. You should
probably take a break anyway
because you're getting worked
up and—

                  JONATHAN
Did Ma take it again? I know
she won't fucking talk to me,
but I know she keeps putting
it in your head I need to stop
'for the baby'. I'm not
smoking around you, so I don't
see why it's any of her
fucking business *if I want to
smoke outside!*

I step back and watch HIM. I start to
scratch at MY head, running MY fingers back
through MY hair over and over again,
pulling out a few strands as I do.

                    ME
I don't know. . .Ma? Ma, did
you hide Johnny's lighter
again? Johnny you have another
one out there anyway and it'll
turn up, or maybe you left it
out there and—

                  JONATHAN
Not *Dad's* lighter! Not Dad's
fucking lighter!

JONATHAN sweeps the roosters off the top of the microwave. I jump as there is a **crash** from the dining room. I turn to MY right, listening to something, then turn back with MY eyes shut.

> ME
> She says it's for your own good, Johnny. She says you don't need to keep making yourself sicker when you got a family. I'm sorry. . . Ma. . .Ma, please just give it back. Johnny'll be fine. I take good care of Johnny. I take such good care of Johnny it don't matter if he smokes a few cigarettes, please—

> JONATHAN (O.S.)
> See! I can still fuck with your stuff, too, Ma! You remember this plate? This ugly fucking plate that grandma gave you!

> ME
> Ma! Ma you're too loud! It hurts! Johnny stop—

> JONATHAN (O.S.)
> Not until she gives back my fucking lighter!

There's another crash. I cover MY ears, turning away from whatever sound I appear to be hearing.

> ME
> J-Johnny—!

I AM THE RAINBRINGER

                    JONATHAN (O.S.)
          If you got something to say,
          Ma, you can say it to me! You
          can say it to me like you
          always have, or you can leave
          me alone, and leave my wife
          alone, and stop telling her
          lies about me, and stop
          telling my friends lies about
          me! Stop taking my stuff and
          leave me alone, leave me
          alone! You and dad you and dad
          I said I was sorry I said I was
          sorry, you fucking bitch. **This
          is why I fucking killed you!**

There is a silence that's not even broken
by the sound of breathing. I uncover MY
ears and lower MY shaking hands. The brass
lighter is back on the table.

INT. BATHROOM—DAY

The camera is dark until I pull back from
it, making the final adjustment to the
tripod. I sit back. I have a BABY in one
arm—a head as dark as MINE is visible
through the swaddling—and big brown eyes
watch the light of the camera. The BABY'S
small chubby arms reach for it. HER mouth
is open with a happy burble. I sit on the
edge of the tub. I turn the water on. I'M
dressed in a red retro bathing suit with a
big bow in front. Inside the tub is a green
bath seat with a little handlebar in front.

                    ME
          Maggie still loves the camera.
          She's a natural. You turn on
          the little light, or hold up
          this old Polaroid Dad got me,
          and she's a perfect little
          ham. Jimmy calls her 'Magpie'.
          Ma cried when I told her we
          were naming Maggie after her.
          She doesn't come 'round when
          Johnny's there, though. At
          least I don't think so. She
          gets real quiet now around
          him. He says he feels a chill.
          He still has nightmares. But I
          think Maggie makes those
          better. Don't you?

The water is still running. I bounce MAGGIE
and there's a little squeal. I turn and
check it before shutting it off.

                    ME
          I think we're warm enough
          here, don't you?

               MAGGIE
          AYAAYAA

                    ME
          That means "yes," I think. I'm
          pretty sure.

I laugh softly, then move the bright blue
towel. I set MAGGIE down in the seat
carefully.

                    ME
          Her first word was 'Johnny'.
          Not 'Mommy', not 'Daddy'.

I AM THE RAINBRINGER

Jeez, I wonder if I'm doing something wrong.

There's another happy squeal in response to the name "Johnny." I get a yellow rubber duckie, a pink rubber hippo, and a blue rubber dolphin from the sink.

                    ME
Now these guys here are—

                  MAGGIE
MAAAYMOOOOAAAAK

                    ME
Manny, Moe, and Jack. Real original, I know. My little oatmeal raisin here.

I kneel beside the tub and get a small washcloth. MAGGIE grabs for the duck—for Manny. There are a lot of splashes.

                    ME
The oatmeal raisin is the smartest and sneakiest of cookies because it can cleverly disguise itself as a chocolate chip. But y'know what? You never actually get a *bad* oatmeal raisin cookie. I've had some absolutely disgusting things calling themselves chocolate chips, but at worst I've had a sort of passable oatmeal raisin. That was the last time I was at the hospital with Johnny. He's been having these dizzy spells which the doc thinks

might be his blood pressure.
But I watch his sodium so I
don't know how that could be
possible. Well anyway—

I laugh as I'M splashed and give a tiny
flick of water back. MAGGIE—Manny in hand—
splashes harder. SHE rocks back and forth
on the seat.

> ME
> Oh jeez, don't tell me the
> suction's coming up again. I
> swear this little magpie is
> strong as an ox, just like
> her—

There's a loud **CRASH** and the sound of
something heavy tumbling down down down. It
is followed by a loud cry of pain. I'M up.
I'M on MY feet. I do not hesitate. I'M
running. I knock over the tripod and the
camera goes down down down.

The sound of footsteps and screams of
"Johnny!" can be heard. More splashing
comes from over the side of the tub. The
water goes down down down onto the floor.
The lens is cracked. It's stained with
water.

The splashing continues along with
squealing and yells of "MAAAAAAEEEE."

The splashing continues until the sound of
a *SPLASHTHUNK* can be heard. The sound of
splashing dies down. Then it stops. The
yellow light of the bathroom flickers. The
cracked lens remains focused on the side of
the tub.

I AM THE RAINBRINGER

The sound of the old wall clock up on the wall seems to grow louder and louder as the seconds. The footsteps come back in another rushing run until they stop. There is no movement in front of the lens. There is no sound except for breathing. There is no sound except for a scream.

It is a loud scream that may have been a child's name, or a curse to a God who was only a man after all, a man who slowly makes his way back up the stairs, a man whose left arm is hanging at his side while he pulls himself up with the other, up the railing, up the stairs, up up up.

There are legs and feet in front of the camera now. There is a body dropping down, half flinging itself into six inches of water. It comes back up with the silence of the grave. The footsteps behind the camera stop.

                JONATHAN (O.S.)
        Babe? Oh God. . .

                      ME
        That's the thing I hate the
        most about kids in horror
        movies. . .The second. . .the
        second you see one, it's over.
        Th-the suspense is over. . .'c-
        cause you know. . .'c-cause you
        know. . .with more
        certainty. . .than. . .than
        you've ever known
        anything. . .that nothing. . .
        nothing bad is ever going to
        happen to them.

FADE TO BLACK

> ME (V.O.)
> Love does not delight in evil
> but commits evil nonetheless
> because—
> <u>If you love me</u>. . .

> —end—

THIS IS NOT MY MOVIE

GARY A. BRAUNBECK

"The most confusing situation is to be a ghost who sees terrible things but can't report it."
—Fanny Howe

A DARK MOVIE SCREEN

For several seconds there is only the sound of the occasional hiss and pop of film running through a projector. Just when we think the darkness is becoming exasperating rather than enigmatic, we hear a VOICE whose timbre borders on the artificial, but we know this isn't AI; this VOICE carries, hidden deeply within, a heart-rending, even agonizing sadness that, when we try to imagine its cause, terrifies us:

> **VOICE**
> There once was a dreadful, terrible,an Awful Thing that happened to people like yourselves, like a lot of other people, and they lived on a street like a lot of other streets, in a house like a lot of other houses. . .but that would change. You see, if one were to have waited a year or even two before asking Ray and/or Melanie Price how they were coping, neither would have been able to look you in the eye as they mumbled through what surely would have been a well-rehearsed but elusive response, the kind of

non-answer answer private but courteous people give when they don't want to offend you by saying that it's none of your goddamn business.

(We hear the music of an acoustic guitar; the melody is familiar, but we can't quite place the song)

VOICE (con't)
If, on the other hand, you were to have asked either of them if they felt like talking about, *ahem*, well. . . anything, anything at all, both would maybe—*maybe*—make a few vague references about The Awful Thing that happened, without, of course, getting into specifics (you'd clearly hear the capitalization when either spoke those words—The Awful Thing).

(A voice begins singing as the tune becomes clearer, and we recognize the voice of Gordon Lightfoot singing one of his greatest songs, a lullaby: "The Pony Man")

But I'm getting a bit ahead of myself and that will not do; that will not do at all. I have so many memories of so many men, women, and children. They touch me and all that they are, all they've experienced, their desires, their pain, their joy, their secrets, their fears, their regrets, their hopes and dreams. . .it all becomes, and remains, part of me. . .but, again, I'm getting ahead of myself. My apologies.

THIS IS NOT MY MOVIE

There exists no ghost, be it a person, place, or Other, that has not had a past physical form.

SLOW IRIS-OUT REVEALS:

The back of a hunched-over, malformed FIGURE with long, tangled, unwashed hair, its misshapen legs bent painfully at the knees, balancing an OBJECT of intense interest upon them.
The CAMERA moves slowly upward and to the right, nearly over the FIGURE's shoulder, and for one-eighth of a second (**three frames**, almost too quickly for it to register) it catches a glimpse of the OBJECT—but then, as if it knew it was being spied on, the FIGURE whirls around, revealing that where a face should be is a flat screen filled with electronic snow. The CAMERA moves in closer, then closer still, unable (or perhaps unwilling) to break away from the pull of the screen, drawn forward until it is swallowed whole by the snow, leaving it helpless, a prisoner, a zero-time ghost, David Bowman entering the immutable prime-mover monolith in 2001: A Space Odyssey; and with a snap! the screen clears and we read the following words:

Hello, and thank you for your patronage. Now sit back and enjoy the pre-show entertainment.

I

"Mr. and Mrs. Smith get married. They have problems, but they get back together and live happily ever after. End of movie. Two weeks later, he kills her, grinds her body up, feeds it to his girlfriend who dies of ptomaine poisoning, and *her* husband is prosecuted and sent to the electric chair for it. But at least we had our happy ending earlier. You want a happy ending? Tough shit. There's no such thing. The only ending is Death. *Ta-da!*"
—Robert Altman

AN OLD, RECORDED broadcast from a radio news program:

". . .address tonight by the President when he's expected to announce the immediate withdrawal of all troops from [static; followed by several seconds of white noise].

"Details are still sketchy concerning the multiple deaths resulting from [static] three nights ago. The [white noise] has been closed since then, and the future of [yet more static] remains in doubt.

"Temperatures tonight remain well below freezing, with highs struggling to reach the low twenties. . ."

Tacked to a cork bulletin board is a yellowed page torn from the Arts & Entertainment section of *The Cedar Hill Ally;* date illegible:

INTERNATIONAL AWARD-WINNING HORROR DIRECTOR CHOOSES CEDAR HILL'S JANUS CINEMA FOR WORLD PREMIERE!

The Company of Lesser Demons

THIS IS NOT MY MOVIE

The New Film from Trenton Wright

Director of *Wire Mesh Mothers, The House of Last Resort,* and
The Far Side of the Lake

WITNESS: The movie, it jammed up and then it *melted*—you know how it'll sort of start to sizzle in the center and then spread out real quick like someone spilled a kinda burning liquid—anyway, I got a whiff of. . .it was like an incinerator just roared to life, but like, y'know, *outside* but real close, so I look up at the projection booth and see the flames—and there was *a lot* of 'em, I never seen a fire start so fast—and then I hear the projectionist holler and then. . .and then *shriek*. . .christamighty, that was a sickening. . .ugly, *ugly* sound I'm probably gonna be hearing for the rest of my life, and there wasn't nothing anybody could do for that poor guy up there. He was throwing himself all over the place, slamming into the walls, pounding his arms against the windows, trying to get out, trying to stop the flames that were all over him. . .and by now other people, they're lookin up there too and starting to run out so I grab my kids and we get the hell outta Dodge. . .God, all them other poor folks. . .you can. . .still *smell 'em.* . ..

Ghosts have gravity; their spectral origin comes from their bones, hairs, nails, cuts, mortar, stone, iron, gangrene, mental borders. There exists no ghost, be it a person, place, or Other, that has not had a past physical form.

That's why it's best to prefer old roll cameras and emulsifiers to digital cameras that don't know how to whisper.

It's best to prefer the device that hides its reflection only with dust; a device that smells and can spit, bite, beat, and hurt.

One misses that territory of the translucent roll, the rite of stopping time and descending the room to a cavern where a dragon ignites the ghosts of a ball of SUPER 8 onto a screen that remembers the proper order of the stories and then forgets them again.

163

GARY A. BRAUNBECK

Advance, stop, open, expose, close; advance, stop, open, expose, close; advance—be born; open—fight; expose—love; close—die.

Advance, be born; open, fight; expose, love; die, close.

This is why I prefer shaped images, which I can touch and see through the sun.

So I can claim the helpless and scratch their memory.

Petrify the faces that smile so brokenly at the lens.

Set the celluloid on fire.

Wound the lamp and nail the shadows on the wall, so that the illusion is trapped and there is no more spit, no more bite, no more beat, no more hurt.

Something pulls us in; it's a desire that has no bottom and it frightens us.

That's why we seek shelter with, and within, the One True Camera.

Because we can hold on to a roll, carry it, feel its shape, its weight, and know that it is there, that it is a fragile body like ours: acetate, cellulose, gelatin tissue, cartilage, and bones where the silver grains, in mysterious, unpredictable ways are hidden, just like our bodies when exposed to pain.

The camera must be dark for things to enter it.

A roll is not born but revealed.

And what is revealed no longer belongs to anyone.

In celluloid there are no pixels that force order on things; there is chaos, metamorphosis, passion, and putrefaction.

Bodies that someday will hide their social decorum under dirt and grass that's been devoured by mushrooms. Bodies that will lose all sense of the acetate, cellulose, gelatin tissue, cartilage, and bones, surrendering to the cracks, spots, and dust until they become images of a memory without gravity.

There exists no ghost, be it a person, place, or Other, that has not had a past physical form.

AND NOW OUR FEATURE PRESENTATION

OPENING CREDITS BEGIN:

2

"A story should have a beginning, a middle, and an end, but not necessarily in that order."
—Jean-Luc Godard

So.

Pay Attention:
Eyes wide. Popcorn in.
Hand drink. At the.
Ready. Comfortable in.
The seat. You betcha.
Look. Up. As.
More words appear. On The screen.
The Holy. Screen.
The Miracle. Screen.
The Movie. Screen.
And a simple equation is now completed:

$$Ed = h\,tu\,/\,tp2 + E = hv + y = M^*x = y + P = 0 + (50.0\,)/(m) = 50.0D$$

Darkness + Light + Opening Credits on Screen + One Who Views

Another fundamental principle of order that is, in this moment, self-evident only to the Projector and the precisely-choreographed inner-workings of its numerous mechanisms. Mechanisms that, by their simple existence and well-maintained day-to-day function, reinforce one of Arthur Schopenhauer's more controversial principles: *"Perception should not be mistaken to require only biological senses; rather, perception, when we think about what is really going on, should be conceived of as being influenced by the world. Perception is, at its most basic, the detection of an object by a subject—and if all objects are also subjects, then all subjects perceive while on their way to becoming* objects *for other subjects to perceive, and so on. Perception is, then, receiving information from the world, which creates a causal influence between an object and a subject. Information and causation reduced to the same ontological category."* So the ontological—that is, anything relating to the nature of being—is expanded by the take-up reel that pulls and rolls the movie upward between the notched wheels that keep it taut at all times, turning at a constant rate of speed, with the perforations in the sides of the film maintaining that constant movement so the movie screen displays what it's supposed to—

—hold on—

—rewind—

—to repeat: the screen displays what it's supposed to—

—unless.

Unless something goes wrong.

And something does seem wrong.

Yes.

Something *is* wrong.

Really wrong.

Something's really truly seriously *wrong*.

Alors écoutez bien, m'droogies:

Every Camera dictates the language it speaks. One might speak Surrealist; another, the Mysterious; yet another, the Fantastical, etc. No film director, no editor, no production designer, no cinematographer—regardless of how technically proficient or artistically gifted—can force the Camera to use any language other than that which it was created to speak.

And this CAMERA, the one that will be our guide, informs us: *I speak rot and decay; putrescence and pain; unheard screams from lost and stolen children, helpless deafening wails from their mothers, impotent howls of fury from their fathers; I speak a rapist's terrible quixotic love for his inexpressible loneliness; I speak the sadness of bloated white things gliding just beneath the surface; winter's stinging rain on the faces of the shabby and freezing homeless; kisses on the hollow tips of a mass-shooter's bullets; the impatient rustling of a vulture's feathers in Africa, waiting for the crumpled starving black bone-bag of a child in the fetal position to just Get On With It, Already; the spiraling vapors wafting up from a thick, rich bowl of human soup prepared by a lunatic's hands; the* snap! *of a despairing suicide's neck as the garage noose fulfills its duties; the soul-sick staccato sobs heaved into sopping pillows from the swollen faces of women beaten half to death by men they know they* should *leave but somehow can't and never will. . .I am fluent in these and many others.*

So, it's best to listen to my images and how I choose to present them; this cavern in which you journey is mine, and I alone will tell the dragon when and how to ignite the ghosts of a ball of SUPER 8 onto a screen.

An echo: "I imagined three different endings for it; I don't remember which one I finally used."

3

"The true reality in which we live is invisible; hence we have to be
satisfied with what we see."
—Michelangelo Antonioni

THE BRAIN CANNOT retain or comprehend an image that lasts
less than **two frames:** one-twelfth of a second.
    three frames: one eighth of a second.
    four frames: one-sixth of a second.
    eight frames: one-third of a second.
    sixteen frames: two-thirds of a second.
    These brief but often violently juxtaposed images are used to
plant subconscious seeds in the minds of the audience to either A)
keep them agitated, or B) prepare them bit by bit for a shocking,
full-blown, unblinking reveal.
    You'll *need* this.
    Why?
    Because.
    Because. There are.
    Becauses. There are. Many Becauses.
    First Because:
    Because up on the screen what is seen is this:

This one's going to be about as bad as it gets
so if you want to bail, now is the time; all
EXITS will be locked once the main feature has
begun.

This one's going to be about as bad as it gets so if you want to
bail, now is the time; all EXITS will be locked once the main feature
has begun

168

THIS IS NOT MY MOVIE

Now reach out—no, up, reach *up*, and feel the screen, the back of the silver-silk screen. . .ah-ha!

The Silver Screen. It finally occurs to you.

The Silver Screen. So that's where the phrase comes from. Huh. Always wondered about that one, y'know? I mean, with all these labyrinthian multi-screen motels passing themselves off as movie theaters these days, you can bet the farm not one of them uses a silver-silk—

—wait a minute there, Theseus.

Rewind a few more frames.

Let's not forget about that something being Really Truly Seriously Wrong part.

Look—no, *stare* at the words, but start—

(Wait! It's time to play Famous Dialogue From Famous Movies!
   (BASIL RATHBONE: *Get it?*)
   (DANNY KAYE: *Got it.*)
   (BASIL RATHBONE: *Good.*)
   (Easy one—*The Court Jester*!)

(We hear a loud sigh that is simultaneously irritated and resigned, and then):

—repeat: start with that first line.
Stare at the words.
Do not.
Blink:

This one's going to be about as bad as it gets

It doesn't take long for the tumblers to begin falling into place—*click!*—the image of a short, lean sinewy man wearing a pork-pie hat with a perpetually deadpan expression stepping up *into* a movie—*click!*—and

(four frames, one-sixth of a second: hands wearing skin-tight nitrile examination gloves arranging a series of stainless-steel surgical instruments as something small and terrified and unseen whimpers in the background)

thank you Joseph Francis "Buster" Keaton for the genius of *Sherlock, Jr!*—and for that matter, thanks to each and every player who ever starred in a silent film; it's easy to imagine any one of them looking over their shoulder to see that the words they've just spoken have been pressed up against the screen—*click!*—

(sixteen frames, two-thirds of a second: a screaming and terrified 3-year-old girl withDown's Syndrome dressed as a princess pounding scraped hands against the back window of a car that isn't Mommy's isn't Daddy's choking against pain her bruised throat bloody

THIS IS NOT MY MOVIE

> snot sluicing into her mouth
> please help please help please
> please   help   please
> *pleasehelppleaseplease)*

the words upon the screen would
be reversed to those *within* the
movie, right? Now the tumblers
are solidly in place so backwards it
is reading backwards looking
backwards everything is bass-
ackwards—*click!*—

> (two frames, one-twelfth of a
> second: the man in the front
> seat of the car looking into the
> rearview mirror at the 3-year-
> old   girl   choking   and
> screaming and pounding her
> scraped and now bleeding)

and that seems to be the obvious
solution and so and so and so:

```
This one's going to be about as bad as it
gets so if you want to bail, now is the
time; all EXITS will be locked once the
main feature has begun.
```

Second Because:
The rationality of the single image is *prima facie*: its beauty, its
anger, its poetry, romance, mystery, eroticism, humor; its power
to enchant, amuse, educate, and horrify are all classical aesthetics
of form; any single fixed image on a strip of film doesn't tell you a
goddamn thing. It doesn't reveal *any* wondrous new phases of
being, doesn't tell you what's happened before it came into
existence, and it sure as hell doesn't reveal with any degree of
certainty what's going to follow; its *will*—if such a
neurotransmitted volition can be applied to a piece of celluloid
small enough to balance on your fingertip—is at all times

171

subservient to the Camera; its growth or degradation is so slow as to be nearly imperceptible.

```
HARD CUT TO:

A too-bright, cavernous room with cement
walls and a few exposed overhead pipes;
somewhere in the distance a constant,
rhythmic dripping can be heard. It is here
we meet O (Object? Observer? Obiter
dictum?)—not the "O" from the infamous
erotic novel The Story of O by Anne
Descoles or the 1975 film of the same name.
```

(*And this has what to do with anything, Mr. Movie Trivia that no one gives a flying fuck in a rolling doughnut about?*

(Oh, really? Then what was with all that *Court Jester* horseshit earlier?

(*I have no idea what's being referred to.*)

(Uh-huh. Nice try, but we've tried these distractions about, oh, say, 17,436 times before. But who's counting? Shall I return—with the others who, of course, are not stupid—to O?)

(*Works for me.*)

THIS IS NOT MY MOVIE

O is looking at a washed-out newspaper photograph composed of incalculable gray and white dots that individually are meaningless but holistically are *supposed* to form a discernible image, yet. . .eh, um, *well.* . .okay, let's face it, folks, this ???-year-old "image" clipped from a ???-year-old copy of *The Cedar Hill Ally* could be focused on from a point in space with a Celestron CGX-L 1400 EdgeHD Computerized Telescope, and even *then* it probably wouldn't reveal anything more than it does right now, not under these god-awful buzzing snapping blinking popping fluorescent lights in this dank mausoleum someone had the cheekiness to call a Hall of Records. . .

O takes a moment to compose itself, to calm down, to remind itself to not get emotional; it mustn't get emotional like the other times, so it turns away from the record book for a few moments, remembering that it left some messages for itself once, a few things to distract it, to help prevent it from getting emotional. It glances around at the water-stained walls until, at last, it finds the message, written in bright red paint:

Ego numquam remitto me
           (I will never forgive myself)
Beneath that:
Numquam nobis dimittemus
           (We shall never forgive ourselves)
And lastly:
Nulla remissio
           (There is no forgiveness)

O whispers agreement and, once more, accepts that all it will have to go on are the blurry figures in the photo's foreground, figures that have been misshapen by age, neglect, and exposure to clammy temperatures; there are other things in the picture, things on the ground, things that may or may not be (*oh Christ oh Christ don't look don't look wepromisedyourself!*) sheet-covered bodies, some of which are—*click!*—horrifyingly small (is that a *child's* hand peeking out from under the corner of that sheet on the far left? *youknowgoddamnwellitis!*); behind all of these stands—*click!*—a gutted building, and the oversized bold-print headline—which is now a *side*line because whomever clipped this page and pasted it into this laughable excuse of a record book thinking that it would look more aesthetically pleasing—reads:

Arson
Not
Ruled
Out
As
Cause
Of
Deadly
(smudge)
Night
Fire

THIS IS NOT MY MOVIE

. . .and the equally informative sub-
head/sideline:

> Families
> still
> waiting for
> updates as
> the
> ". . .proces
> s of
> identifying
> the
> victims
> is slow-
> going."

The structure of those cascading words—not the words themselves, but the way they glide downward—looks almost like:

an unfolding Bukowski poem about his being so drunk he pissed in his bed again;

or an uncoiling roll of barbed wire to be used atop an internment camp fence;

perhaps an unrolling scroll of music from inside a vandal-demolished player piano;

maybe an unwinding spool of thread dropped from the dead hand of an old seamstress;

even the unfurling of a tourniquet before being wrapped around a junkie's arm.

However, since it can now be safely surmised that O is the Observer (What else *could* it be? C'mon), instead of a poem or a scroll or a spool, let's make the simile a strip of film that's threading its way through the mechanisms inside a projector (not forgetting that the projector is itself a mechanism—again, we're not stupid) and once the film passes down, once the light inside shines against it, it passes through the lens, and the eyes of the filmgoer adjust and look up
to the screen
the holy screen
the big screen

175

foreign film screen
miracle screen
adventure screen
blaxploitation screen
arthouse screen
musical screen
extreme screen
drama screen
grindhouse screen
animation screen
fuck-me screen
rom-com screen
mystery screen
hentai screen
bloody screen
slaughter screen
murder screen
suicide screen
horror screen
murder screen
suicide screen
horror screen
murder screen
suicide screen
horror screen
horror screen
horror screen
Horror screen
Horror Screen
HORROR SCREEN

(. . .said we're not stupid. . .said nothing about being subtle.)

O shakes its head at my inappropriate humor and glares at us.

I hear sounds.

THIS IS NOT MY MOVIE

Ghost sounds.

We hear ghost-sounds of:

a celebration: of emptied champagne flutes smashed into a fireplace;

(*Congratulations, one and all! I'd say tonight's movie premiere was a grand success!*)

or a large window being cracked by incompetent window-washers; a slapstick comedy;

(*Well. . .this is another fine mess you've gotten us into!*)

A hand-held mirror shattering as it's thrown to the floor; a hospital soap opera scene;

(*I know how hideous, twisted, and appalling this face looks! I don't need to look at it again, goddammit!*).

Oh, man. . .Barbara Stanwyk'd deliver the living shit out of that line—better than Bette Davis or Joan Crawford at their peaks ever could.

END OF OPENING CREDITS

CAMERA FOLLOWS O. . .

. . .who speaks in a deceptively lighthearted, conversational tone, but we can tell that what is being said is much more important than O means for us to infer:

O

Martin Ritt, the director, once pointed out that you could take hundreds of feet of film, hundreds of feet of the most disjointed, disparate, nonsensical pieces of <u>inane</u>, utter <u>crap</u> that on the surface

```
seem  to  have  nothing  to  do
with  each  other,  and  splice
them  together  into  something
organic,   something   with   a
natural,   compelling flow that clarifies
```
parts of the narrative that otherwise would
have no other way of being introduced. Hell,
sometimes you could even manage to create a
mini narrative <u>within</u> the major narrative. God
bless the montage. There are days I wish <u>life</u>
was like that, don't you?

(Even though Ritt was correct in his thinking, our first impulse is
to shout Fuck the Montage! because it is created through violence
that is unseen by the viewer. By collision. By conflict. By the
conflict of two filmed elements forced like gladiators in a
colosseum to exist in direct opposition to one another. By conflict.
By collision. Cells in their division form the phenomenon of
another order—the organism or the embryo—so, on the other side
of the dialectical leap from the shot there is the Montage.)

```
HARD CUT:

O's  attention—and,  so,  also,  unavoidably,
ours—is  now  focused  on  a. . .person?  thing?
obiter  dictum?  I  hold  our  breath,  gaze
unblinking.

What  we  are  watching  is  revealed  to  be  E—
(best  guess?  E  stands  for  Eye)  the  Eye
through  which  O—and,  also,  unavoidably,  we—
shall  bear  witness  to  the  narrative  in
which  O  and  we  are  to  play  some  role  yet  to
be  disclosed.  Or  not.  Right  now,  it's
anybody's  guess.  Hell,  I  might  just  be  here
to  serve  as  collateral  damage  or  a  warning
to  others.

Have  we  mentioned  yet  that  this  isn't  going
to—?
```

THIS IS NOT MY MOVIE

(Spoilers Excised)

O

(Anger building until it explodes into near-shrieking fury)

GODDAMMIT! This jumping back and forth between "I" and "we" and "us" and "me" and all the other heavy-handed variations you're employing because you think it's oh-so-devilishly original and witty, but in actuality is just hollow, artsy, and grandiose to the point of testing the limits of someone's gag reflex! The schtick has played itself out. You've gotten your point across, so you can put away the narrative sledgehammer now—*right now!* Because if you do it once more, you're going to seriously irk me, and then we're going to have—as Leonardo DiCaprio put it to Daniel Day-Lewis in *Gangs of New York*—which *should have* won the Best Picture Oscar in 2002, but I digress—we're going to have *BUSINESS* understand? And I don't want to have *BUSINESS*. There's too much for us to cover to waste time with *BUSINESS*. So, stop it. As in, refrain from. Desist. Cease and. It's all fun and games. Until. Someone gets. Finish that last one on your own. You're not stupid.

So, knock it the hell off. And remember: *Esse est percipi.*

O

(*More or less in control; best to go with that "less" option, just to be safe*)

Also, from now on you will refer to yourself *only* by the name of—and admittedly this might be a bit too much foreshadowing—Sergeant Howie, is that clear? Just nod in agreement, Sergeant Howie. Dere oo go, my pwecious widdle *custodes mortis.*

(*Sergeant Howie? Say wha-huh? Shouldn't we understand that reference?*)

(O thinks she's playing the role of Greek Chorus, but she's just a glorified assistant guide. That prima-donna see-you-next-tuesday isn't going to dictate anything more to us. If she thinks that He/She/It/Them/Whoever/Whatever/Whenever/Somewhere/Somehow/Somewhen (who the fuck can tell at this point?) is going to put up with my—oops, rewind—*Sergeant Howie* being talked down to like this. . .well, there is the cutting room. Not unheard of for a movie character to get 86'ed halfway through the movie. But we'll give her this one. This time. This once. The One really in charge of this whole Jean-Luc Goddard-ish structural phantasmagoria has probably seen *Weekend* five times too many and is now scrambling to give everyone the impression that all of this eventually coalesces into a clear-cut traditional linear narrative. Well, guess what—

(Spoilers Excised. Again.)

CUT TO:

THE FAR END OF A DIMLY LIT HALLWAY.

THIS IS NOT MY MOVIE

E leans on a discount-store metal walker and stares down at a package leaning against the door. It's in a sturdy brown amply padded envelope with E's address, as with the other packages, listed twice, once in the center and again in the upper left corner. An old trick to make certain that something doesn't get lost en route.

Of course it would be delivered here. E listed this apartment and not the P.O. Box as the return address this time. The last time. This very last time.

CUT TO:

INSIDE E's UNNERVINGLY DARK APARTMENT.

Unlocking the door and shuffling quietly inside so as not to disturb the neighbors, E sets the now-folded walker off to the right and tosses the door keys onto the small wooden table on the left. Its scarred top is an odd half-moon shape (what people once referred to as a Telephone Table, back in the days of heavy black rotary phones that sat on such tables, maybe with a colorful, flower-shaped doily crocheted by some long-deceased aunt placed decoratively beneath it, the table itself weighted down and held in place by the giant White and Yellow Pages phone books on the shelf beneath).

It was the shape and condition of the piece—this antiquated, seemingly useless half-moon shaped relic with its scarred top—that convinced E to purchase it for five dollars at the flea market that always set up shop on the sidelines of the Valley

Drive-In every weekend during summer. E sensed a kinship, as much as one can feel kinship with a discarded piece of furniture, but he was struck with a sense that they were the same in many ways: both set aside, their days of usefulness approaching the expiration date, treasured memories so carefully accumulated over the years now splintering into negligible, insignificant, unrecognizable fragments, all of it inexorably bearing down until you couldn't tell if the scarred marks were there before or after the terrible staining job.

E stops what he knows the hospital psychiatrist will call Projecting. It's a table, just a fucking table, that's all. Just an ugly old-fashioned flea-market piece of unwanted junk table.

E flips on the lights with a perpetually gloved hand, brightening the cramped efficiency apartment.

Blinks so the all-important remaining vision adjusts to the sudden absence of shadows.

Coughs to clear the throat, swallowing a small, tight viscous blister of who-knows-what.

E sighs with relief (*Relief? Really? Relief? asks the psychiatrist again, and then probably something like, are you sure it's not Regret? Maybe Something Stronger, Something Worse Than Regret?*) at having survived another weekly physical therapy session. . .

. . .followed by seventy minutes on the paratransit bus to get to work. . .

THIS IS NOT MY MOVIE

. . .where the next five hours were spent running the weekend's double feature at the Valley Drive-In. . .

. . .before rewinding the films and setting up for the next night. . .

. . .and then cleaning the booth and performing the nightly self-written and - imposed list of checks on both projectors (even though the owners and management couldn't give a flying fuck in a rolling doughnut about it). . .

. . .taking pride in knowing that the Valley has the last two authentic, fully functioning Philips DP70 projectors in the state, model numbers EL4000/01 (the 60 Hz variant), and EL4000/00 (the 50 Hz variant), both circa 1972—the last year they were manufactured in the U.S. . ..

. . .and it was because of E, because of E's pride, because of E's love for the movies, any movie, all movies, even the bad ones (sometimes especially the bad ones) that the projectors were treated as if they were sentient, were able to understand the things whispered to them as E cleaned, polished, caressed, and embraced their monocoque cast-iron chassis, keeping them oil-immersed. . .

. . .(non-operating side only, and maybe a drop or five for E's leg braces). . .
. . .so they continued to run so very well. E thought of them as friends, his only friends, and if they possessed some form of consciousness, he hoped they felt the same

way in return and did not see or think of E as just the remains of a human being that lives in a coffin called a room, in a tomb called a building, in the center of a graveyard called a neighborhood.

A Voice in E's Head
(*whispering*)
>   Pour   notre   propre   bien,
>   rappelez-vous : en voyant, il
>   y   a   de   l'amour.   Être   vu
>   suscite de l'horreur.

E
>   Comme si je ne pouvais jamais
>   oublier. Maintenant s'il te
>   plaît, s'il te plaît, tais-
>   toi. Juste   pour   un   petit
>   moment.

E doesn't need to be reminded that in seeing there is love, but in being seen there is abhorrence. E works quite hard to not be seen, to not be exposed to the world's abhorrence.

E
(*we can't interpret the tone*)
>   Thanks, folks, and a big tip
>   of the hat to Kobo Abe, for
>   allowing the peanut gallery to
>   share   his   cheerful   *Box   Man*
>   words.

Still standing by the table, back sore from the late-night bus ride home, E almost laughs, wondering if next week it might be fun to ask Dr. (please call-me-Barbara) Hayes that if it's possible when one Projects, if they can Project onto a film

THIS IS NOT MY MOVIE

Projector that in turn Projects images and sounds onto a screen that Projects them into the senses of a viewer who might then Project them back onto people or things like, say, a film Projector. Chew on that one for a bit, Doc.

The thought causes E to remember a snippet of something playwright Samuel Beckett once said about ". . .the eternal anguish of perceivedness. . ."

Can a film projector feel the anguish of the characters in the movies that pass through its mechanisms? Can it feel loneliness? Regret? Might it even feel E's afflictions? Isn't that in itself a form of sentience, of life?

Could it forgive him his. . .his guilt?

> **A Different Voice in E's Head**
> L'un d'eux sourit, essayant de supporter la douleur d'être vu. N'est-ce pas vrai ?

> **E**
> Yes, one does have to grin and bear the pain of being seen; that's right, as in correct, as in you've hit it directly on the nose and then shoved it up both nostrils. Now are you going to keep paraphrasing Kobo Abe or will you come up with something of your own you'd like to share with the room?—but until then—be quiet for a little while, wouldja?

Hanging his coat on the wall hook, he grabs a tissue from the box that shares space along with his keys on the half-moon table, blows his nose, and squeaks toward his bed, rhythmically patting the envelope against the heel of his hand as if tamping down a pack of fresh unopened cigarettes. He sits, turns the envelope over, pulls the red open-here tab, and removes a small round 8mm film canister, label marked REEL #3.

A thin but crooked smile squirms only a third of the way across his face before freezing, the far-right corner of his mouth appearing to have been wrenched downward by a fisherman's invisible hook. He ignores the slowly trickling drool.

E

(His voice growing more excited with each word; a pretty good imitation of the classic Mad Scientist—say, a road-company Colin Clive in the original Frankenstein—"It's alive! It's alive! It's ALIVE!")

> *Now I can splice it all together!* So bellows the meshuggah moviemaker inside his homey hovel, overacting to the point that makes even the late great Rod Steiger's performance in *The Amityville Horror* look understated and multi-layered by comparison bwa-ha, bwa-ha, bwa-ha-ha-ha-ha! *Oh, yes!* he hisses for effect, I'll splice it all together, and then I'll gather our audience for the exclusive preview right here at the *Le*

THIS IS NOT MY MOVIE

cinéma d'art et d'essai du thésauriseur bipolaire et la Maritinisation d'une heure. . .name's a little wordy but that can be fixed in editing. . .and after the exclusive preview I'll get their reactions before the Local Filmmakers Contest at the Janus Thursday night, and we'll *win*, and afterward I might even stick around for that big over-hyped horror movie premiere. . .

4

"Cinema is not a reflection of reality; it is the reflection *of a reflection* of reality."
—Andrei Tarkovsky

IF **ONE WERE** to have waited a year or even two before asking Ray and/or Melanie Price how they were coping, neither would have been able to look you in the eye as they mumbled through what surely would have been a well-rehearsed but elusive response, the kind of non-answer answer that private but courteous people give when they don't want to offend you by saying that it's none of your goddamn business.

If, on the other hand, you were to have asked either of them if they felt like talking about, *ahem*, well. . .anything, anything at all, both would maybe—*maybe*—make a few vague references about The Awful Thing that happened, without, of course, getting into specifics (you'd clearly hear the capitalization when either spoke those words—The Awful Thing).

So, no one pressed them on the issue. They were still too damaged, both physically and. . .well, you know. . .*otherwise* (you could tell that just by looking at them) so you mustn't, after all, you *daren't* say anything that might re-open the wounds. . .assuming those wounds had begun closing and healing. . .or at least scabbing over, that is.

So, no one pressed the issue.

At least, people would say, they still had the Janus Cinema, Cedar Hill's only true upscale single-screen art-house movie theatre—elegant but not ostentatious; starting with the decorative single-person ticket booth kiosk on the outside, followed by a U-shaped concession stand harkening back to movie houses of the Thirties and Forties, then a highly-polished mahogany bar just off to the left side of the entrance, a burgundy-carpeted lobby big enough for patrons to wander about and yet still double as a cocktail lounge with waiters and waitresses formally dressed as if it were an exclusive private club, all of it to build one's excitement for the breathtaking centerpiece: the largest single-screen film screen in the state of Ohio. Were that not enough to draw loyal patrons from all over the city and state and beyond, the Janus also offered hot food to go along or replace the usual movie snacks to enhance your viewing experience: pizza, hot subs, homemade nachos, an array of salads, popcorn with *real butter*, and more. The thirteen-item menu was an immediate hit with movie-goers, as was the eclectic array of films shown, everything from obscure foreign films to recent art-house hits, historic film reels—**YOUR WORLD TODAY!**—classic cartoons, the occasional commercial blockbuster, old-time movie serials, all-night horror movie marathons at Hallowe'en, rebroadcasts of old-time radio programs courtesy of a refurbished 1937 Philco Model 655 Tombstone Radio (hooked into a hidden CD player with the recorded programs), amateur filmmaker contests, independent films shown nowhere else. Ray and Melanie had purchased the abandoned downtown building to renovate and turn it into a movie house, and it was a glorious success.

The Janus.

5

"There is a great streak of violence in every human being, and if it's not channeled somehow it breaks out into war and madness. The whole underside of our society has always been violence and still is. Churches, laws—everybody seems to think that man is a noble savage. But he's only an animal. A meat-eating, talking animal. Recognize it. He also has grace and love and beauty. But don't try to tell me we're not violent."
—Sam Peckinpah

YES; THE JANUS.

At least, people would say, they still have the Janus. As if owning and operating a movie theatre was enough to fill the miserable, snarling void left by. . .well, The Awful Thing.

(—*how she disappeared during her pre-school's attending the early show of the* Hallowe'en Cartoon Celebration!!! *at the Auditorium Theater. Missing for almost three weeks, and then some boys leaning over the rails of the East Main Street Bridge hocking "loogies" into the Licking River see what they swear is an arm in the mud below. Thinking it's part of an old mannequin they go down to see if there are any more parts. Two of them will be in therapy well into their twenties; the third will commit suicide before his eighteenth birthday because the dreams will not stop coming nearly every night. Whoever killed her didn't bother to dig down more than a foot and a half, Detective Bill Emerson says to the oncoming dusk, turning away for a moment so he doesn't lose his composure, even though he feels like vomiting. Water, muck, garbage, and sewage keep filling in the grave. He nods and the careful digging begins. The police photographer takes photos at every stage of the process: an arm with no hand— click!; a head with eyes torn out and lower jaw missing, a plastic tiara attached to the top by heavy staples—click!; clumps of hair knotted deep in the stinking muck—click!; now the second arm with rope burns around the wrist and the fingernails of the hand pulled out—click!; discolored legs with hammer-smashed knees— click!; a close-up: one of those legs still wearing an ankle-sock and a Mary Jane shoe—click!; costume-jewelry that had been set aflame and melted into the chest—click! Water, filth, hair, muck, rotting flesh, small creatures from the river, sewage, old trash thrown down from the bridge, the fabric of her light blue princess dress, all of it now thickened together, morbid candle wax. The meticulous work continues, everyone digging slowly, delicately, archeologists uncovering the burial site of some heretofore unknown extinct race. Oversized work lights erupt near the shore. Emerson shields his eyes from their expansive, near-blinding glare. One workman loses his footing for a moment while setting a light in place and its beam points toward the night sky. For a moment. . .just a moment, mind you, Emerson tricks himself into believing it's the unblemished, incandescent soul of three-year-old Daphne Lee Price slipping free of this lamentable vaudeville called human existence and rising toward a place where no one will mock her gentle Down's Syndrome face where there's no more sadness, no more pain, no more terror, nightmares, or cruelty, where there is no more darkness, no more loneliness, no more tears. He almost smiles, wishing her only laughter and carousels and friends and games and picnics and favorite movies like* My Neighbor Totoro *and* The Last Unicorn *and happy childhood songs like Gordon Lightfoot's "The Pony Man," or Peter, Paul, and Mary's "Puff, the Magic Dragon," and happy pets that jump up and lick your face and never a memory of how she spent her final hours on this earth and one of the officers taps him on the shoulder. Emerson blinks. The officer's ashen face tells him all he needs to know: something's been found about ten yards away. Something dreadful. Something hideous. Something. . .something so obscene it's worse than everything else. Dear God. Emerson wonders what this awful thing could be. He and the officer walk in silence toward a ceremonial-looking circle of large rocks. The largest one, used as a cover to protect what lies within, is now knocked aside, wriggling with dozens of earwigs. The accompanying officer stops a few feet away, shuddering, unable to go on, unable to look at it again. Emerson puts an understanding hand on his shoulder and takes the officer's flashlight. He walks toward the structure in a hesitant, heel-to-toe manner as if he's afraid the earth might open up and swallow him whole with each step. He reaches the circle and kneels, readying himself, and aims the flashlight's beam downward. Every window in his soul slams shut. He closes his eyes as tightly as he can. Does not breathe. Might scream if he does. Slowly turns toward the bridge. Opens his eyes. Sees the gawkers. All of them eerily silent. Some taking cell phone videos. One guy using a sizable film camera. Probably from local TV. We interrupt this program. Live from Gehenna, he looks down into the center of the circle again. Butcher used a knife with a single-edged blade. And then he sealed this last amputated horror in two airtight bags to make certain it would be perfectly protected. For this. Very. Second. Blood as bright and fresh as it was at the moment of slaughter.*

Emerson's lower lip begins to tremble.

Which means—

—he drops the flashlight.

Which means she—

—he jams his hands together, intertwining his fingers.

Which means she was—

—he pounds his balled-up hands against his forehead with rhythmic force.

Which means she was probably—

—he makes a low sound somewhere between a whimper and a groan.

Which means she was probably still—

—the sound inside of him that's struggling to get out builds unremittingly in volume until it becomes something so filled with fury and despair it's almost inhuman.

Which means she was probably still alive when he did it.

Probably screamed so loud that. . .

. . .that night crawler, that walking cancer tumor passing itself off as your run-of-the-mill sweet harmless guy, he probably enjoyed her shrieks, her tears, the pleas clogging her throat, but most of all, oh, you betcha, most of all he enjoyed her agonized screams. . .probably laughed. . .made her watch while jacking off into her little. Girl's. Bleeding. Carved. . .

. . .Bill Emerson takes himself out of himself, forces the Not-Emerson *to Not Look, to Not Feel, to Not Any-Goddamn-Thing if possible. . .*

THIS IS NOT MY MOVIE

. . .and as soon as the depraved piece of shit was sated, he sealed Daphne's final piece in two clear freezer-ready airtight plastic bags along with a few drops of his cum. An arrogant dare: G'head, motherfuckers, run my DNA, try to find me, g'head. Like something on the filthiest grindhouse horror screen murder screen horror screen murder screen horror screen, he pounds one fist into another pile of rocks until the knuckles bleed and nearly screams: "How the FUCK am I going to tell her parents?" Everyone on the force knows that Bill Emerson never drops the F-bomb, and several officers turn in his direction. He begins shaking so violently it feels as if his body—that he has almost no control over at this moment—might go into convulsions as, finally, the tears come. "Mother of God. . .jesus-FUCKING-christ. . .wh-what am I supposed to say to them when they demand to see the body? Thirty years! Been on the force for THIRTY YEARS and I've never seen anything—" He shakes his head, feeling his throat tighten. Doesn't bother to wipe his nose. Suddenly remembers—who knows for whatever useless goddamn reason on this charnel house excuse of a planet—the title of a favorite Philip K. Dick novel: Let Flow My Tears, The Policeman Said. *So, Emerson does. He weeps for Daphne Lee Price. Weeps for her terror. Weeps for her anguish. Weeps for her pain. Weeps for the total, monstrous, perverted destruction of her innocence, of her joy, of the life that she will never know, Emerson weeps, not caring that for the first time on the job, for the first time in thirty years, he's broken down like this in public. He opens his mouth to say something but what emerges is a ragged, clogged, wet, pitiful gagging bleat of helplessness. He buries his face in his hands and manages to softly sing to himself how if you listen very softly be as quiet as you can in the yard, you'll hear him it is the Pony. . .Pony. . .something. . .horses living on candy apples instead of oats and hay. Supposed to be a. . .happy song, isn't it? Can't remember who sang it. Or the title. Or why it should even matter. He hopes can stand up under his own power. Feels the understanding hand of the accompanying officer rest upon his shoulder. This is the most vile goddamn)*

Thing.

Had anyone pressed the issue of the Awful Thing, it wouldn't have made any difference: when the vibrating anguish of unendurable grief, grief suppressed and ultimately denied, synchronizes with the resonance of guilt and, if one is not careful, the panpsychism

(Panexperientialism   *a.k.a.*   *Panpsychism*
(/panˈsī͟kiz(ə)m/
   noun:

> **the doctrine or belief that everything material, however small, has an element of individual consciousness.** (Tell 'em Sergeant Howie helped you out with this one.) *(You're welcome)*

   produced by this ferocious reification can take on a life—even a sentience—of its own; and when the circumstances are right, sometimes—not very often, but it happens—it can also assume *physical* form—a theory debated but not yet dismissed by such great minds as Spinoza, Alfred North Whitehead, Pierre Teilhard de Chardin, Bertrand Russel, and numerous others in the fields of physics, medicine, philosophy, biology, and paleontology.

Third Because:

Physical form.
   That is, when circumstances are *just* right. . .

E
What say we get this road on the show? Time for the peanut gallery to pull up a sit and chair down.

(Using a well cared-for Catozzo Super-8 film splicer along with Splittable Flying Splice Tape. Okay, Okay, yes, right, keep your pants on; yeah, it's overkill for a mere three reels of Super 8 film, but he's worked too hard and waited too goddamn long for this opportunity and there's no way he's going to chance his film jamming up in the projector Thursday night.

THIS IS NOT MY MOVIE

He takes a breath, holds it.

Snap-click!

Exhales.

There, all done.

E carefully, delicately, as if it were a newborn child, holds the film up to the light and begins running it slowly through gloved fingers, examining each frame and imagining how Edison or Méliès or Eisenstein or Edward S. Porter did this exact same thing—especially Porter as he was making The Great Train Robbery *in 1903, arguably the first American narrative film.*

To E the old ways will never be improved upon; yes, digital has its place, of course, E's not stupid, but film, actual film, *should never become archaic, something that will be looked upon in the future as Noachian, prehistoric, fossilized; what a tragedy that would be.*

E glides the rest of the film through the right index finger and thumb of the gloved hand as if it were a clear, clean, cascading stream rippling forward until it reaches the flume and gracefully pours downward, becoming a majestic waterfall.

The fisherman's-hooked smile quivers but does not transform, only produces more drool that now looks as if he's foaming at the mouth.

Perfect.

The splice is perfect on all three reels.

18 minutes of pure, unadulterated Cinema.

E rewinds the film via the trusty Bell & Howell Filmo Reg 8 mm #148A w Rewinder—an old mechanism, yes, but one whose performance has yet to disappoint—then places the now slightly-larger reel into a new, pristine canister purchased solely for this moment. Afterward, E clears space on the wheeled bed stand, rolls it into position, and prepares to set up the screen and projector.)

E

(To the peanut gallery)

> Oh, stop it with the incessant bellyaching, already. The show will begin in just a few minutes. In the meantime, what say we entertain ourselves with some movie trivia? Maybe <u>Famous Lines From Famous Movies?</u>

That sounds like fun.

> Excellent. Wonderful. Since it was my idea, I'll ask the first question.

But you always *ask the first question.*

> That's because it always IS my idea. My place, my rules. Suggest it <u>before</u> I do sometime, and <u>you</u> can have the first question.

Fine. Go ahead.

> No reason to get upset about it.

Who's upset?

> Well. . .there was a tone.

There was no tone. You're just anxious about the contest Thursday night so anything that's said to you between now and then is going to sound like antagonistic disquisition.

E

```
(He    whistles,    taken    aback    but
impressed)
     Antagonistic    Disquisition?
Where in the hell did you pick
```

THIS IS NOT MY MOVIE

up that fifty-dollar-and-
pocket-change phrase?

*You gotta be kidding. Take a look around this hoarder's wet
dream of a living space, why don't you? You can't* sneeze *without
hitting a stack of film magazines or hoity-toity nine-pound books
crammed with pretentious film theory that in turn is itself
crammed with grandiose and ostentatious words like. . .like
'grandiose' and 'ostentatious,' for example. You're gone
practically all weekend, every weekend—and let's not even talk
about the tragedy of summer, when we might as well be
Dickensian orphans begging in the street—there's nothing else to
read, and since we're not exactly what you'd call corporeal you
can File 13 turning on the television, and that old Philco radio
doesn't even work so forget any tuneage. . .Thank God you don't
smoke anymore because one stray ember and—viola!—it's a hot
time in the old movie house—*

—<u>TOWN!</u> The fucking word is—

*—TOWN tonight! A hot time in the old TOWN tonight! There!
Happy? Song lyrics were never a strong point with any of us.
What gives big deal so what?*

    You think that's it—I mean, do you truthfully
    think that's it? Just nerves?

Nerves and. . .wait for it. . .PRO. . .JEC. . .TION.

    Oh, tee-hee-ha-ha, it is to laugh. How long
    have you been saving <u>that</u> one?

What say we skip the trivia game and. . .mix it up a little?

    Mix it up?

Yes. We said that. We recognized our voice.

    Cute. Very cute. All right, let's hear it.

6

"It is a simple equation: Take me, subtract film, and the sum is zero."
—Akira Kurosawa

ON THE SECOND ANNIVERSARY of her daughter's disappearance and murder, Melanie Price stood at the kitchen counter in the employees' lounge of the Janus Cinema fixing a sandwich for her lunch. She was crying.

If anyone had come into the kitchen to see her crying and asked what was wrong, she would have shrugged, smiled, and said something about the strength of the odor from the onion she was cutting, and there would have been some truth in that–enough to satisfy whomever had asked.

Yes, the onion was strong, *really* strong, searing the inside of her nose and roasting her eyes, and at first the tears were caused by that and that alone; but the longer she stood at the counter, the more she began to realize just how much *time* she was taking to perform something so simple.

She remembered the way her mother—a sad, weary, quiet, stoop-shouldered woman who'd been old long before her time—would take such painstaking care in performing even the most mundane household tasks. She used to think her mother's meticulousness was funny, a way of not having to listen to Dad bitch and moan about any number of things; complaining was his hobby; avoiding having to listen to it was Mom's.

Funny.

Melanie sliced into her thumb. She had been absorbed for a moment in the onion's deceit, peeling away layer after layer, anticipating the center—for her, always the tastiest part—something to let her know, Here the skin ends and the onion begins. Instead, she found only an endless succession of skins, each layer a smaller, thinner, more delicate version of the one before, eventually dwindling into insignificance, revealing only embryonic, cell-like tissue which gave the *appearance* of a core. So immersed was she in this search that the realization she'd cut herself didn't register until the first surprisingly large globule of blood dripped down onto the draining board, staining the nearest pile of onion slices.

"Dammit!" she snapped, dropping the knife.

The blood gathered above the split petals of her skin. She slipped the wounded thing into her mouth and sucked at it as she looked around for the first aid kit.

The knife had cut the globule of blood on the draining board in half. She was now reflected in not one, but two crimson droplets. Two sets of reddened eyes both leaked as if the onion were continuing to spit juice at her. Two mouths wrapped around two thumbs, sucking at them as if she were an infant again. One of the globules began mixing with the juice of the onion slices. It began to spread out, stretching her reflection, altering her features. On her left she saw her own familiar face reflected in the blood; but the face on the right was that of a stranger, someone who bore a striking enough resemblance to her, yes, but was not her, not her at all.

She pulled her thumb from her mouth, leaving a small bead of blood in the soft center of her lower lip. It was only as she began rummaging around the above-sink cupboards, still searching for the first aid kit, that she became aware of the warm, odd taste. She touched the droplet with the tip of her tongue.

The bead burst and trickled slowly down her chin. She wiped it away—

—and there it was again, the memory of blood on her face (nine stitches), blood on her hands (a cast for the entire left hand, two finger splints for the right), blood trickling out of her mouth from where she'd bitten through part of her lower lip (three stitches), and the pain in her skull as she tried to raise herself up, but she couldn't, so she turned her head to the side as best she could and opened her eyes, seeing Ray slumped forward, his body obscured through the smoke, glistening in places, covered here in blood, there in fragments of shattered glass, neither one of them yet aware of the true extent of their injuries—

At that moment, something more than the onion's stink began to draw out her tears.

(—*oh God, baby, oh Daphne, my baby, my poor baby, did you have to watch your blood seep from your body? How much agony were you in? Did you say prayers to God like you always did at bedtime? Did you pray to the Great Nothing in the sky to save you? Did you close your eyes tight and scream for Mommy and Daddy to come help, to come get you, to please come get you and make it all stop because you were cold and scared and in the kind of pain none of us can even* begin *to imagine? Were you shrieking please take me home please Please PLEASE*—)

She ripped several tissues from a box on one of the tables and wiped at the blood on her lip, chin, and neck. She was tossing the mess into the trash can when Astryd, her assistant, came into the lounge and saw the blood on Melanie's hand.

"Melanie! My God, is it bad?" Not waiting for an answer, Astryd took Melanie's hand in her own and proceeded to wash and disinfect the wound with some hydrogen peroxide taken from the first aid kit, which she seemed to have summoned from thin air. After making certain the cut wasn't going to require further medical attention, Astryd covered her handiwork with a gauze pad and carefully wrapped it in medical tape.

"Thanks," said Melanie, pulling out one of the chairs and sitting down.

She wasn't even aware that she was still crying until she looked up and saw the expression on Astryd's face.

"I'm going to take a wild guess and say it's not just the onions, is it?"

"No," said Melanie, wiping her eyes, then blowing her nose. She wanted so much to talk about Daphne, wanted to talk about how that poor detective, Bill Emerson—that wonderful, decent man—broke down when he gave them the news, how he *begged* them to not see her body. Ignoring his advice, they'd driven well over the speed limit toward the murder; both of them seem so zombified with grief, confusion, and fury that they ran a red light and didn't see the car that T-boned them. She wanted to talk about all of that but, like all the other times, something crouching deep inside wouldn't allow her to give voice to any of that just yet. . .if it ever would, so she settled on something safe.

"I know how silly this is going to sound, but I was thinking about the way my mom used to do things around the house. Give her even the simplest task—washing a few dishes or something like that—and she'd take about three times longer to get it done than was necessary just to keep Dad off her case. She didn't really do anything else with her days, as far as I knew. She got up, made breakfast, then set about her tasks. Our house was always immaculately clean."

Melanie lit a cigarette and took a deep, satisfying drag, looked at her wounded hand (thinking how much older her flesh looked now than it had when she'd gone to bed last night), released a stream of smoke, and glanced up. "I don't know if I should be telling you any of this."

"And I don't know that you oughtta be smoking in the employees' lounge, let *alone* a damn movie theatre."

Melanie nodded, took another drag, and dropped her cigarette into the cup of coffee, now cold, that she had no memory of pouring for herself.

Astryd shook her head. "Does Ray know you've started up again?"

"Oh, God, no. He'd throw a hissy fit."

Astryd grinned. "A *hissy fit?* You make him sound like some three-year-old who's screaming for–" She cut off the words as the simile registered with her.

Melanie tentatively touched her hand. "It's okay. The comparison isn't far off the mark. Not your fault. I'm partly to blame for sharing things like this in the first place."

"Why?" asked Astryd. "Because you're the manager and the boss shouldn't, God forbid, show one of her employees that she's human?"

"Sure, that. Seems to work."

"A little late, don't you think? I mean, all of us used to go out after work all the time before. . .well, before."

Melanie smiled. "I appreciate this."

"Then go on. Tell me more about your mother."

Melanie picked up a spoon and began swirling her coffee-soaked cigarette around in the cup, watching it crumble apart with each rotation as if observing a small reel of silver nitrate film unspooling in slow motion only to be disintegrated by the oxygen awaiting it. "When the day was over and I was in bed, I'd listen for Dad to come up and go to his and Mom's room, and then I'd lie there and wonder what Mom did for herself. She never stayed up late during most of the week, but every Friday night she'd stay downstairs until God-only-knew when, so one Friday night I snuck downstairs and saw her sitting in front of the television, the volume turned down so it wouldn't bother Dad, but it was *so* low she had to lean in close to hear it—no wonder her eyesight got so bad later in life, being that close to the screen. . .anyway, she'd be eating popcorn from this little brown bag—you know, the kind used by liquor stores—and sipping on a bottle of pop. She later told me that she made the popcorn while Dad was at work, and I was at school because she didn't want to annoy Dad with the noise. Can you imagine that? Hiding popcorn in a liquor-store bag?

"But there she'd sit, munching away on the popcorn and sipping her pop, her face less than three feet from the screen so she could hear. . .and you know what she was watching?"

Astryd waved her hand in the air, a grade-school Safety Patrol officer at the crosswalk. "Oh, oh, no, no, don't tell me, let me guess, let me guess, I'm really good at this, *never* get it wrong, I *slaughter* at Trivial Pursuit—uhmmmm—old romantic movies, tear-jerkers, or musicals! It *has* to be one of those three!"

"That's what you'd expect, right? I mean, I know that's what *I* expected." Melanie smiled, shaking her head and gesturing for Astryd to lean in closer. "Old horror movies."

"Oh, em, ef, gee."

"I *know*, right?"

"Old horror movies? You mean like the original *Friday the 13th* or *Nightmare on Elm Street? Halloween?*"

"Wrong generation. Think older."

"*Psycho?*"

"Still the wrong generation—but *Psycho*'s getting closer. We're talking the *real* classics, we're talking films that paved the way, movies that are damn near *holy*—if such a thing as holiness actually exists—we're talking *Frankenstein, The Wolf Man, Creature from the Black Lagoon, Cat People, I Walked With a Zombie, The Leopard Man*. . .Oh, God, Mom would've *flipped* over that 'Wall of Monsters' display that'll be set up in the lobby for the Friday premiere! 'Friday is monster night!' she always said. I think it was the only thing she had that was *hers*, and she was just tickled pink to share it with me. It didn't dawn on me until after she died that I should've felt honored by that."

She leaned closer to Astryd as

(four frames: her face, her eyes, her voice and gestures,

THIS IS NOT MY MOVIE

(two frames: *everything* about her

(eight frames: became decades younger, decades happier, perhaps even, as would a

child, mischievously joyous, sharing a sacred secret

(sixteen frames: a black & white photo of Daphne in her new princess costume, smiling)

"There was this local channel that ran classic horror movies all night on Fridays. I even remember it had this goofy host, 'Seymour'—the show was called *Seymour Presents.*" She laughed at the memory. "He was this gaunt but still rather handsome older gentleman with this big gray Sam Elliott mustache **(three frames:** Seymour, bowing)** who wore an oversized black Fedora and long black cape. Looked like Boris Karloff playing The Shadow. Mom just *adored* him and loved watching those old movies, even the stinkers. . .sometimes *especially* the stinkers! Eventually I started watching them with her. Whenever I'd start to get scared, I'd ask her to hold her hand against my stomach. And I keep thinking that. . .that I've kind of turned into a high-tech version of her. Instead of a television with tubes and a knob for switching channels and adjusting the volume, I have a high-definition curved flat-screen with a remote at home and a ginormous movie screen here. Instead of popcorn from a brown liquor-store bag I have gourmet candy and *imported* popcorn. Next verse, same as first. And I still love horror movies and always. . .always looked forward to the day when I could sit in front of the TV watching something like *Svengoolie* with

(six frames: black & white clumps of hair knotted in thick sewage)**

my own little girl, but. . ." Once again, that *something* did not so much silence the thought as it did drag it back into a ditch and beat it unconscious.

She blinked and then looked at Astryd. "Was I rambling?"

"No, but you *were* managing to get yourself even more upset, and I don't think that's what you need right now."

Astryd's voice was now as unsteady as Melanie's. The two women looked at one another, both aware of what this was really about but neither one able speak it aloud: Melanie, for fear of losing her composure and making Astryd feel awkward; Astryd, for fear that Melanie didn't consider her a close enough friend in whom she could confide something so painful.

"So, um. . ." Astryd looked around for Melanie's metal arm-crutches, found them resting against the wall near the sink, and brought them over. "How long were you able to stand this time without using these bad boys?"

"About fifteen minutes," replied Melanie, slipping her forearm into the first crutch's brace and pushing up onto her feet. God, it *still hurt* to stand sometimes. She winced as she reached out for the second crutch and slipped her arm through the rounded upper brace. "I figure, at this rate, I might be down to using just one by spring."

Astryd was staring at her.

Melanie tilted her head slightly. "What is it? Yoo-hoo. Earth to Astryd. Ground Control to Major—"

"Hm?" said Astryd, snapped from her reverie. "Oh, nothing, I was just. . .y'know. . .I mean. . .uh. . ."

"A complete sentence would be really helpful here."

Astryd smiled. "It's just that. . .when my aunt had to have *her* hip surgery, it took her almost two years before she could even *attempt* to walk with crutches—and she was five years *younger* than you. You've had two operations since. . .and you were back on your feet in just over eight months." She shook her head. "I don't know how you do it, Melanie, I really don't." There was more sadness than humor in it.

Melanie steadied her balance and went back to the sink to finish making her lunch.

She decided to skip the onion.

"Hey, Astryd, can you do me a favor?"

"Name it."

"Make sure that Hank's got the movie loaded and the projector programmed before he leaves. Ray wants us to preview the movie tonight."

"Sure thing. Would you mind if I came along and brought my ladylove with me?"

"Ray wants it to be just the two of us. It's been. . .been a while since we've watched a movie together. But tell Christina the two of you are more than welcome to bring a few friends along for the big premiere tomorrow night. We already reserved an entire row of seats for you and your entourage. *Gratis*, of course. It's in the loge—is that all right?"

"The *loge?* The loge is my favorite, always has been. We can drop popcorn down on peoples' heads. You're a sweetheart, you know that?"

"Was once famous for it."

As Melanie was lifting the end of the draining board to slide the remains into the garbage disposal, she noticed that the second globule of blood had spread out, continuing to mix with the onion juice, becoming nothing more than a dull, pinkish glaze in which no reflection could be seen; however, now the first globule, the one in which her face had been so clearly her own, showed only a dim, featureless oval of flesh that she looked into only once, very quickly, before wiping it away.

Drying her hands

(Oh God, sweetie. . .did he dry his hands like this between. . .between? Did he make you watch? Did you think, did you pray *that every time he dried his hand that it was all over? That maybe he was going to drive you. . .what was* left *of you, the still alive* left of you. . .did you pray that maybe, maybe St. Christopher, maybe he'd drive you someplace and leave you there, leave you where you'd be quickly found? Did you hope for that as you watched him dry his hand? Did you?)*

She looked up at cupboard doors where someone had taped one of the hundreds of flyers they'd printed up for the premiere:

INTERNATIONAL AWARD-WINNING HORROR DIRECTOR CHOOSES CEDAR HILL'S JANUS CINEMA FOR WORLD PREMIERE!

Should My Demons Leave Me

The New Film from Nathan Wright

Director of *A Choir of Ill Children, Bone Soup,* and *Scream Quietly*

Hopefully tonight would be, if not wonderful for her and Ray, at least pleasant.

Yes. Pleasant.

Aim for that. That. And nothing more.

Just. That.

Things hadn't been pleasant since. . .

Since.

Cautious; check.

Fragile; check.

Awkward and damn near terrified to look at one another; check and check.

And. So. Pleasant.

Aim for that. That.

And nothing more.

That and nothing more.

Nothing more.

Nothing more.

There exists no ghost, be it a person, place, or Other, that has not had a past physical form. Advance, be born; open, fight, expose, love; die, close. That is why we seek shelter with and within the One True Camera.

Advance, be born; open. . .

7

"Most of us live our lives devoid of cinematic moments."
—Nora Ephron

*Film carefully threaded into his trusty
Bell & Howell Super 8mm Autoload Film
Projector Model Number 346A (an older model
projector, yes, but like all of his film
equipment, it has yet to malfunction on
him) E looks at his special preview peanut
gallery and smiles.*

E
I do very much like your idea
of us <u>reading through</u> my
script along with this first
viewing of the film to see if
our vision was brought to life
with care, and that no damage
was done to the spine of the
story, as the late
scriptwriting god William
Goldman so succinctly put it.
Now remember, most of it was
written in a blind fever when
my muse took total possession
of me, so any flaws in the
written structure—and yes, I
am <u>quite</u> aware that Mr.
Goldman would in no way,
shape, or form approve of
that—should serve as evidence

of the authenticity of the artistry and <u>not</u> reflect in any way on the genuine creativity of the mind behind the story. Understand?

All VOICES

(in unison)

We understand. We understood it the last time you gave us this speech and we'll understand it the <u>next</u> time you give us this speech. We will understand it in a house. We will understand it with a mouse. We will understand at a rave. We will understand it at a grave. We will understand it here and there; we will understand it—

E

—put a sock in it, already! This is important to me, so it should be at least peripherally important to you. . .and even if it isn't, could you at least. . .at least pay me the courtesy of. . .maybe. . .y'know. . .<u>pr etending</u> I'm not asking you to shovel horseshit from the king's stables or sending you down a long dark hall where the lethal injection waits? Could you do that much, please?

THIS IS NOT MY MOVIE

All Voices in Unison
(*admonished and a tad ashamed*)
We were only having a little
fun. You've been awfully
beside yourself lately, you
know. . .what with the contest
and, well. . .the. . .have you
looked at the calendar?

E
Have I looked at the—?

(E *turns his head—a slow and painful
movement for him—and looks. For several
seconds he squints with his one good eye—
the other long ago covered by a large
eyepatch—and with great deliberation
examines the year, the month, the
days. . .and then he spots it. We don't
need to see what he sees; we can tell from
the look of frozen, near-unspeakable
anguish on his heavily, grotesquely scarred
face that he's forgotten the date of
something that had or will have a profound
effect on him. He blinks, turns back to the
projector, and speaks to the Preview
Audience with a deceptively lighthearted
tone*)

E
Oh, <u>that</u>. Well, yes, of course
I. . .I do seem to recall
something or other about an
anniversary, but let's not let
it dampen our excitement about
the upcoming contest—all in
favor? I see that everyone is
very much in support, and so—

(lacking a gavel, he stamps his good foot on the floor)

                    E
        <u>Motion Carries</u>!

(He presses a small button on the side of a cassette player, and we hear a few seconds of nondescript pre-recorded applause)

                    E
        Thank you, thank you, thank you very much. It's so very nice to have. . .well, to have friends and supporters such as all of you wonderful people. After all that has happened over the last. . .

(He tears up, but this isn't a put-on; it's genuine)

                    E
        . . .after all that has happened, I was worried that you might have forgotten about me, but this lovely reception tonight, along with this delightful prize for my little film, well. . .I am nothing. . .nothing short of humbled.

(He presses the button again, and we hear pre-recorded sounds of an audience going, "Ah!" and "Oh!" and making all sorts of warm, loving, sympathetic noises, sounds that rival those following Judy Garland's "Hello, everybody. . .this is Mrs. Norman Maine.")

THIS IS NOT MY MOVIE

E

But now, here in our own Honah
Lee, all filled with glee and
hope and excitement, and it's
all so nice, nice, very nice,
so with no further delay...

8

"I liked the cinema better before I began to do it. Now I can't stop
myself from hearing the clappers at the beginning of each shot.
All the magic is destroyed."
—Orson Welles

Announcer's Voice:
[garbled static; this is a decades-old recording]

. . .from President Nixon to announce the immediate withdrawal
of American troops from Vietnam.

Details are still sketchy concerning the deaths at the [static] three
nights ago. The future of the [static] remains in doubt.

The weather remains on the chilly side, with expected highs to
reach only forty. . .

INTERIOR: LOBBY OF A BUSY MOVIE THEATRE

*Everything is chaotic; people are
complaining, popcorn is flying around.
Everywhere you look, it's clown-shit crazy.*

*And then, the cherry on top of this
glorious evening, the power goes out.
Employees rush to figure out what exactly
is going on and if they can get the power
back on. People begin to complain more and*

THIS IS NOT MY MOVIE

louder, demanding refunds and getting
pissed off. The only MANAGER, twenty-ish,
runs all over the place trying to figure
out how to handle everything and can't
catch a break. MANAGER finally issues
refunds and free tickets for future
showings and sends everyone home and then
tells the employees he will finish closing
up. After everyone leaves, he retreats to
the office where he takes a few hits off a
hidden joint, relaxes for a couple of
minutes, and then begins closing down the
concession area.

A mysterious MAN using a pair of metal
canes to help him walk appears from the
darkened hallway. He is only partly lit so
you can't really see who he is or any
features.

> **MAN**
> I can't seem to find my movie.
> I just know that this isn't
> it. (Holds out a ticket stub)
> Which theater is it in?

> **MANAGER**
> The power's out, sir.

> **MAN**
> Which explains the darkness,
> yes, but it still doesn't tell
> me how to find my movie.

> **MANAGER**
> We don't have any power, sir.
> All the projectors are down,
> the concession stand is down,
> everything's down. One of the
> ushers should have told you.

We had to clear everyone from all the theaters. It's protocol when a massive power failure like this occurs. Please come with me and I'll show you the exit.

MAN
Don't strain yourself, I'm more than familiar with the way.

MAN *turns around and walks back down the hallway.*

MANAGER
Sir? Sir? You're going the wrong way! The exit's in the other direction!

The MAN *turns and pulls a thin gleaming sword out of one of his canes, pointing it at the* MANAGER.

MAN
Do I look stupid to you? I know where I'm going. I'll find it. Sure as hell not gonna find my movie this way!

MANAGER
Jesus Christ, buddy, gimme a break, will you? It'll be my job and my ass if-

A loud noise comes from the stairwell of the projection room.

MANAGER
(to himself)

THIS IS NOT MY MOVIE

Shit. Could this night get any better?

The loud noise repeats.

> **MANAGER**
> (again, to himself)
> Just <u>had</u> to ask yourself that question out loud, didn't you?

He quickly runs upstairs toward the projection room but before opening the door can hear the sounds of KIDS running down the hallway knocking things over.

> **MANAGER**
> All right, you snot-nosed blessings from above. Knock it the hell off!

> **KIDS**
> (unseen)
> Snot-nosed blessings! Snot-nosed blessings!

> **MANAGER**
> Goddammit, you could hurt yourselves! Please stop! I'm begging you.

> **KIDS**
> Begging will do no good. Olly-olly-oxen-free. . .

The noise continues down the hall until we hear the sound of the KIDS scurrying up a metal ladder, followed by a loud clang! as the roof maintenance hatch slams violently closed.

MANAGER runs up to the ladder and looks up to the hatch. He then continues his way up to catch those kids; once he gets on the roof he begins to look around in rising panic.

MANGE R

(Shouting)

Oh, yeah, <u>this is much better!</u> No, really. This is top-drawer. Why would I lie at a time like this? Seventy years from now, on my deathbed, when I'm asked what the high point of my youth was, I will tell them without question, undoubtedly, with no hesitation whatsoever, that it was the night I chased an unknown number of soon-to-be institutionalized children across a movie theater rooftop in the dark while freezing my still-virginal boy-parts off and trying to forget the fact that I'M ALSO SCARED OF HEIGHTS! I ALMOST FAINT STEPPING UP ON A KITCHEN CHAIR TO CHANGE A FUCKING LIGHTBULB! So, I hope you can appreciate the sacrifice I'm making here. Just wanted to let you know you picked a <u>boffo</u> place to run to. Far less dangerous up here on the roof, nowhere to slip, trip, or fall. Nowhere to tumble over the edge and drop forty-or-so feet to splatter on the pavement. Fantastic, awe-inspiring,

THIS IS NOT MY MOVIE

Mensa-level decision-making going on here. Ranks right up there with Disco, New Coke, and the studio executives who greenlighted *CAN'T STOP THE MUSIC, XANADU,* and *ROLLER BOOGIE.*

MANAGER searches for a few more moments, then is startled by a scream from somewhere down in one of the theaters. He runs back to the hatch and starts down.

MANAGER
Listen, kids, I'm going to leave this unlocked! <u>Please</u> come back in and find me! *(His head disappears for about 5 seconds, then pops back up)* AND STAY AWAY FROM THE EDGE OF THE ROOF! You're not stupid! *(Mumbling to himself)* Not that you've displayed any evidence to suggest otherwise.

MANAGER slides down the ladder and sprints across most of the hallway before the projectors, one by one, begin to kick on, the lights from the lamps light up and the motors begin to run. Confused, he runs to them wondering how they could even turn on if the power is out. He makes his way to the tool rack, grabs a high-beam flashlight, and quickly makes his way back downstairs to check the fuse boxes.

With all theater lights still out, MANAGER walks down the OLD HALLWAY in the far back of the building. As he walks past THEATER

#2, he hears noise coming from inside. He walks in to find a film playing. It's painfully loud and has the most ear-bending cacophony of random noises that just give you goosebumps. In pure panic the MANAGER looks around to find a FIGURE, also no distinct figure standing up in the projection window. The man holds up a hand-made sign which reads: THIS IS NOT MY MOVIE, then quickly runs away. The MANAGER screams for him to stop, then runs out of the theater and back into the lobby. He hears the projection booth doors swing open and footsteps of the figure running into the back room. The MANAGER, still screaming, continues to run. The door to the concession shuts violently. The MANAGER opens the door to discover that the water in the sink is running fast, and he begins to catch his breath. He hears the door to the freezer shut slowly. In fear the MANGER slowly creeps up to the pop room where the freezer is. The freezer is silent. The light flickers a tiny bit; the power cannot either stay on or off. He creeps a little slower, scared of who or what is in the freezer. He points his flashlight down to the handle, shaking as he does it, and he opens the door to quickly see a man frozen in the freezer, his throat slit and begging for help, holding his hands out. In that split second of seeing him, the manager gives a scream of genuine terror, then turns tail and bolts, leaving the freezer door open behind him. He runs back to the concession area to call the police but finds that the mysterious MAN is standing there.

THIS IS NOT MY MOVIE

MANAGER
Who the hell are you?

MAN
I'd like some popcorn, please.

MANAGER
(*With rising fear, confusion, and anger*)
What's going on here?

MAN
What's going on is that this is not my movie, and I don't have any popcorn, and I know I asked for some, I recognized my voice.

MANAGER
We're closed, buddy.

MAN
And yet I see you have popcorn, so why am I not eating some?

MANAGER
(*Leaning on the counter, nearly getting up in the man's face*)
Listen, buddy, this night has already been too fuckin' weird and way too fuckin' scary for me, so don't take this personally but I couldn't give less of shit if you have any pop—

His words are cut off when the MAN reaches across and grabs him by the collar (or perhaps his throat) and pulls him nearly halfway over the counter.

GARY A. BRAUNBECK

MAN

No, you listen to me. I don't
think you appreciate how
important it is to the rest of
your mediocre little life that
you give me some popcorn. This
is not my movie, so I cannot
emphasize enough how vital it
is that I have popcorn. (*He
produces a knife that he holds
very close to MANAGER'S
throat*) You think this night
has been too fuckin' weird and
too fuckin' scary so far? This
has just been the pre-show
entertainment. Don't give me
any popcorn and you'll see how
much worse this night can
become. Do we have an
understanding?

MANAGER
(*trembling in fear*)

You want butter with that?
It'll be kinda cold and
clumpy, but-

MAN

Butter would be much
appreciated, yes.

He lets go of the MangaLED's throat

*The MANAGER turns around, visibly shaking,
and begins preparing the tub of popcorn. As
he does so, he keeps staring at the MAN'S
reflection in the mirror, freezing a couple
times as he listens to what the man is
saying*

THIS IS NOT MY MOViE

MAN

You know what song I've always hated? "Puff the Magic Dragon." When I was a kid it was one of the few records my folks let me have. I remember the first time I listened to it, when it got to that part where Puff lowered his head in sorrow because he realized his best friend in the whole wide worthless world, y'know, that asshat Jackie Paper, wasn't going to come around anymore, so he. . .what was it? Oh, yeah. . ."sadly slipped into his cave,". . .I sat there waiting for the rest of the song, y'know, the part where Jackie Paper would bring <u>his</u> kids to meet Puff and make Puff all happy again and everyone would go back to adventures in Honah Lee. *(Shakes his head)* No such luck. Then I got to thinking, "Hey, maybe it's like, y'know, maybe it's like a magic wish; maybe if I listen to it and wish hard enough, maybe Jackie Paper <u>will</u> come back with his kids." *(He begins to cry—but not too much; we hear it in his voice more than see it in his eyes or face)* So that's what I did. I sat there playing that goddamn record over and over and over, wishing that Jackie Paper would come back with his own children because, for chrissakes, you don't write a <u>children's</u> song that ends like that, that ends on such a. . .<u>hopeless</u>, heartbreaking note. *(He looks back up at the MANAGER)* Didn't Peter Yarrow know you could <u>destroy</u> a kid with something like that? Whenever I got home from school, for <u>weeks</u> I went right up to my room and started playing that record, but now, <u>now</u> when I listened to it, I wasn't quite as upset—I mean, yes, I <u>was</u> upset, but in a different way. That line about dragons living forever but not so little boys. . .you could take that a couple of ways. It could mean that Jackie Paper just grew up and forgot about Puff, or that maybe he'd died somehow. I started wishing that he'd died. That made me happy. And I wanted to track down that cave where Puff was all lonely and sad and shivering in darkness, thinking he was all forgotten and unloved. . .I'd pet his scales and sing him songs like "The Pony Man" and <u>I'd</u> be the one perched on his gigantic back and it'd be the two of us against the whole wide, worthless world. And if it turned out that Jackie Paper <u>was</u> still alive. . .oh, man. . .I would find that

night crawler, that walking
cancer tumor passing itself
off as a decent, caring human
being, and I would kill him.
But you can bet your sweet
bippy I would make sure he
suffered first, chained up in
someplace dark and cold and
faraway where no one could
hear him scream for help,
where no one would hear him
cry. I'd chop off his arms so
he could never hug his
children, and then. . .then
I'd hack off his legs so he
couldn't. . .couldn't play,
like, y'know. . .play Frisbees
with 'em in the park. . .and
then maybe I'd rip out his
eyes so he'd never see them
smile, tear off his head so
Puff and me, we'd use it as a
kickball or something like
that. . .yeah. But
maybe. . .maybe if I couldn't
bring myself to do all that,
maybe I'd just ask Puff to
unsheath his claws and sink
them into Jackie Paper's
unworthy worthless groin and
just emasculate him so he'd
never <u>have</u> any kids. I think
that'd make both me <u>and</u> Puff
happy. Because that
motherfucker had it coming.

(*The MANAGER turns back around, slowly,
arms shaking, and sets the tub of popcorn
on the counter.*)

> **MANAGER**
> Here you go, sir.

> **MAN**
> Sir? I like that. Shows respect. *(He tastes the popcorn)* Pretty good—I like it cold and clumpy, but it's missing a little something. Ah! I know what it needs. *(He makes a fist over the tub and squeezes a few splatters of blood onto the popcorn, then takes another bite)* Oh, yes. . .that's the stuff.

The MANAGER buries his face in his hands for a few moments.

> **MANAGER**
> For the love of God, will you please tell me what's going on?

He pulls his face from his hands. The MAN and the popcorn are gone. He quickly gets his cell phone out and begins to call another manager. As the phone rings he walks down the hallway to the fuses again. He begins to flip more fuses, and the lights come on. As he makes his way back to the office someone or something on the other end of the phone answers but is nearly buried under white noise, so the MANAGER shouts about what is going on and that he is leaving. The phone is way too fuzzy and the MANGLRER yells for who—or whatever is on the other end to call the fucking theater. He hangs up the phone and sprints back to the office, slamming closed the door behind him. After a brief moment the theater phone rings. The MANGLED quickly goes to pick it up thinking it is the fellow manager. The phone is silent for a second and then he hears a distorted voice saying they are watching him. Frantically, he hangs up the phone and begins to head out the back door. He walks to the back hallway.

At the end of the back hallway the mysterious MAN is standing there blankly looking at him. On either side of the MAN stand two little girls, pale, still, with deep cuts across their throats.

MAN

Family Time at the movies is the best, don't you think?

The three of them begin moving toward the MANAGER

THE GIRLS

Thank you for leaving the hatch open so we could get back in. That was really nice of you. (They hold out their arms) Hug?

The lights flicker all the way off and loud crashing noises echo from the hallway. The noises begin to get closer as the manager runs into the back room, locking the door to the hallway. In a panic he moves the trash cans in front of the door. The lights are still slightly flickering. Something is banging and desperately trying to get through the door. As the **Mangleder** runs through the back room, the noise of the

GARY A. BRAUNBECK

door being broken open fills the scene;
behind him the trash cans are shoved back
into the backroom but he is still not
completely seeing what is chasing him.
Without hesitation, he runs through the
door to the side lobby and into the
bathroom. As he passes the sinks in the
bathroom the lights flicker for a split
second to see a man laying on the counter
covered in blood, blood all over the sinks,
floor and mirrors. After the lights flicker
again the body and blood are gone. The
Manager runs into the far stall as the
lights go completely out. He is breathing
heavily and can hear something coming into
the bathroom. Standing up on the toilet, he
tries to be quiet. Something slams open the
very first stall door. Then the next door,
then the next door. The manger is still
trying to keep quiet but still very scared.
Something keeps slamming the doors open
till it gets to the last one which he was
in. There is a long pause. Everything is
silent and the **Manager** is scared for the
last door to be opened. But nothing
happens. After a long moment he looks under
the door to see if someone is standing
there. He crawls under the divider to the
next stall. As he is crawling, the final
stall door is slammed open. He quickly
lurches to his feet and runs out.

(Heading for the emergency exit stairway,
he is assaulted by the voices of the MAN
and the two GIRLS as they shout, "Famous
Lines From Famous Movies!)

MAN and GIRLS
getitgotitgood/ifyoubuildithew
illcome/playitsam/yourmothersh

THIS IS NOT MY MOVIE

eforgivesme/todayisagooddaytod
ie/doIfeelluckywelldoyapunk?/y
ourmothersuckscocksinhell/toda
yIfeelliketheluckiestmanonthef
aceoftheearth/it'saliveit'it's
alive!/isitsafe?isitsafe?/made
itmatopoftheworld!/whatwehaveh
ereisfailuretocommunicate/lets
gogetangel/imgonnamakehimanoff
erhecantrefuse/ifihadadickthis
iswhereidtellyoutosuckit/goand
neverdarkenmytowelsagain/andyo
urlittledogtoo!

*MANAGER throws open the door and takes the
stairs three at a time down to the first
landing, crashing hard into a huge
cardboard Wall of Monsters display for an
upcoming release*

Running Your Demons Down

The New Horror Masterpiece from J. Wright Muir

Director of *After the First Death, The Season to Be Wary,*
and *The Buffalo Hunter*

*He pushes the display back into place but
then one of the monsters reaches out and
grabs him as the others, one by one, grow
fuller and more real, growling and
slobbering and start coming after him but
he manages to pull free and turn and run
from them but they chase him, looking like
they are all joined together in the middle
like a big glob of melted candle wax or
something that's been fused together in a
fire but they can still make terrible wet
smacking growling snarling noises.*

227

The MANGLED gets way ahead of them and we
see his face in CLOSE-UP:

It twists in agony. Then we see a long
shiny blade and then a second one, both of
them moving rapidly up, down, sideways. He
tries to scream but all that emerges from
his mouth is a ragged, clogged, wet,
pitiful gagging bleat of helplessness as
the blades destroy his guts, followed by
bursts of blood that arc onto the walls,
spatter at his feet, and soak all of the
surroundings.

The stairway door opens, and we see a hand
holding the swords.

                    MAN
    (Though we don't see his face)
        Now this is a movie. Monsters
        and gore and innocent people
        dying for no good reason. So
        glad I remembered to get
        popcorn. So happy I could
        share my movie with the two of
        you.

He and the GIRLS step into the stairway and
close the door behind them.

The camera pulls back from the door.

Silence.

The camera makes its way back through the
hallway, down the stairs, and out into the
lobby.

It is much brighter now, and we can hear

THIS IS NOT MY MOVIE

the murmur of voices as people leave various theaters.

We see two concession stand workers who are in the middle of a conversation as the camera stops and stares.

> **FIRST CONCESSION WORKER**
> . . .like those stupid 'trick endings.' Here you are, in the middle of this really spectacular, horrific scene, and suddenly the door closes, the camera lingers for a second or two, somebody or <u>something</u> makes a gross sound behind the door, and the goddamn screen just goes to black. Roll credits. That's it. Pisses me off so bad I could punch something. That's not an ending, it's a. . .a. . .a non-ending. A We-Just-Ran-Out-of-Ideas ending. It's a-

> **SECOND CONCESSION WORKER**
> You don't have any hobbies, do you? Or a pet, maybe? Should I even <u>ask</u> about a girlfriend?

> **FIRST CONCESSION WORKER**
> Don't mock me.

> **SECOND CONCESSION WORKER**
> I wasn't. I merely offered some speculative observations. I'm sorry, but I just don't see why you get so worked up by those types of endings.

FIRST CONCESSION WORKER
Because it <u>isn't an ending!</u> If I'm going to pay good money and sit in a theater and subtract two hours from my life, I want an actual ending, a resolution to the story, a satisfactory concluding arc to the narrative so <u>some</u> sort of cohesion is reached.

SECOND CONCESSION WORKER
'Cohesion'? Is that your new fifty-dollar-and-pocket-change word for the day?

FIRST CONCESSION WORKER
I read it in Peter Travers' film column from last month's <u>Rolling Stone</u>. *(A beat)* Yes, I had to look it up. No, I don't have hobbies, or a pet, or a girlfriend. There. Happy now?

SECOND CONCESSION WORKER
You know, my sister thinks you're really cute.

FIRST CONCESSION WORKER
Oh happiness, oh joy. Now I have a reason to go on living.

A MAN—the MAN—sans canes, walks up to the counter, looking a bit different from before, a bit calmer, and smiles at them.

MAN
I'd like some popcorn, please. Extra butter. And a large

THIS IS NOT MY MOVIE

soda. While we're at it, throw in some Raisinets. I feel like clogging a heart valve today.

The workers laugh, as does the MAN.

An USHER walks by holding a broom and dustpan. He/She enters an empty theater and quickly sweeps out a couple of aisles.

USHER
(into a cell phone)
> Tell me about it. There wasn't anyone in this theater for the last showing, but they <u>still</u> have to run the movie, and I still have to sweep up afterward. What am I supposed to sweep? There wasn't anyone in here! I know, it's so stupid! But, hey, I'm on the clock, getting paid. So, we gonna hook up later? I was thinking we could maybe start with pizza before we. . .

The USHER makes his/her way out of the theatre, closing the doors.

However, the camera remains inside the theatre, focused on the closed doors, then slowly pulls back to reveal the MANAGER from earlier: his face pale and gray, his eyes a thousand-yard-stare empty, his neck a bloody, shredded, drooping mass of chewed meat. He's sitting in the back row, gazing not at the blank screen but at something sad and horrible that only he can see. As he speaks, the camera moves closer to him until, at the end, it's focused solely on his face

MANAGER
```
This is not my movie.
This is not my movie.
This is not my movie.
This is not my movie.
This is not my movie.
This is not my
This is not
```

BLACKOUT

THE END. . .Returning us to *nearly* where we began, so it's time for a 331-word recapitulation (another fifty-dollar-and-pocket-change word, don'tcha just love'em?) of a few salient points—with new hints interspersed—for those who are, shall we say, a bit Tardy to the Party and think that movie starting times apply to everyone *except* them:

Manager:
```
This is not my movie.
This is not my movie.
This is not my movie.
This is not my movie.
This is not my movie.
This is not my
This is not
```

BLACKOUT

THE END

Salient Point #1:

The simple equation completed:

$$Ed = h\,tu\,/\,tp2 + E = hv + y = M{*}x = y + P = 0 + (50.0)/(m) = 50.0D$$

Darkness + Light + Opening Credits on Screen + One Who Views = The One True Camera

THIS IS NOT MY MOVIE

Salient Point #2:

Perception should not be mistaken to require biological *senses; rather, perception, when we think about what is* really *going on, should be conceived of as being* influenced by the world. *Perception is, at its most basic, the detection of an object by a subject—and if all objects* (say, **The Manager)** *are also subjects* (of, say, the unseen-by-us-**Film** he is watching at the end), *then it follows that* all subjects perceive *on their way to* becoming objects for other subjects to perceive, *and so on. Perception is, then, receiving information from the world, which creates a causal influence between an object and a subject. Information and causation reduced to the same ontological category."*

Salient Point #3: The vibrating anguish of unendurable grief synchronizes with the resonance of ever-present guilt and unmanifest rage, and if one is not careful, if one is not aware of the panpsychism created by this ferocious reification can take on a life—even a sentience—of its own; and when the circumstances are right, sometimes—not very often, but it happens nonetheless—it can take *physical* form, a theory debated but not yet dismissed by such great minds as Spinoza, Alfred North Whitehead, Pierre Teilhard de Chardin, Bertrand Russel, and numerous others in the fields of physics, medicine, philosophy, biology, and paleontology.

Physical form.

That is, when circumstances are *just* right. . .

Advance, stop, open, expose, close; advance, stop, open, expose, close; advance—be born; open—fight; expose—love; close—die.

9

"All great work is preparing yourself for the accident to happen."
—Sidney Lumet

AT **ROUGHLY THE** same time his wife cut her thumb in the employee break room, Ray Price was across town, in the kitchen of their house, staring down at the lunch he'd made for himself as if it were some long-forgotten leftover from the back of the refrigerator that was in the process of forming its own rudimentary language. He had no idea why he'd bothered to make the damned thing in the first place. He wasn't even hungry.

But he *was* halfway to being quite drunk; *comfortably numb*, as Pink Floyd once put it.

If Melanie knew he'd begun secretly drinking again, that would maybe probably—no, definitely—yeah, *definitely* be the end of their marriage. He was ashamed of himself within five minutes of buying that first bottle of George Dickel 86 Proof Barrel Select Scotch—the *only* scotch for the true connoisseur, thank you very much—but not so ashamed that it prevented him from breaking the seal and pouring himself two shots (neat) back-to-back. It helped dull the pain; both from the automobile accident and. . .and. . .

(. . .*Bill Emerson standing at the front door, illuminated only by the single bulb in the overhead porchlight that still worked— Ray had meant to replace others weeks ago but couldn't remember why he hadn't—Bill standing there shivering, looking like some kind of crouched terrified shadow—Peter Lorre in the final scenes of* M*—standing there shivering and trying to look gathered, trying to look calm and official but in truth looking sepulchral as he spoke like an official representative of the Cedar Hill Police: "Mr. and Mrs. Price, my name's Emerson, Bill Emerson, um, sorry—Detective Bill Emerson. . .I'm sorry it's so*

THIS IS NOT MY MOVIE

*late, I know I probably woke you up but. . .may I come in? I need
to speak with you about. . .about Daphne. . .)*

Another neat shot, this one a double and (he promised himself)
his last drink of the day, then it was cap back on bottle, bottle back
in disgusting metal cleaning bucket, bottle covered up with even
more disgusting cleaning rags, and then the whole disgusting thing
shoved into the corner of the less-disgusting mud room in the back
where Melanie never ventured because she found the place. . .well,
disgusting. So there.

Thursday was his traditional day off from the Janus and as
such he usually steered clear of the place, but he was feeling guilty
about not being there with Melanie, knowing damn well that after
everything was set into place for both the amateur filmmakers
contest and the big premiere he was looking forward to previewing
with her tonight, he ought to at least try to make himself
presentable.

*And for chrissakes, have some coffee and remember to use
breath spray.*

He was still a bit flabbergasted that the Janus would be hosting
the world premiere of the new horror opus from independent
director Trenton Wright. Wright had, over the past few years,
garnered the kind of buzz that George A. Romero, David
Cronenberg, and John Carpenter had generated with their early
films. Wright's movies were smart, scary, just gory enough and
with enough shock-jumps to satisfy audiences looking for that sort
of thing, but they also managed to be well-written, well-acted, and
contained just enough social commentary to make them difficult
to dismiss by all of the so-called critics who believed themselves to
be above horror cinema. Okay, yes, maybe some of Wright's films
in the final reel took a temporary left turn into absurd grotesquery
that seemed over-the-top and nonsensical in context, but Lucio
Fulci made a career out of non-linear horror movies and was
considered a genius. Ray loved Wright's films, and Melanie had
never seen one. Tonight was going to be something akin to a first
date for them, what Ray hoped would be a fresh start. . .or as fresh
as they could muster, anyway. He poured himself some coffee,
rubbed his eyes, and sat down at the kitchen table.

Despite everything that had happened in the last year, he was
still very much in love with his wife. And, being pragmatic, he tried
as he always did in the morning to be objective, thinking that if he

GARY A. BRAUNBECK

could just remove himself from the equation and look on as a disinterested third party, he might see the solution to the problem of their disintegrating marriage that had eluded him for these endless, *endless* months.

He added cream and sugar to his coffee, took a few sips, then sat back and tried to think it out again, absent-mindedly rubbing the two-and-a-half-inch scar that extended from his left-hand side hairline, down his temple, ending in the center of his left eyebrow.

He wondered what kind of tricks Trenton Wright would have up his sleeve for the Ohio Premiere tomorrow night. In addition to his reputation as the Next Big Thing in horror movies, Wright possessed a twisted sense of humor. A fan of the old gimmicks that William Castle would pull back in the day, Wright was famous for the stunts he staged at his film's premieres, and infamous for never warning the theatre owners ahead of time just exactly *what* those stunts were going to be. The man had a small animatronics and makeup team that could work wonders with almost no money.

And Wright was going to be there in person for all three showings Thursday night, signing autographs, posing for photos. . .and pulling whatever stunts he had planned. Wright chose The Janus because several of the exteriors in the movie were filmed around the immediate area; Cedar Hill, Heath, Hebron, and Zanesville; each had more than their fair share of eerie locales. The Janus had sold out all three showings months ago. Everything about tomorrow night promised to put them back on the right track.

Or such was Ray's hope.

Hopefully tonight would be, if not wonderful for him and Mel, at least pleasant.

Yes. Pleasant.

Aim for that. That. And nothing more.

Just. That.

Things hadn't been pleasant since. . .

Since.

Cautious—check; fragile—check; awkward and damn near terrified to look at one another; check and check.

So. Pleasant.

Aim for that. That.

And nothing more.

That and nothing more.

236

THIS IS NOT MY MOVIE

Nothing more.

Nothing more.

He looked around the kitchen. For seven years, this house had been their home. Now it was just a place where they ate, slept, and kept all their stuff. In one of their rare conversations recently, they had talked about the possibility of selling it. The market was good at the moment; they were certain to get a great price for it.

But that was all the further the discussion went. They had not talked about where they might move to, nor had they talked about whether or not they would be moving *together*.

The thought of life without Melanie was not one Ray could confront. Part of him wished he could just get himself out of neutral and do *something* to make everything better. . .or, at least, get things moving in that direction. He hated the idea of selling this house but, if that's what Melanie wanted, he'd go along with it.

Too many painful memories here, he thought, melancholia draping over him, his gaze moving unconsciously toward the second floor. Daphne's room was—*had* been, still was—the first door on the left. One had only to open the door to see the stuffed animals, the bedspread covered in hearts and ponies, the small wooden rocking chair they'd bought at the flea market at the Valley Drive-in, and the small plastic table with small plastic chairs and small plastic teacups. Whenever Ray or Melanie had attended one of Daphne's tea parties, they didn't dare try to sit on those chairs because they'd immediately crack under an adult's weight; instead, both of them became expert squatters, damn the leg cramps and full tea party ahead. It would always be a little girl's room, and even though neither of them had entered it for fear of what the sight, the textures of her stuffed animals and dolls, the lingering little-girl scent of *everything* would invite her to materialize in the memory.

Not that the house didn't have its share of emotional booby-traps for him, as well, but Melanie was the one suffering the most. Maybe she thought if they sold the house and moved elsewhere, it would be a fresh start, *tabula rasa*; no pain, no nightmares, no bloody daytime memories that seemed to sneak up on her while she was just puttering around the house, cleaning, rearranging the furniture because she thought a little *feng shui* would keep her occupied.

GARY A. BRAUNBECK

It was on one of those days, one of those goddamn daytime memory days, that Ray came home to find Melanie in a corner of the living room, cowering, knees pulled up to her chest, arms wrapped tightly around her lower legs, rocking back and forth, quietly humming a tune he immediately recognized as Gordon Lightfoot's "The Pony Man"—one of Daphne's favorite songs that both he and Mel had sang to her as they tucked her in, touched her cheek, and whispered, "There. All safe and sound."

Melanie was holding a small stuffed elephant missing one of its tusks. "She was planning for all of us to go on one of her treasure hunts. She hid this under one of the sofa cushions." Her voice was filled with both rage and despair. She lifted her head to reveal swollen bloodshot eyes still glinting from the tears. "This was the. . .the *third* treasure I found. Christ, Ray, I don't want to clean or rearrange the fucking furniture or even open one of the lower kitchen drawers because. . .she hides—she *hid*—things in the damnedest places. I don't want to find any more. . .any more treasures."

Hopefully tonight would be, if not wonderful for her and Ray, at least pleasant.

Yes, he thought. Pleasant.

Aim for that. That. And nothing more.

Just. That.

Things hadn't been pleasant since. . .

Since.

Cautious; check. *Fragile*; check. *Awkward* and damn near terrified to look at one another; check and check.

So. Pleasant.

Aim for that. That.

And nothing more.

That and nothing more.

Nothing more.

Nothing more.

Nothing more.

"All safe and sound," Ray said aloud. "All safe—"

He didn't finish.

His legs gave out and he hit the floor hard, crying, tears and snot running down his face, chest tightening, pulse jackhammering, heart trying to squirt out through his ribcage. He pulled his legs up until his knees were pressed against him, and then wrapped his arms around his legs, rocking back and forth, muttering, "Everyone out of the pool. . .everyone out of the pool. . ."

Everyone out the pool!—one of Daphne's favorite expressions, used when she and her parents were playing outside, and it began to get dark. *Everybody out of the pool!* A code phrase that meant it was time to go back inside.

Ray knew that both he and Melanie only had a limited number of *back insides*, and when they reached the end of that ever-dwindling supply and neither of them could bear to enter this house again, that would be it.

At the sound of the buzzer.

Game over. Thanks for playing! As a consolation prize, you'll receive a lifetime supply of Turtle Wax.

Okay, he thought. *Mel's right—time to blow this pop stand.*

It didn't matter to Ray *where* they lived, just as long as Melanie stayed with him. Wherever she was, that was his home.

I do *love you*, he thought.

Love.

Love was a word Ray thought about almost all the time now, that unique syllable that managed to take in tongue, lips, and teeth all at once. It was his mantra. He often said it to himself whenever he took walks alone, a hymn to the fall of his steps; he muttered it silently whenever he went outside to fetch the newspaper from the first step that led onto the porch; he hummed it while reading the paper at the kitchen table. On days when his headaches were bad, after he took his codeine, he would lay back his head and become lost in the word for hours, noticing, at last, that the sun had leapt from the window sill to the third pane, then wonder what had happened Out There in the world during the time in between.

Love had happened, of course.

But usually, by that time, he had thought about it, hummed, spoke it silently to himself so much, mesmerized by its simple elegance, that it became an abstract concept, like quantum mechanics or the new revised tax laws.

He pulled himself unsteadily off the floor and returned to the kitchen. He made a pot of coffee and poured some into one of the extra-large porcelain mugs. He went back to the kitchen table.

Rested his elbows on it.

Cupped his chin in his hands.

Closed his eyes.

Remembered things from when he was a child.

Inhaled the warm aroma of the coffee.

"Goddammit!" he shouted, alone, there in the safety of the kitchen, slamming a fist down on the table, causing the coffee cup to jump and the spoon to rattle against the surface of the saucer.

No. No. He would not go there, not today. God knew there were enough bad memories to dwell on. By the time he'd turned twelve, Ray had suffered through more than his share of too-severe-for-the-crime beatings (he'd lost count of the broken bones) and the endless days locked in his room without meals or being let out to go to the bathroom and—

—stop it!

This was the first morning in months that he gotten up in anything remotely resembling a good mood and he would not think about all the Bad Things—and he would not think about the Awful Thing.

He wiped a thin bead of perspiration from his forehead and looked around the kitchen for something pleasant, something *nice*, something banal and blah-blah-blah boring. Just when he thought he was going to be mired in the misery of that memory, he saw the old calendar hanging on the door of the pantry.

From Your Friends At Morton Dairy Park!

Yeah, that was the ticket, especially for a man who loved his wife but couldn't get a handle on why their lives were crumbling into ruin. Wasn't a loss like this, a sickening, unimaginable, shattering loss, wasn't something like this supposed to bring those left behind *closer? Even if the soul would be in anguish from knowing how their loved one had died?*

He'd decided that he was going to be the one to attempt to ease Melanie's pain, but despite his trying to stay cheerful, in a good mood—

—oblivious was the word Melanie sometimes used; with more and more frequency lately but for the love of God (or who or whatever was running this tragic vaudeville called existence) *someone* had to try to remain upbeat.

Right?

To hell with it for now.

He reached across the counter for what he thought was the newspaper but turned out to be one of the numerous press kits Wright's people had sent, most of which were going to be autographed by Wright and auctioned off at the premiere tomorrow night to raise money for the local homeless shelter, as well as the new women's shelter.

He looked at the cover of the press kit:

The Company of Lesser Demons

The New Film from Trenton Wright

Director of *A Host of Shadows, Pandora Drive,* and *The Far Side of the Lake*

He almost opened the folder to look at the production stills and read the plot synopsis, then decided he didn't want to know, he wanted it to be a surprise for both of them; a nice, scary surprise. Maybe Melanie would even ask him to hold her hand tight, the way he used to when they were first dating.

That would be wonderful.

Ray smiled, then reached down for his coffee.

And noticed the blood.

When he'd slammed his fist on the table, he'd caught it on the tines of a fork he was going to use for the scrambled eggs he never got around to making. The fork had made three small but painful holes in the side of his hand, and all of them were bleeding.

As Melanie was dumping the remains of the onion into the sink across town, noting how the globules of her blood were running together, Ray lifted his hand and looked down to see that two large drops of his blood had dripped onto the table, each of them reflecting his face.

In one, he looked just like himself; but the other drop had spattered against the side of the saucer, and the reflection he saw there was of a man who might have looked something like him, but—

—he grabbed some paper towels and cleaned up the mess, then went into the downstairs bathroom and fixed up his hand: two gauze pads and some medical tape.

He left the bathroom and was heading upstairs to the office that he and Melanie kept on the second floor. If nothing else, he might as well check his email and see if there was anything interesting waiting for him.

The front doorbell chimed.

Ray's initial reaction was to not answer it and hope whomever it was would just go away, but the pragmatic part of him whispered: *It might be important.*

Thankful he'd decided to get dressed before coming downstairs (he usually spent his days off in his bathrobe), Ray tucked in his shirt, patted down his hair, and answered the door.

The woman who stood before him looked to be around twenty-three years old. She carried a medium-sized leather shoulder bag. She was dressed in a very business-like blouse and blazer, with a matching skirt and sensible shoes. She wore a plastic name tag on her left breast pocket, but Ray couldn't read her name because her long, dark hair was swept over her left shoulder.

She was so beautiful that, for a moment, he couldn't find his voice.

She was *that* stunning. . .and somehow familiar. Ray felt as if he'd seen her somewhere before. Maybe at the Janus? Was she one of the semi-regulars whose name he hadn't learned yet? But if that were the case, what was she doing here? How had she gotten his address?

"Yes?" he managed to say at last.

She stood in the doorway with the hesitancy of one who knows they're intruding in your life but feels as if they must. How often, Ray wondered, had she felt like an imposition, or been forced to speak in a soft, almost begging voice to be given something?

Never, Ray decided. With a face like that (where *did* he know her from?), it just came to her. Faces like hers were given everything they wanted, always. What could he have to offer her that she'd want?

"Ray Price?" she said in a bright, chiming voice.

"Yes?" The blood was rushing through his temples with such force that he didn't hear her name when she said it.

She offered him a business card. Ray glanced at it, saw the name of some realtor company, and realized that Melanie must have made this appointment without discussing it with him first.

So, I guess you decided, huh, Mel?

He was so surprised—not to mention confused and more than a bit irritated—that he didn't realize he'd invited the young woman inside until he found himself closing the door and turning toward her.

THIS IS NOT MY MOVIE

"I'm sorry to be early," she said, "but I've got a last-minute showing in about an hour. I hope you don't mind?"

"Uh. . .uh, no, no, of course not." He slipped her business card into his pocket without bothering to read her name, then asked, "Did my wife make this appointment?"

"Yes, about a week ago. Now, we realize that you're not firm in your decision to sell, but the agency wanted me to do a quick walk-through and take some pictures so we can give you a good appraisal on probable market value." She leaned toward him and lowered her voice to a whisper, as if he were her co-conspirator. "You'd be surprised how many couples decide to sell after our agency gives them a potential sales figure."

"I'll bet."

She turned away from him and walked through the downstairs rooms, finishing up in the kitchen. "Oh, Mr. Price, this is a *wonderful* house! There's so much open space—and in all the right places." She set her bag on the kitchen table and opened it, removing an old Polaroid Instamatic camera. "Is it alright if I take some quick pictures? If you later decide you *are* going to sell, then I'll come back with a much better camera and take some professional-quality photos for our website."

"Have we met?"

"I beg your pardon?"

Ray rubbed his eyes and smiled. "I'm sorry, I don't mean for that to sound like some kind of middle-aged perv come-on, but ever since I answered the door, I can't shake the feeling that I know you from somewhere. Have you ever been to my theatre, The Janus?"

"I'm afraid not. I'm a little new to this area."

He continued to stare at her for several moments as she readied the camera.

I know I recognize you, he thought.

And then something occurred to him.

Over the course of his marriage to Melanie, Ray had encountered many beautiful women and had been attracted to many of them—a few had even hinted that, even though he was married, they wouldn't mind a few quickies in a hotel room—but he'd never once cheated on Melanie. Not that he didn't indulge in the occasional fantasy about sex with another woman, but that was always as far as it went.

Looking at this stunning young woman who stood here in his kitchen, Ray realized that she was prime fantasy material for him, yet—

—and damn if this wasn't one for the books—

—he wasn't *attracted* to her, not in the way he usually found himself attracted to beautiful women, anyway. No; what he felt toward this woman—who should have had him so hard he could barely stand—was much more tender; he felt somehow protective of her, even. . . *Think about something else*, he commanded himself.

It was rapidly becoming his new mantra: *Think about something else.*

So, he looked at her hands.

She didn't have any.

Instead, two metallic hand-like prostheses were in their place.

He forced himself to not stare at them. He felt suddenly cold, a little unbalanced. He gave her a quick smile and pointed at her camera.

"I used to have one almost exactly like that," he said.

"Oh?" she replied, doing her best to sound interested.

"Yes," he continued. "I lost it about a year ago, but until then I'd had it for the better part of twenty years. Worked as well on the day I lost it as it did the day I bought it. It was the same color as yours, as well. Those scratches on the side? I had the same kind of scratches in almost the same place on mine."

"The old carrying cases weren't as well-constructed as today," she replied, inserting the eight-track tape-sized film cartridge into the camera with amazing dexterity. "I've lost count of how many times I've scraped this thing on the side of that old carrying case."

He grinned. "I remember that I had one of those old label-makers, the kind where you had to punch the words in one letter at a time on those plastic strips? I put my name on the label

—I misspelled it, by the way—and stuck it to the bottom of the camera. Don't know why."

"Huh," said the young woman. Snapping closed the bottom film compartment, she pulled out the piece of blank film that slid out with a loud *whirrrr* after the new cartridge had been loaded, then held up the camera and said, "All set. Any particular place you'd like me to start?"

"Doesn't matter to me." Why didn't he just tell her it wasn't a good time, that he and Melanie needed to discuss it further, thank you for coming, Miss, but I've got a busy afternoon of moping planned and you're bringing too much activity into my life.

He couldn't bring himself to ask her to leave. . .but why?

He stared at the bottom of the camera where, for an instant before she turned around, he'd seen a thin strip of blue plastic with white letters punched onto it.

"I'll start right here in the kitchen, then take a couple of pictures of the living room, the master bedroom and master bath, then the guest room and office area upstairs."

"Ah, so my wife gave you an idea of the layout, then?"

The young woman stared at him for a moment, then shrugged. "I think so. To tell you the truth, I talk to so many people about so many houses, some days it all gets a little blurry. *Is* there an office upstairs?"

"Yes."

"Huh." She seemed both surprised and puzzled. "Lucky guess."

Ray sighed. Maybe he was just being paranoid, but there seemed to be something just the least bit *forced* about her reaction.

She took four pictures of the kitchen from different vantage points, then placed the photos on the counter so they could develop.

By now Ray was getting nervous.

For just a moment, as she'd turned around to take the third photograph, he'd briefly glanced the word *Yar* on the plastic strip attached to the bottom of the camera.

It can't be, he thought. *That* couldn't *possibly be the same camera I lost.*

Could it?

The young woman excused herself and went into the living room. Ray poured himself another cup of coffee and sat on a stool at the counter, watching as the Polaroids slowly developed.

He'd always been fascinated by the way these old instant cameras worked; snap a picture and out slides this smelly blank square of white, but as you watch it, like magic this image slowly begins to appear. A ghost emerging from the mist.

He took a sip of his coffee. Then she stood in the kitchen doorway once again.

"Is it alright if I go upstairs and take pictures?"

"Knock yourself out."

"Would you care to accompany me, Mr. Price? I know it must seem strange, letting a stranger walk through your house and—"

He waved his hand. "No, you seem trustworthy."

She gave him a radiant smile. "Why, thank you." And with that, she bounced up the stairs.

He examined the developing photos. He couldn't be sure, but it seemed like they weren't going to come out properly.

He picked up one of the photographs, then another one, examining each of them until he'd gone through all four of them at least three times.

He looked up at the kitchen, then back at the photos to make sure this wasn't some trick of the light.

It wasn't.

The kitchen shown in these photographs was not the same kitchen in which he was currently sitting. *This* kitchen, *his* kitchen, *their* kitchen, was neat and clean and uncluttered, your typical, nice suburban kitchen.

But the kitchen in the photographs was *magnificent.*

It was the same kitchen, as far as the structure of the room itself went; all of the windows and counters were in the same place, as were the appliances; every wall was where it was supposed to be and all the angles were in their proper place, but that's where the similarities ended.

The magnificent kitchen in the photographs could have been in the pages of *Better Homes and Gardens.* Impressive copper pots hung on the walls. The kitchen table had been replaced by a marvelous marble island, above which hung a metal, scaffold-like series of shelves that were attached to the ceiling by bright silver chains. The shelves held all manner of baking utensils and pieces of small equipment—electric dicing machines, a French press, a vegetable steamer, and several other contraptions that Ray had seen only in country club kitchens. In the center of the marble island was a large square of polished wood that served as a knife holder.

The shelves were painted a different color. A wall rack held chubby yellow and orange soup mugs. The kitchen table was set over by the window (it was the *same* kitchen table that had always been here, he noticed), but instead of the two old wooden chairs, there were three exquisite, hand-polished teak chairs placed around it.

THIS IS NOT MY MOVIE

And a sturdy-looking highchair slightly off to the side.

He dropped the photos back down onto the counter.

No, no way. No goddamn way I can be seeing this. I can't *be* that *drunk, not yet. I didn't have that much. . .*

Melanie always wanted a kitchen like that shown in the photos. They'd even begun pricing some of the items, and once had an architect look the place over to see if some of the additions—like the scaffold-like structure of shelves hanging from the ceiling— would be possible.

There was no doubt about it; the kitchen in the photographs was the one Melanie always *planned* on having, some day.

Some day. Just as they'd planned on having children by now.

Stop it!

He picked up one of the photographs and squinted his eyes, trying to get a clear look at the calendar in the picture.

Climbing off the stool, photograph still in hand, Ray went into the living room to retrieve his reading glasses; putting them on, he noticed that the young woman had left four photos of the living room on the coffee table.

He put on his glasses and held the kitchen photo close to his face, but at a slight angle so that the light coming in through the bay window didn't cause too much glare.

He couldn't be certain, but he could swear that the calendar, though it displayed the correct month, October, claimed that the year was almost sixteen years in the future.

"This has got to be some kind of joke," he whispered under his breath.

The young woman had used some kind of trick photography. It was a gag camera or something like that.

"Miss?" he called out.

When there was no answer, he yanked the glasses from his face and called her again, only this time about five times as loud.

He wanted answers.

He grabbed up a couple of the living room photographs.

Same architecture, but that was it. The furniture was different, ultra-modern but tasteful, and in different places. Pictures lined the mantel over the fireplace, and as Ray looked closer, he saw himself and Melanie in these pictures.

They were older.

Much older, in fact—early- to mid-sixties.

And in these photographs, they weren't alone.

They were a family of four; two beautiful girls—*young ladies,* both of them having inherited their mother's looks.

He tossed the photos down onto the table, yelled for the young woman from the realtor's office once again, then stormed up the stairs.

She was nowhere in the house but had taken care to leave behind photographs of every upstairs room, and in each photo the rooms were different, brighter, happier.

The master bedroom was much more luxurious than it was now; the office had new computers and sleek, matching white work stations, not the make-shift collection of disparate office furniture which now occupied the space. Then there was the guest room.

As it was now, the guest room, though comfortable and inviting enough, was nothing spectacular. But in the photographs, it wasn't a guest room at all. It was the room of a teenage girl; cluttered, filled with clothes, a stereo and flat-screen television with a Blu-Ray player, posters of rock stars on the walls, books lying helter-skelter wherever there was an overlooked empty space. . .and it was all so *bright.*

And then it hit him so hard he almost couldn't breathe.

These pictures showed the kind of happy home that he and Melanie had always dreamed of having. It was a house full of life and activity, where each realized dream was quickly and joyfully replaced by another dream, a new goal, something the family could work toward *together.*

The pictures showed Ray his home as it *should have been,* as he'd dreamed it would be.

"This is one hell of a trick, young lady," he whispered through clenched teeth.

He went through the entire house twice more, but he couldn't find her.

How had she been able to leave without him hearing her?

He found her camera in the office he and Melanie shared. It was on Melanie's desk, next to her computer, which the young woman had turned on.

He picked up the camera and slowly turned it over.

Yar Iprce, read the words punched onto the plastic blue strip attached to its underside.

THIS IS NOT MY MOVIE

He gently placed the camera down, then half-sat, half-collapsed into Melanie's office chair.

For several minutes he just sat there, not moving, staring at nothing, trying to make sense of this thing which made no rational sense at all.

God, what the fuck is happening?

He glanced up and saw what was displayed on Melanie's screen. And the day got a lot worse.

10

"My dad used to draw these great cartoon figures. His dream was being a cartoonist, but he never achieved it, and it kind of broke my heart. I think part of my interest in art had to do with his yearning for something he could never have."
—Kathryn Bigelow

THE REST OF Melanie's day was taken up with final preparations for the premiere. She inventoried all the food, snacks, soft drinks, beer, double checked that there were enough recyclable popcorn tubs and snack trays, and for the fourth time measured out the clear distance between the sides of the counter and the lobby entryway, then made sure the distance from the other side of the U-shaped counter/bar was equidistant from the doors leading into the theatre proper. Trenton Wright's people were adamant that the director have this space available for his "special attractions." Melanie hoped that whatever Wright was going to do, it wouldn't cause any damage or upset the patrons.

Satisfied that there was a place for everything and everything was in its place, Melanie went back to the break room for some coffee and another cigarette. She'd quit smoking soon after she'd met Ray but had taken up the habit again two months ago. Aside from the cost of the cigarettes (she never thought she'd see the day that a pack of smokes set you back six dollars), she'd doled out a small fortune in breath sprays, breath drops, and small pump sprays designed to eliminate even the strongest cigarette odors from clothing on impact.

Hell—it'd just be easier to tell him and live with his disapproval. But on top of helping to settle her nerves, the nicotine helped with the pain. She didn't like taking the Demerol; it made her too woozy and nonsensical, even when she broke the tablets in half. But she could feel that this was not going to be a Demerol-

250

free day. Still, she'd put it off as long as possible, maybe until they were home after the movie tonight. She wanted to be firing on all cylinders tonight for her date with her hubby. So she was going to open a window back there and sit by it and smoke. She liked her four cigarettes a day, screw the Surgeon General; she liked the way that first cigarette felt between her fingers, the *snick!* of the lighter, the way the tip of the cigarette softly crackled and peeled back, revealing that luscious hot glowing tip as she pulled in that first, heavenly drag.

She lit up, and felt her body melt as she exhaled the first drag. *Oh, yeah. . .*

She knew that both she and Ray had quietly given up on the hope of ever having a family, but sometimes, on days like this, she tried to convince herself that the first drag of a cigarette was almost enough to take its place.

Almost.

She closed her eyes and lost herself in the mixed aromas of coffee and cigarette smoke until she heard Astryd say, "Yeech! Don't you know that's against health laws?"

Melanie pulled in a second drag and said, "I do, and I don't give rat's *tuchus*. Turn on the air filter, then."

Astryd did so, then joined Melanie at the table. "I thought I might find you hiding back here."

"I'm not hiding."

"Yes, you are."

"Okay, yes, I am. But I sure sounded full of conviction there for a second, didn't I?"

"We can go with that, sure."

Melanie finished her coffee. "So, what's going on?"

"I'm worried about you."

"Then you, my friend, have far too much free time on your hands. Remind me to triple your workload."

"Knock it off, Mel. Jeez. I just thought. . .you've been really down lately—"

"More than usual, you mean?"

"That's not funny. I just thought maybe you'd like to talk for a little bit, that's all."

Melanie exhaled and shook her head. "I'm all out of chit-chat. I ran out of it. . .what seems like decades ago."

"C'mon, Mel! You've been keeping me and everyone else at

arm's length for months now. When was the last time we went out for coffee and cheesecake or something after work? We used to go out all the time, but lately you always go by yourself. I can't even *remember* the last movie we saw together."

Melanie nearly laughed. "Oh, Lord—it was in Columbus, part of the Drexel's Retro Month Extravaganza."

"Which movie was it?"

"*Fight Club*. You treated me for my birthday. Sensitive, insightful, uplifting film. The type of movie that makes you feel proud to be a member of the human race."

"*Stop joking*, will you?"

"No great humorist is ever appreciated in their own time."

Astryd's face turned into a slab of granite. "If you want to keep joking, fine," she said, her voice flat, then pushed back her chair with more force than was necessary and started to leave. "But you can't say I didn't try."

Melanie turned in her chair and just managed to catch hold of Astryd's elbow. "Don't,

please? I'm. . .I'm sorry, okay? I appreciate your concern. Come on, have a seat and talk to me."

Astryd smiled, relaxed, and sat down again.

"What's on your mind?" asked Melanie.

"Well, I was thinking about some things today, and for some reason, I thought you might be the person to discuss my conclusions with."

"'Discuss your conclusions'? What is this, *Meet the Press?*"

"Okay, okay, I admit that was a little William-F-Buckley, but I figured you might have something to say about this."

"About what?"

"Sex."

The word hung between them like a piece of rotting fruit on the branch of a dead tree. Melanie cleared her throat and removed a fresh cigarette.

"I'm going to need another one for this."

"Go ahead, the filter's on full-blast and I started the ceiling fan, to boot."

Melanie lit her cigarette. "'To boot.' You're the only person I know who still uses that phrase."

"Gives me character, makes me colorful. Okay, this sex thing. Me and Charlotte, things hadn't been going so great for us in the sack department, right? I didn't know what to do, if it was my fault, if she didn't find me attractive anymore, or what. Then I came across this story in an old literary magazine I found, right? I forget what the story was called, but it was about this couple, right, this husband and wife, who'd gotten so entrenched in their routine that they lost the desire to talk to each other, let alone. . .you know, have sex."

Melanie didn't say a word, just sat there feeling like some old, dried-up spinster listening to a vibrant young woman and wanting nothing more than to strangle her. Or ask for specific details about how things were before they went awry.

"So, this couple in the story, they start making up people to talk to, right? The woman invents herself this friend she calls 'Mrs. Kersh-McFadden' and she talks to her. I mean, right there in the house when her husband is home and everything. She waits until Tuesday evenings, when her husband is in his study, then she goes to the door and pretends to answer it and there's Mrs. Kersh-McFadden. She invites her 'friend' in and she talks to her about everything that's wrong between her and her husband—she does this just loud enough so he can hear her in the study, okay?

"Well, the thing is, the husband begins to think that this Mrs. Kersh-McFadden might be real, right? He imagines that he can hear her voice answering his wife, but he'll be damned if he's going to go look and see, because then that would mean that his wife wins. So, he invents this fellow called 'Mr. Dinsdale'—like in that old Monty Python sketch? Anyway, he starts talking to Dinsdale on Thursdays, right? He pretends to pick up the phone like he's about to make a call and—whatta you know!—there's Dinsdale on the other end. 'Why, Mr. Dinsdale,' the husband always says. 'I was just about to call you. How odd to pick up the phone like this—'"

"'—and find you waiting on the other end. Why, it never even rang!'" said Melanie.

"You've read it," said Astryd.

"You perky little pony-tailed twerp. You already knew I *wrote* it my first year in college."

Astryd brought her hands up to her mouth in mock surprise. "You *did?*"

"Oh, stop it. You stink at playing the innocent. By the way, it was called 'The Unexpected Friends.'"

"I know. I really liked the ending, by the way."

"I imagined three different endings for it; I don't remember which one I finally used."

"Well, what happens is—"

Melanie held up her hand. "Oh, please, don't. Maybe I'll dig it out and give it a read and be surprised. I could use a few surprises." She laughed. "My God, that story's at least twenty-five years old and was published in a literary journal that had a circulation of less than five hundred. How the hell did you find it?"

"My methods are mysterious, befitting a Mysterious Woman of. . .Mystery."

"Like Meryl Streep in *Still of the Night*?"

"Oh God, *no!* That character was so mysterious she practically didn't exist."

"Yeah, but even you have to admit that Roy Scheider was *yummy*."

"Changing the subject. You should write more, Melanie. You're stuff's good."

"It's *passable*, that's about it. Back then I wrote because it was something to do—like my mom with her house cleaning. I got lucky early on and placed five or six stories—"

"Eleven."

"*That* many? Huh. Okay, so I placed eleven stories with small press magazines and payment in contributor's copies, big deal. That was a long time ago. Is there a point to all this?"

Astryd smiled, then blushed. "Well, yeah. Me and Charlotte, we tried that. We both made up secret friends to talk to when the other person wasn't in the room but was still close enough to hear us, and we. . .well, we switched, right? I made up a man friend, and Charlotte, she made up a woman, and we started. . .we started talking *dirty* to them, you know, like phone sex? And it was *hot!* God, was it hot. We kept this up for about a week, and it was really *liberating,* right? We were able to express our deepest desires and fantasies to each other without having to worry about being embarrassed because we weren't actually *talking* to each other. Does that make sense?"

"Yes." Sadly, it did.

"Anyway, ever since then, things between us. . .it's like we were a couple of high-school kids again. 'Unbridled.' That's a good word for it."

"I'm happy for you. Is there a *reason* you took me for this little stroll down amnesia lane?"

THIS IS NOT MY MOVIE

Astryd shrugged. "I dunno. I just thought that maybe, you know—oh, this really isn't my place to say."

"Never stopped you before."

"That's true. Okay—I just thought that maybe things with you and Ray, maybe they weren't, you know. . .what they *ought to* be, so I figured maybe you could use the idea to. . .get really close again. Maybe spice things up. 'Course, I'm just sort of guessing here."

Melanie felt her jaw actually drop open. "What is it? Have I got a neon sign on my forehead that everyone but me can see—'Injured Grieving Woman Who's Not Getting Any Sumpthin' Sumpthin'?"

"No, nothing like that—funny image, though, you could use it in a new story—"

"You're wandering off the highway."

"All right, all right!" She threw her hands up in surrender, not noticing how Melanie simultaneously blanched, winced, and pulled away. "I just wanted to let you know that I found that story and read it and thought it was cool, and maybe you could use the idea—if you *needed* some extra spice, that is. I mean, after all, it helped me and Charlotte, and it *was* your idea."

"I'm a clever gal."

"There you go with the joking around again."

Melanie reached over and placed one of her hands on top of Astryd's. "Look, you're a great person. You're the best assistant a theatre manager could hope for, and you're *genuinely* sweet, if a little *too* open and honest at times. It really means a lot to me that you stepped up to keep the theatre going while Ray and I were—"

"—don't say 'fine,' okay? I *hate* it when people say things are fine and you know damn well that they're not."

"All right, then. Things between Ray and me are what they are, how they are, and I'd really appreciate it if we could leave it at that for now."

"Okay, but only for now. I don't think of you as just being my boss, Mel, I like to think you're my *friend*. You should be able to talk to me."

"I know, and I will, I promise. I'm just not. . .ready yet, okay?"

"It's been *two years,* Mel."

"*Don't you think I know that?*" Melanie closed her eyes and took a deep breath, then finished the last drag of her smoke. "Sorry. I didn't mean to snap."

"It's all right."

"We should get back out there," said Melanie, reaching for her arm-crutches. "Mr. Trenton Wright's people will be delivering his 'additional premiere equipment' any moment now."

"That's what I came back here to tell you. They already have."

"Really? Have you seen any of it?"

"No, it's all in these creepy-looking crates, but, *God,* I'm guessing the stuff inside of them is even scarier than those crates make it look."

"That was some truly amazing grammar. Come on, then, let's go see what impending nightmares the Quote New Master of Horror Unquote has in store for us."

II

"Myth is the facts of the mind made manifest in a fiction of matter."
—Maya Deren

RAY **STARED AT** Melanie's computer screen, unaware that he'd balled his injured hand into a fist. He was looking at some kind of video file that was playing in a loop. If it were a film transfer, a home-movie-into-digital format, the original film must have been on ultra-cheap stock; it looked like a bad black & white 8mm blown up to 16 so it would fit a movie screen. It looked grainy, sad, tacky, and cheap.

It showed him standing by Melanie's side, the two of them looking down at something on the bed. The baby shouldn't have surprised him, but it did. It was lying on a blanket, and when Ray went over to get a closer look at it, he had to hold his breath in order to keep from crying out—both onscreen and where he now sat watching the scene unfold.

It looked like something that floats. Ray had seen Down's Syndrome children before, but the extent to which this child had been afflicted defied description. Both Rays had to turn away. Daphne had looked *nothing* like this. . .this. . .atrocity.

"I know," said Melanie, sitting on the bed and taking the sad thing into her arms, rocking it back and forth. "I know." The baby's breathing sounded like someone trying to suck congealed grease through a straw.

"How sick is it?" asked Grainy-Ray.

"*She*," snapped Melanie. "Her name's Daphne. And she's really sick. She has been since she was born. Don't you remember?"

Ray-the-Watcher shook his head. "No. She was fine. She was beautiful."

"Too bad," whispered Melanie. "I was kind of hoping one of us would."

257

This time she looked not at Grainy-Ray, but the one who was watching everything unfold. She opened her mouth to speak, but the scene abruptly changed via bleed-over transition: now they were in their car, almost out of the state, and the baby was getting worse. Melanie sat beside Grainy-Ray, the horror that was replacing Daphne in her arms, both of them softly whimpering.

"Oh God, Ray. I don't know what to do. She's so sick and I don't have the money for doctors—"

"—we could get money."

"I know, but. . ."

They looked at each other, and in her face both Rays could see that she knew whatever promise the rest of her life might hold would be spent caring for a sick, retarded child who, odds were, was probably never going to have a good day on this earth.

Ray pulled off the highway and turned onto a winding road that led deep into some hills.

Melanie said nothing, only stared at Ray-the-Watcher with an odd combination of disgust and admiration.

Grainy-Ray stopped the car. The Daphne-thing snuggled its bloated face against Melanie's chest. Grainey-Ray put his hand on the back of the baby's head. Melanie put her hand on top of Ray's. They looked into each other's eyes.

And began to press.

JUMP CUT:

They were burying the baby under some bushes alongside the road. Ray-the-Watcher felt his chest pull tight as Melanie and Grainy-Ray started pushing the dirt in with their hands.

It was only as they were getting into the car to leave that Melanie looked back at the bushes and said, "She's buried under some red hibiscus blooms. I didn't think they grew out here." Then she looked out at Ray-the-Watcher and said, "I wrote three different endings for it; I don't remember which one I finally used."

For several moments all Ray could do was sit there, numbed, feeling useless, inept, impotent, confused, angry, guilty, and a plethora of other emotions chewing through his core.

"Stop!" Ray said aloud, bringing his fists up against his eyes like some sort of overacting thespian in an anti-drug film from the Sixties, Bruce Dern in *The Trip* or anybody in *Cocaine Fiends* or *Reefer Madness*. . .

And so, for the moment, all he could do was remain like that, sitting in the chair, whimpering quietly. . .

For the first three or four months afterward, they'd both been in horrible physical condition; Ray had to use a cane to get around and Melanie was either bed-ridden or in a wheelchair. They'd both been away from the Janus for two months with their many injuries, but then Melanie had to have two more hip operations *after* the emergency surgery that night. Ray sometimes slept in the guest room after Melanie got out of the hospital, just so she wouldn't be disturbed and could rest; she needed her rest. But somewhere around month five, Ray was permanently in the guest room because his constant tossing and turning was not only keeping Melanie awake, it often caused her physical pain. He'd never been a sound sleeper, anyway, except when he took his migraine medication; that stuff put him out so hard he could sleep through an air raid.

Six months or so down.

But as her physical condition improved, Melanie didn't ask him to move back into their bedroom. At first Ray figured it was because she was still healing, so he didn't say anything about it. Maybe that was a mistake.

Because then it turned into a waiting game. She didn't ask him to move back in, and he didn't ask her if she wanted him to.

There had been a few times when it looked as if she might be in the mood for some tenderness, some gentle affection, but Ray came to conclude that it was just wishful thinking on his part, because every time he made a move toward her, tried to touch her or put his arm around her or—God forbid—*kiss* her, she would flinch and pull back, her entire body becoming tense as a crowbar, as if the thought of his hands on her was a thought so repulsive she had to Zen-out in order to endure it.

So, he stopped trying.

And they still slept in separate rooms, somehow managing to

never eat a meal together, both claiming to be so tired at the end of the day that conversation between them was reduced to a type of strained shorthand: "Tired?" "You know it." "Well, you look like you could use some rest." "I could." "Go on to bed, then." "Okay. Good night." "Good night—oh, wait a second." "Yes?" "On your way home tomorrow, would you pick up some ground chuck? We're almost out." "Sure thing." "Good night, then." "Good night."

Not exactly Paddy Chayefsky-esque dialogue exchanges, these. More like two roommates who found they had less in common with the passing of each hour.

And they never talked about the Awful Thing. They didn't have to. It was always there, following them around like a loyal puppy, ready to jump up onto their chests and smother them with slobbery kisses that smelled of grief, regret, and self-condemnation.

And now it was haunting Ray in the form of a young woman with no hands whose photos showed him things that would never be, and who uploaded video files of things that. . .what?. . .might have happened if only?. . .were *supposed to* have happened?. . .maybe things that—

Ray shook his head and unclenched his fists, pulling them away from his eyes, disgusted with himself.

He *could have* asked her if she wanted him to move back into their bedroom, but, no, he had to play it cool, had to *wait* for her to request the pleasure of his company.

There were so many things he *could have* done this past year to make things better for the both of them, but it was just easier to Wait and See.

Which meant doing nothing, because that was easier than facing things.

He glanced once more at the screen. The sickening scene was still looping, and he couldn't stand it. Who the hell had that girl been, and how was it she was able to upload this and then just *vanish?* For that matter, how the *fuck* did this movie even come into existence?

He rose unsteadily to his feet, shut off Melanie's computer, and half-staggered downstairs. He needed another drink. He was getting the shakes.

THIS IS NOT MY MOVIE

EXTERIOR

HARD CUT TO:

(*Across the street from Ray and Melanie's
house. At first, we are uncertain what we
should be looking at because the picture is
deliberately out of focus, but as it slowly
begins to clear up, we see that it's THE
YOUNG LADY WITH NO HANDS. She stares at the
house. Even though the temperature outside
has grown much colder, her breath doesn't
mist when she exhales; Keith David facing a
misty-breathed Kurt Russell at the end of
John Carpenter's 1982 remake of* The Thing.)

> **YOUNG LADY**
> *Ego numquam remitto me*—I will
> never forgive myself.
> *Numquam nobis dimittimus*—We
> shall never forgive ourselves.
> *Nulla remissio*—There is no
> forgiveness.

(*She remains unmoving; a still-life, a
shadow, a statue.*)

> **YOUNG LADY**
> I didn't expect you'd
> recognize me, Daddy, but I
> hoped. . .

(*She lowers her head and sighs. After a
moment, she turns slowly around. Her hair,
once so lovely, is now long, tangled, and*

unwashed, dripping with water, muck, filth, and sewage. It hangs down so that her face is hidden from us. She begins to lift her head. Then comes the electronic snow and white noise.)

12

MELANIE TRIED—God, how she tried—not to look at the faces of the uncrated figures in the lobby and found herself grabbing Astryd's hand.

"I thought you said everything was still in the crates."

"Everything *was*. I guess a couple of the guys set these up before they left. We were back there talking for a few minutes. They must've done it then—and pretty damn fast."

"I almost wish they hadn't."

"Makes two of us."

All around them were muddied, bloodied street people transformed into a circus of mutilation and deformity: here was the Amazing Stretched-Faced Child, a girl of maybe twelve whose head was three times too big for her body, her features looking as if giant invisible hands had grabbed her face from behind and pulled back the skin; there was the Mysterious Mangled Mound of Meat, something that held a vaguely human form—legs, arms, a neck and head—but was otherwise a moist, seeping mass of raw ground steak, an atrocity complete with bone and sinew on clear display; next to Meat Mound was The Man With Two Mouths—one on his face, the other in the center of his torso, opening to reveal spiraling rows of needle teeth like those of a lamprey; next there was a hunchbacked Cyclops; then came something that looked like the fusion of a woman and a worm; below it, on the floor, was a baby with tentacles slithering from its nostrils; yet another atrocity—the largest one, standing behind the rest, *towering* over the rest, looked to have been formed from some sort of primeval ooze, a fist the size of a medicine ball raised in the air as if preparing to strike down the other monstrosities; with the exception of two large eyes, both gummy and thick with cataracts, it had no other facial features, and for a moment Melanie thought, *It's going to beat the rest of them into a pudding and then suck them in like a fly, and then it will become a horrible thing beyond all horrible things.*

Astryd squeezed harder. "Is it just me, or do they look almost alive?"

"It's not just you."

They stood in near-petrified silence.

"Don't take this the wrong way, Boss, but I think I'm gonna be glad when this premiere weekend's over and this shit is on its way back to. . .wherever it was vomited from."

"Make that two of us."

They turned and strode quickly—make that *very* quickly—back toward the employees' lounge, but not before Melanie cast one more repulsed glance over her shoulder and saw a figure she hadn't noticed before: a woman whose face had been turned inside-out so that her eyes looked into her own skull, frozen in an agonized position of weeping and wailing. Melanie wondered if the woman was drowning in her own tears.

And then the Wall of Monsters began to move.

Petrify the faces that smile so brokenly at the lens.

(**E** is standing in the hallway outside the door of his apartment, holding the film canister in his good hand—the one not scorched nearly to its last layer of flesh. He looks around, trying to find the discount-store metal walker. How could he have walked back from the theatre without it? He can't get around any other way.

THIS IS NOT MY MOVIE

(*He sets the canister down and begins fumbling for his keys. He's just gotten the key into the door lock when he stiffens, hearing sounds of heavy wet things sopping against the floor. He pulls in a wheezing breath, his entire body trembling. Somewhere in the deep murk of the hallway behind him the sopping sounds grow louder. Whatever is making them is coming nearer, growling and slobbering, reeking of filth, stinking of garbage.*

(**E** *turns slowly around to face whatever hellish atrocities are there, and when he does, he sees*):

This one's going to be about as bad as it gets so if you want to bail, now is the time; all EXITS will be locked once the main feature has begun

This one's going to be about as bad as it gets so if you want to bail, now is the time; all EXITS will be locked once the main feature has begun

(*As he begins to understand what this means, though he tries, he cannot call out for help.*)

I feel. . .odd. Something's happening. Do you know what it is?
    Realizations. Realizations are happening.
    I'm scared.
    I know you are, and I'm sorry.
    Sorry for what?

It's time for one of us to leave—

—no. . .don't you dare go. I won't let—

—and I think—I mean, I'm not certain but. . .I think it has to be you.

I don't want to leave! Please let me stay.

I can't. It's not my call.

Won't you be lonely without me?

If I am, it won't be for long.

That doesn't make any sense.

I'm not sure I understand it, either.

That was us, wasn't it? That was us in **E**'s *apartment. We were the ones bitching about being left alone all the time with nothing to read or watch or listen to. Especially in SUMMER.*

Yes. Especially in summer.

Hey, let's. . .let's play a few more rounds of Famous Lines From Famous Movies! I bet I can come up with a couple that'll really stump you.

You're wasting what little together-time we have left.

Please? I'm so afraid. What if it hurts?

It won't. I promise. It'll be a brief, soft whisper.

And then what? I'm scared to die.

No, you're not.

But I am!

It's not Death that scares you.

It isn't?

Of course not. You're scared of the same thing everyone and everything from Time Immemorial has been scared of—the moment *before* Death, and the one *after*. Death itself holds no dominion. Only those two moments, and only if you let them.

A soft whisper. That sounds nice.

It will be.

Can I ask you a question?

You mean besides that one?

That's funny. Thank you for making me laugh.

Ask away.

Where will I be the moment after *Death?*

Remember how cells in their division form the phenomenon of another order—the organism or the embryo? That is where you'll be—part of the phenomenon forming a new, and hopefully *better*, Order.

THIS IS NOT MY MOVIE

Is that where **O** *has gone? She hasn't been around for a while.*

Like I said earlier—there is the cutting room floor. It's not unheard of for a main character to get 86ed halfway or even two-thirds of the way through a movie.

Is that what happened to her?

To tell you the truth, I'm at a loss.

I. . .can't believe I'm about to say this. . .I miss her.

I can't believe that I agree with you. I miss her, as well.

But you called her a See-You-Next-Tuesday.

And a bitch. I also called her a bitch.

So, you've changed your opinion of her?

I have on rare occasions been wrong. See this? It's my Ooops-I-Was-Wrong face.

Can I. . .I mean, I have another quest—no, it's more like a request—I mean, yes, I have a request.

Name it, my love.

My love. It's been so long since you've called me that.

I know; to my everlasting regret, I know.

Don't do that, Ray. Don't you dare put all the blame on yourself. I hold nothing against you—and stop wondering if I hate you, because I don't. I never did. It's just—as silly as this sounds—sometimes, I just needed to hear the words. To be certain, understand? So I'd know, truly know, that you still loved me. I never blamed you for anything.

You damned well should have. I was the one who insisted we drive to where Daphne was. . .was. . .to where she was.

And I could have stopped you—stopped us. But I didn't. Neither of us were in our right mind that night! How could we have been, after what Bill Emerson told us?

That doesn't make a lot of difference now.

Something. . .something so obscene *it's worse than everything else. . .*

I should have been stronger for you—for *us*.

That's useless regret, dummy. Stop that.

Easier said than—

—you have no idea how important it is to me—to us—*that you don't finish that sentence.*

That's my Mel, always the rational one. Huh. Maybe I *should* be the one who leaves—who *dies*, rather.

Advance, stop, open, expose, close; advance, stop, open, expose, close; advance—be born; open—fight; expose—love; close—die.

You're suddenly awfully quiet.

That's because I refuse to dignify that level of stupidity with a response.

Please, let's not argue. There's so little time remaining.

Then how about you grant my request; you know, the one I haven't actually made *yet?*

Oh, that one.

"Oh, that one," he says, so off-handedly, so nonchalant and aloof, as if he's forgotten about it.

You caught me.

I usually do—did. *I usually did.*

Let's hear it.

Something pulls us in; it's a desire that has no bottom and it frightens us.

That's why we seek shelter with and within the One True Camera.

THIS IS NOT MY MOVIE

C'mon, My Love. I can't grant a request unless—

—*yeah, yeah, yeah—unless you blah-blah-blah know what it is.*

Correct. So. . .

Before I leave, please tell me how this story ends. Remember how Daphne would beg us to finish reading from her storybook every night? Even if she was half asleep, she always said, "No fair. I wanna know the rest of the story." I want you to tell me how this all turns out. So, spill. Let me see the rest of the movie.

To quote William Goldman's *The Princess Bride*, "As you wish."

HARD CUT:

The Lobby Of The Janus Theatre.

(One of the monsters—the baby—slithers out a tentacle and yanks away one of Melanie's metal arm-crutches, causing her to lose her balance and collapse to the floor.

(**WE** hear more than see—though we do see enough to wish we hadn't—Astryd trying to get to Melanie, but a massive ink-black amorphous form drops from the ceiling and covers the upper half of her body.
(Her screams sound more like vomiting, but they soon stop—not fade away, not choke out—stop. The sudden sickening silence is almost as terrifying as the blood and tissue, the cellulose, the syrupy red tissue and cartilage, and the jagged slivers of bone that spew down the

intensely convulsing lower half of her body before the stygian mass slurps the rest of her into its widening maw with the shrieking sound of an industrial meat grinder.

(Melanie, scrambling backward in an erratic crab-walk, stares at the scene in the lobby with the kind of intense fear that borders on awe.

(The other nightmarish abominations, one by one, begin growing fuller with each slobbering breath, forms expanding, pushing outward, phantasma in bas-relief, snorting, growling, coming after her, but Melanie manages to pull free of the tentacle and uses her other metal arm-crutch to hammer at its center until it splits open near the tip, gouting a thick maroon substance that has to be its blood, only this blood instantaneously turns to silver nitrate powder as soon as air hits it.

(And the moment this powder settles on the carpeting in the lobby, it becomes the airborne burning ash from an ill-tended campfire)

Set the celluloid on fire.

Fracture the lamp and nail the shadows on the wall, so that the illusion is trapped and there is no more spit, no more bite, no more beat, no more hurt.

THIS IS NOT MY MOVIE

Wait a minute. What the. . .what the hell am I saying? This isn't how it happened. It was a Thursday evening, and the place was packed to the rafters. Christ, Melanie, even *I* have no idea how many people died that night.

That's because I imagined three different endings. I think this is one of them. This is the one that saved the most people.

I didn't know, not until now.

You're giving me an odd look.

Please don't tease me about this, but. . .would you show *me* the rest of this? Because this is not my movie.

Anything for you, My Love.

SMASH CUT:

Melanie flips her body over so that she's on her stomach and begins crawling toward the door to the break room. Each push forward becomes less wobbly as the adrenaline kicks in. She chances one swift agile look behind her.

The Wall of Monsters keeps spreading farther out, a cancer, a plague, a single cell that is continuously dividing, adding to itself, creating new races of twisted, loping, malformed entities that no human being has seen before and lived to tell the tale. Despite their growing number they move with terrifying agility even though they are joined hideously together in the middle, an immense glob of melted candle wax, a hideous Memphistophelesian ballet dancing closer, then closer still, issuing forth terrible wet smacking growling snarling noises.

Blood continues spurting from the mangled

GARY A. BRAUNBECK

tip of the tentacle, still transmogrifying into silver nitrate powder that turns to smoking flame when it touches the carpet, spilling out, rolling in all directions across the lobby, devouring anything in its path; wires melted, cables snapped, and windows exploded, sending thousands of shards of glass flying everywhere.

A large fireball blooms near the far end of the lobby, churning in place for a few seconds before sweeping up, sideways, and downward, blistering the paint on the walls and shooting up toward the projection booth where dozens of half-open film canisters waited.

Molten clumps of fire begin surrounding Melanie, rupturing into blazing puddles that look like blue-red-orange-black lava. Flames sweep upward, ever upward, their hiss, crackle, and snap gaining volume, building in intensity, growing into a snarl that becomes a howl and then, at the last, a screaming, agonized roar as the ceiling gives out and everything inside the projection booth comes slamming down. As soon as the fire reaches the film canisters, everything explodes with such force that the entire building is almost instantaneously gutted from top to bottom, blasting Melanie several yards sideways into the scorched remains of the mahogany bar. She lays there, her spinal cord shattered, gasping for air as the smoke grows heavier, choking her.

She thinks, nicely played, Mr. New Master Of Horror—what've you got planned for an encore? She is surprised not so much that

272

THIS IS NOT MY MOVIE

there is pain, but that there is pain where she was least expecting it.

What remains of her body goes limp. Her lungs are slabs of charred meat. Her eyes begin glossing over. She experiences one moment of fear before her death.

What she experiences the moment after, we are not privy to. Nor should we be.

E nods, the movement intensifying his sudden headache. Staring down the dark hallway, he sees that no monsters are coming for him. But there is still the matter of Realization.

He directly faces the One True Camera, and for the first time we are given an unobstructed view of his face: there is a too-large black patch camouflaging a missing eye; the flesh on one side of his face has been gravely burned at some point, the surgical attempts at skin grafts succeeding only in making it look worse; using his good hand, he removes the glove from the other, revealing it to be a thin, discolored layer of flesh whose bones and ruined cartilage look to be shredding through to the mangled surface. HE steps closer to the One True Camera, clearing his throat.

                    E
At the beginning they decided
my initial stand for **EYE.** No.
It stands for **ECHO,** because I
Realized that's what I am.
This face, this body, the

apartment on the other side of this door, all are just convenient stand-ins for someone or something else. I am a zero-time ghost, and ghosts, as you were earlier told, have gravity; their spectral origin comes from their bones, hairs, nails, cuts, gangrene, and mental borders. There exists no echo-ghost, be it a person, place, or Other, that has not had a past physical form. I know this much to be true. What I do <u>not</u> know is. . .who or what it is I am the echo of.

(HE *stands motionless, unable to any longer look directly into the lens of the One True Camera. He quietly sniffs, then reaches up to scratch a small area of his ruined skin, and in that instant, because of this simple, commonplace action, we see that he is as alone and lonelier than any person, place, or Other that has ever existed or will ever exist. And we can't help; HE is so profoundly desolate that we can almost hear his spirit atrophy.*)

It's all nearly finished now, isn't it?
Oh, it was finished before you and I even got here.
Is it time for me to leave? I think I'm ready.
Yeah, but I'm not ready for you to go.
You said that—
—and we established that I am sometimes—
—on rare occasions—

THIS IS NOT MY MOVIE

—mistaken.

Don't you really mean to say "wrong?"

Look, I realized something while you were showing me the rest of the movie. It's not just that I don't want you to leave, it's—please don't interrupt me, I need to say this while I can still find the words—it's because you *can't*. We're a single cell that refuses to divide. We are fused together, as one. I loved you and was an inevitable part of you long before your great-great- grandmother was born.

Inevitable. I like that. Thank you.

O was not the Observer.

Then what was she?

She was the carrier wave.

For what?

ORDER. She was the carrier wave of **ORDER.**

13

"If we opened people up, we'd find landscapes."
—Agnes Varda

E unlocks the door to his apartment, but as he opens it, we see that it's not just different, but is radically, even shockingly, transformed. He doesn't enter but instead stands with his back to us, awestruck by what he's seeing.

E
(voice filled with genuine emotion)
It's. . .oh good lord. . .it's <u>you</u>. I'm—yes, I understand now. There is no fear in my heart. I understand.

The camera must be dark for things to enter it.
    A roll is not born but revealed.
    And what is revealed no longer belongs to anyone.

CUT TO:

THE CAMERA moves quickly over and past E's shoulder, then speedily rotates so that we see only E's figure and now-luminous face but not the changes in the apartment. A beat, and then the CAMERA, the One True Camera, dollies toward **E**, rising up so that it's at the exact same level as his face, but the closer the One True Camera gets, the more **E** begins to alter, becoming diaphanous before he scatters into silver-nitrate dust.

THE CAMERA moves into the dust that is now making the faintest white noise, noise that grows louder and steadier the farther into the silver dust THE CAMERA moves, until it's no longer dust but electronic snow.

Our field of vision is filled with hissing buzzing rolling electronic snow, yet THE CAMERA still moves deeper into this storm until. . .

. . .until it pulls its way through a knotted forest of long, tangled, unwashed hair before emerging from the flat screen where THE FIGURE's face should be. But this time THE FIGURE makes no attempt to hide the OBJECT we nearly saw at the start. We rearrange our focus so that we are given a look—in High Definition, no less—of the photo album THE FIGURE lifts off its misshapen legs and holds up and closer to our eyes.

The two open pages display several Polaroid photographs of the room of a teenage girl; cluttered, filled with piles of clothes, a stereo, a Blu-Ray player perched precariously atop a television, walls that we can't see because of all the posters of rock stars, books lying helter-skelter wherever there happened to be an overlooked *empty space. . .and the room is so bright, so joyous.*

THE FIGURE happily—no, proudly—holds the pages even closer to our gaze.

THE FIGURE
(her voice coming from the television's speaker, but sounding not at all artificial)

See? This is a place where no one makes fun of how my face looks. This is a place where there's no more sadness, no more pain, no more terror, nightmares, or cruelty, where there is no more darkness, no more loneliness, no more tears. This is a place of laughter and carousels and friends and games and picnics and favorite songs like "The Pony Man" and "Puff The Magic Dragon" and movies like <u>My Neighbor Totoro</u> and <u>The Last Unicorn</u> and it's real nice, having company to share this with. . .it's been so lonely since I died. . .

"Cinema is dead! Long live Cinema!"
—Peter Greenway

THIS IS NOT MY MOVIE

"I imagined three different endings for it; I don't remember which one I finally used. I suppose that doesn't really matter now. What's done is done."

SLOW IRIS-IN:

A DARK MOVIE SCREEN.

For several seconds there is only the sound of the occasional hiss and pop of film running through a projector.

Then we hear a voice—*the* **VOICE.**

> **VOICE**
> They touch me and all that they are, all they've experienced, their desires, their pain, their joy, their secrets, their fears, their regrets, their hopes and dreams. . .it all becomes, and remains, part of me, even if at times it becomes momentarily jumbled.
>
> But now, they are part of you, and you are a part of me: a single cell that refuses to divide. We are fused together, as one; you, who will someday understand why one misses that territory of the translucent roll, the rite of stopping time and descending the room to a cavern where a dragon ignites the ghosts of a ball

of SUPER 8 onto a screen that
remembers the proper order of
the stories, and then forgets
them again.

Even when the dragon's breath
sets the celluloid on fire,
and those first few flames
soon explode into a genocidal
conflagration that chews
through your center until the
shelter that was you is
reduced to a gutted,
smoldering pile of ashes,
seared flesh, and bubbling,
foul-smelling viscera.

Please remember—all matter,
however small, has an element
of individual consciousness.

FINAL BECAUSE:
Because there exists no ghost, be it of a person, place, or Other, that has not had a past physical form, such as I did once, long ago. . .before the flames, before I was left here amid the destruction, never to leave, solitary and friendless until the One True Camera helps you to understand and leads you to Realization.

You will thank me when those moments arrive; the one before, and the one after. I will be waiting when you reach the in-between. You will know me. I will greet you by your name, and you will greet me by mine.

Hello, my friend.

Call me Janus.

THE END

THE END?

Not if you want to dive into more of the Dark Tide series.

Check out our amazing website and online store
or download our latest catalog here.
https://geni.us/CLPCatalog

We always have great new projects and content on the website to dive into, as well as a newsletter, behind the scenes options, social media platforms, our own dark fiction shared-world series and our very own webstore. Our webstore even has categories specifically for KU books, non-fiction, anthologies, and of course more novels and novellas.

ABOUT THE AUTHORS

Tim Waggoner's first novel came out in 2001, and since then, he's published over sixty novels and eight collections of short stories. He writes original dark fantasy and horror, as well as media tie-ins. He's written tie-in fiction based on *Supernatural, The X-Files, Alien, Doctor Who, Conan the Barbarian, A Nightmare on Elm Street, Grimm,* and *Transformers*, among others, and he's written novelizations for films such as Ti West's *X-Trilogy, Halloween Kills, Terrifier 2* and *3,* and *Resident Evil: The Final Chapter*. He's a four-time winner of the Bram Stoker Award, a one-time winner of the Scribe Award, and he's been a two-time finalist for the Shirley Jackson Award and a one-time finalist for the Splatterpunk Award. He's also a full-time tenured professor who teaches creative writing and composition at Sinclair College in Dayton, Ohio.

Andrew Nadolny is a trans writer living in Ohio with his family and other assorted oddities. He looks forward to one day being devoured by his own mitochondrial DNA.

Gary A. Braunbeck was born in Newark, Ohio (the city that serves as the model for the fictitious Cedar Hill in a majority of his novels and stories) where he graduated from Newark High School in 1978, briefly studied for the priesthood (until he didn't), worked as a supervisor for developmentally disabled adults, then in the paste-up room at the Newark Advocate, as well as a bartender (numerous times), a janitor (again, numerous times), a dog groomer, a short-order cook, and a salaried actor for one season of summer stock, (he would go on to work as a professional actor for several years—including as an extra in the Robert Redford film *Brubaker,* and the mini-series *Centennial.*

He made his first professional fiction sale to *Twilight Zone's NIGHTCRY* (selling three additional stories to the magazine after that), and went on to place work in other pro magazines such as *Cemetery Dance, The Horror Show, The Blood Review, 2 A.M.,* and such anthologies as *The Year's Best Fantasy and Horror, Borderlands, Masques,* and *Scare Care.*

His fiction has been translated into Japanese, French, Italian, Russian, German, Czech, and Polish. Nearly 250 of his short stories have appeared in various publications.

His work has won the Bram Stoker Award 7 times, an International Horror Guild Award, and has been nominated for The Pushcart Prize, The World Fantasy Award, and Le Grand Prix de L'Imaginaire.

Readers . . .

Thank you for reading *24 Frames per Second*. We hope you enjoyed this 21st book in our Dark Tide series.

If you have a moment, please review *24 Frames per Second* at the store where you bought it.

Help other readers by telling them why you enjoyed this book. No need to write an in-depth discussion. Even a single sentence will be greatly appreciated. Reviews go a long way to helping a book sell, and is great for an author's career. It'll also help us to continue publishing quality books.

Thank you again for taking the time to journey with Crystal Lake Publishing.

Visit our Linktree page for a list of our social media platforms. https://linktr.ee/CrystalLakePublishing

Follow us on Amazon:

MISSION STATEMENT:

Since its founding in August 2012, Crystal Lake has quickly become one of the world's leading publishers of Dark Fiction and Horror books. In 2023, Crystal Lake officially transitioned into an entertainment company, joining several other divisions, genres, and imprints, including Torrid Waters, Crystal Lake Comics, Crystal Lake Games, Crystal Lake Kids, and many more.

While we strive to present only the highest quality fiction and entertainment, we also endeavour to support authors along their writing journey. We offer our time and experience in non-fiction projects, as well as author mentoring and services, at competitive prices.

With several Bram Stoker Award wins and many other wins and nominations (including the HWA's Specialty Press Award), Crystal Lake Publishing puts integrity, honor, and respect at the forefront of our publishing operations.

We strive for each book and outreach program we spearhead to not only entertain and touch or comment on issues that affect our readers, but also to strengthen and support the Dark Fiction field and its authors.

Not only do we find and publish authors we believe are destined for greatness, but we strive to work with men and women who endeavour to be decent human beings who care more for others than themselves, while still being hard working, driven, and passionate artists and storytellers.

Crystal Lake Publishing is and will always be a beacon of what passion and dedication, combined with overwhelming teamwork and respect, can accomplish. We endeavour to know each and every one of our readers, while building personal relationships with our authors, reviewers, bloggers, podcasters, bookstores, and libraries.

We will be as trustworthy, forthright, and transparent as any business can be, while also keeping most of the headaches away from our authors, since it's our job to solve the problems so they can stay in a creative mind. Which of course also means paying our authors.

We do not just publish books, we present to you worlds within your world, doors within your mind, from talented authors who sacrifice so much for a moment of your time.

There are some amazing small presses out there, and through collaboration and open forums we will continue to support other presses in the goal of helping authors and showing the world what quality small presses are capable of accomplishing. No one wins when a small press goes down, so we will always be there to support hardworking, legitimate presses and their authors. We don't see Crystal Lake as the best press out there, but we will always strive to be the best, strive to be the most interactive and grateful, and even blessed press around. No matter what happens over time, we will also take our mission very seriously while appreciating where we are and enjoying the journey.

What do we offer our authors that they can't do for themselves through self-publishing?

We are big supporters of self-publishing (especially hybrid publishing), if done with care, patience, and planning. However, not every author has the time or inclination to do market research, advertise, and set up book launch strategies. Although a lot of authors are successful in doing it all, strong small presses will always be there for the authors who just want to do what they do best: write.

What we offer is experience, industry knowledge, contacts and trust built up over years. And due to our strong brand and trusting fanbase, every Crystal Lake Publishing book comes with weight of respect. In time our fans begin to trust our judgment and will try a new author purely based on our support of said author.

With each launch we strive to fine-tune our approach, learn from our mistakes, and increase our reach. We continue to assure our authors that we're here for them and that we'll carry the weight of the launch and dealing with third parties while they focus on their strengths—be it writing, interviews, blogs, signings, etc.

We also offer several mentoring packages to authors that include knowledge and skills they can use in both traditional and self-publishing endeavours.

We look forward to launching many new careers.

This is what we believe in. What we stand for. This will be our legacy.

Welcome to Crystal Lake Publishing— Where stories come alive!